SPQR XIII

THE YEAR
OF CONFUSION

Also by
J O H N   M A D D O X   R O B E R T S

The Gabe Treloar Series

SPQR XIII

THE YEAR
OF CONFUSION

JOHN MADDOX ROBERTS

MINOTAUR BOOKS
New York

A THOMAS DUNNE BOOKS FOR MINOTAUR BOOKS.
An imprint of St. Martin's Publishing Group.

SPQR XIII: THE YEAR OF CONFUSION. Copyright © 2010 by John Maddox Roberts. All rights reserved. Printed in the United States of America. For information, address St. Martin's Press, 175 Fifth Avenue, New York, N.Y. 10010.

www.thomasdunnebooks.com
www.minotaurbooks.com

Library of Congress Cataloging-in-Publication Data

Roberts, John Maddox.
    The year of confusion / John Maddox Roberts.—1st ed.
        p. cm.—(SPQR ; 13)
    ISBN 978-0-312-59507-4
    1. Metellus, Decius Caecilius (Fictitious character)—Fiction.
2. Private investigators—Rome—Fiction.   3. Caesar, Julius—
Fiction.   4. Calendar reform—Fiction.   5. Murder—Investigation—
Rome—Fiction.   6. Rome—Fiction.   I. Title.
    PS3568.O23874Y43 2010
    813'.54—dc22

                                                    2009039832

First Edition: February 2010

10 9 8 7 6 5 4 3 2 1

For my granddaughter, Meagan Fiona Viola
Olmstead, who used to sit on my lap and tour
the ancient Rome of SPQR, and who is now engaged
in her own creative endeavors in art, music, and dance,
with much love from Granddad.

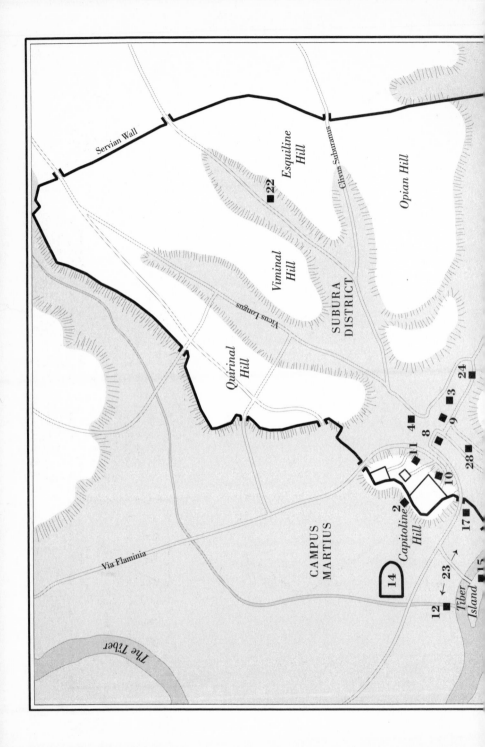

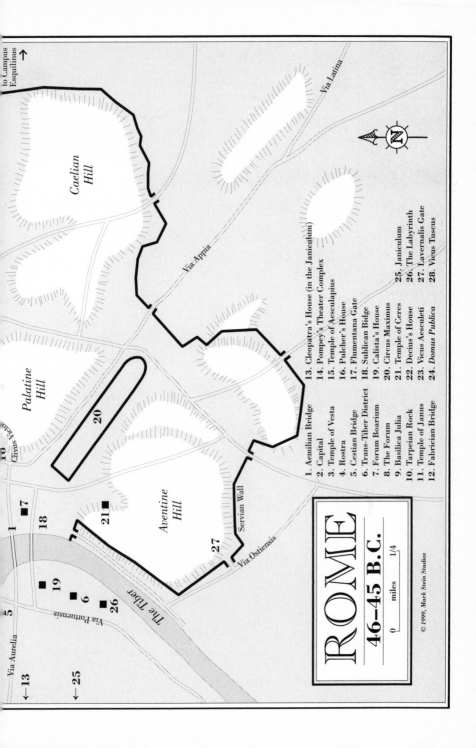

ROME
46-45 B.C.

0   miles   1/4

© 1999, Mark Stein Studios

1. Aemilian Bridge
2. Capital
3. Temple of Vesta
4. Rostra
5. Cestian Bridge
6. Trans-Tiber District
7. Forum Boarium
8. The Forum
9. Basilica Julia
10. Tarpeian Rock
11. Temple of Janus
12. Fabrician Bridge
13. Cleopatra's House (in the Janiculum)
14. Pompey's Theater Complex
15. Temple of Aesculapius
16. Pulcher's House
17. Flumentana Gate
18. Sublican Bridge
19. Calista's House
20. Circus Maximus
21. Temple of Ceres
22. Decius's House
23. Vicus Aesculeti
24. *Domus Publica*
25. Janiculum
26. The Labyrinth
27. Lavernalis Gate
28. Vicus Tuscus

Caelian Hill

Palatine Hill

Aventine Hill

The Tiber

Servian Wall

Via Latina

Via Appia

Via Ostiensis

Via Portuensis

Via Aurelia

Clivus Victoriae

to Campus Esquilinus →

N

SPQR XIII

THE YEAR
OF CONFUSION

1

THERE WAS NOTHING WRONG with our calendar. I didn't think so, and the Roman people didn't think so, but Caius Julius Caesar thought so. Besides, he was dictator and that was that. He was also pontifex maximus, therefore in charge of the Roman calendar, and this was one of his pet projects. When you are dictator, you can indulge your pet projects and hobbies and so forth and if anyone disputes your right to do so you can have them killed. Not that Caesar would kill people over anything so trifling. Quite the contrary. He pardoned persons eminently deserving of execution and might have lived for many more years if he had just killed a few men that I, personally, told him he needed to kill or exile. He wouldn't do it. This lack of foresight got him killed.

That was Caesar for you. Always happy to exterminate whole nations of barbarians for the glory of Rome, or, rather, for the glory of Caesar, but ever reluctant to have Roman citizens put to death, even those who had proven themselves his enemies. Instead, he pardoned those who had taken arms against him, called back exiles, and would even have restored Cato to honor and position if he had just agreed to acknowledge Caesar's primacy. When Cato so splendidly committed suicide rather than live under a Caesarian dictatorship, Caesar mourned him, and I happen to know that his grief was genuine, not a political pose—I was there.

Now back to the calendar. Caesar was master of the world, but one of the problems with conquering the world is that it tends to distract you from other tasks. One of Caesar's tasks, as pontifex maximus, was keeping our calendar in order. By this time, when he was dictator and had (though he did not know it) but a very short time to live, it was terribly out of order with the natural year. It was as if we had lost three months. We were celebrating midwinter rites in late fall. We were sacrificing the October Horse in the middle of summer. It just seemed incongruous and made us embarrassed before the gods.

Caesar's remedy to this situation was characteristically drastic. He was going to give us a whole new calendar. Not only that, but it was to be devised by *foreigners*. It was that last part that rankled the Roman public. They were used to taking instruction and orders from our priesthoods and our magistrates. To be told by a pack of Chaldeans and Egyptians how to conduct their duties toward the gods was intolerable.

Nevertheless, there were worse implications to this long-overdue reform, as I was soon to find out.

"DECIUS CAECILIUS!" CAESAR shouted. I rushed to see what he wanted. There was a time when no senator rushed in this fashion to see what another Roman wanted, but that time was past. Caesar was king in all but name. I ran.

"Caius Julius?" I said. We were in the *Domus Publica*, the house in the Forum that was his official dwelling as pontifex maximus and overseer of the Vestals.

2

"Decius, I have a momentous change in the offing. I want you to administer this matter."

"Of course, Caesar," I said, "presuming, naturally, that this isn't something likely to get me killed."

"And why should that be?" he enquired.

"Well, Caius Julius, over the many years we have known one another, you have concocted more ways to get me killed than I can readily calculate. I could start with Gaul but that would be an almost random starting-point. . . ."

"Nothing like that," he assured me. "This is just a trifling matter concerning the calendar."

"Caius Julius," I said, "the first word you used was 'momentous.' Now you use 'trifling.' I detect a certain rhetorical disjunction here."

"I merely meant that, while my reform of the calendar will be far-reaching and its effects will be felt for all time to come, its implementation is a matter of the merest routine."

That was more like it. I always like things to be as easy as possible. "What will be involved?"

"Sosigenes is supervising the project and you will be working with him."

Sosigenes was Cleopatra's court astronomer, and generally acknowledged as the most distinguished stargazer in the world. He was head of the school of astronomy at the Museum in Alexandria. By "supervising" I presumed that Caesar meant that the project was Sosigenes' from beginning to end. That was fine with me. I had known the little Greek for many years and we got along splendidly. Caesar, on the other hand, was always an unsettling man to deal with.

"I know him well. Where am I to find him?"

"I've established offices for the astronomers in the Temple of

Aesculapius. I want you to go there. Sosigenes will explain the project and you may decide whether you will require assistants to help you."

"Help me do what?"

He waved a hand airily. "Whatever needs to be done."

This did not sound good, but I could not imagine how the institution of a new calendar could be the occasion of much trouble.

I was soon to understand the poverty of my imagination.

THE TEMPLE OF AESCULAPIUS ON the Tiber Island is one of Rome's most unique places, the inevitable goal of the ailing and sightseers alike. The temple itself is beautiful and the island is uniquely disguised as a ship. I have always wondered whose idea that might have been. On the island I found a priest and asked where the astronomers were to be found.

"Those Alexandrians?" he sniffed. He wore white robes and a silver fillet around his temples. "The dictator has given them quarters at the downstream end."

"You seem to disapprove of them," I noted.

"Not just of them, but of their project. Nothing good can come of changing our ancient calendar. It is the sort of presumption that displeases the gods. It is an affront to our ancestors, who bequeathed our calendar to us."

"I see no point in it myself," I told him, "but I am not dictator, whereas Caesar is. Disputing with the master of the world is both futile and hazardous."

"I suppose so," he grumbled.

At the downstream end of the island I found that a courtyard formerly used as a venue for lectures had been converted into a small observatory, a miniature of the immense one I had seen at the

Museum in Alexandria. It had a number of those mysterious instruments necessary to the art of astronomy: long wedges of stone, blocks with curved cutouts and bronze rods, everything carved all over with cryptic symbols and calibration marks. Sosigenes had tried to explain these marvels to me, but I found the municipal sundial quite complicated enough.

The astronomers were clustered on a platform at the "stern" of the island, the part that is carved to resemble that part of a galley. I recognized Sosigenes immediately and one or two of the others looked vaguely familiar. Not all wore the usual Greek clothing. There were Persians and Arabs, and one man who wore a fringed, spirally wrapped robe that looked Babylonian. I had been in that part of the world and had seen such clothing only on old wall reliefs. I caught Sosigenes' eye and he beamed broadly.

"Senator Metellus! You do us great honor. Have you come to refresh your study of astronomy?" He flattered me by referring to my discussions with him years before in Alexandria as "study." I took his hands and exchanged the usual pleasantries.

"Actually, the dictator wishes me to work with you on implementing this new calendar. Exactly what he intends by that, I confess I cannot imagine. My ignorance of astronomy is vast, as you know."

He turned to the others. "The senator is characteristically modest. You will find that he has a sharp and subtle mind, a quick grasp of new facts, and a very superior inductive style of reasoning." Greeks are terribly prone to flattery. "Now, Senator, allow me to introduce the gentlemen with whom you will be working."

There was an old fellow called Demades who hailed from Athens, along with several other Greeks whose names I no longer remember, an Arab whose name I could not pronounce, three Persians, a Syrian, a dark-skinned fellow in a strange yellow turban who called himself Gupta and who claimed to be from India, and the man in Babylonian clothing who called himself Polasser of Kish, but who, from his looks and speech, was pure Greek. I decided to watch out for that one. In my experience, people who affect the clothing of an exotic land that is not their own are usually religious frauds of some sort.

"I really believe," I told Sosigenes, "that my true task has nothing to do with helping you with the calendar, which I could not do anyway, but rather to convince the Roman people that it will be beneficial. We are very attached to our ancient institutions, you know."

"All too well. Well, let me explain a bit." He took my arm and began to stroll among the instruments and the others followed us. Like a great many Greek philosophers, Sosigenes liked to expound while walking. This originated with the Peripatetic school of philosophy, but spread to many of the others. Among other advantages, it saved the rent of a lecture hall.

"For all of your history you Romans, along with most of the world, have been using a calendar based upon the phases of the moon."

"Naturally," I said. "It is a measuring of time observable by everyone as the moon waxes and wanes and disappears and reappears."

"Precisely. As such it is what we might call an intuitive way to measure the year, and it works after a fashion, but far from perfectly. The moon has a phase of twenty-eight days, but, alas, the year cannot be divided into a certain number of discrete twenty-eight-day segments. It is always off by a number of days because the year is 365 days long."

"Are you sure? I always thought it was some number in that area, but I could never be sure exactly how many."

"It is not easy to determine and a great deal of study went into ascertaining exactly that fact. It is now agreed by all astronomers that the year is about 365 days long."

"'About'?" I said.

He looked at the others. "Did I not say that the senator is extremely quick of apprehension?" Then, back to me, "Yes, no matter how many experiments were done, it was found that the year is never quite exactly 365 days long. It is always a few hours longer than that, about one-quarter of a day."

"So it cannot be divided evenly into any number of days at all?" I asked.

"Not with perfect precision. However, we have worked out a new calendar based upon the solar year, using the winter solstice as the beginning and ending point."

"Everyone starts the year at the beginning of January or thereabouts," I said.

"Yes, but using months of twenty-eight days, taken together with the fact that there are a few extra hours every year, means that if you use a certain number of months to the year, you always end up with a number of extra days. You Romans have made up this anomaly by having the priests give varying numbers of days to the months and by adding an extra month from time to time."

"We've found it a useful political tool," I told him. "If you have an in with the pontifexes, you can get them to extend your term in office by an extra month or two."

"Well, yes. Useful for politicians and for generals looting provinces, I am sure, but terribly inconvenient for everybody else."

"You'll find that Romans of the ruling class don't care much what inconveniences other people."

"It seems that Julius Caesar is an exception, then," he said dryly.

"I can't argue with you there, but I still fail to see how this can be an improvement. It is impossible to divide the year into an even number of months and the year in any case can't be measured to the last hour."

"That," he said, "is where subtlety and unconventional thinking are called for. You see, people have been so fixated upon the lunar phase of twenty-eight days that they have always wanted each month to contain the same number of days, even knowing that that is impossible. Upon reflection, though, there is no necessity for this. Why should a month not be twenty-nine days? Or thirty days? And why should each month have exactly the same number of days?"

"Eh?" I said brightly.

"Think about it. Why should each month have the same number of days?"

"Why, because it would be convenient, I suppose."

"Exactly. People are bound by custom and tradition and convenience. It is this sort of thinking we must avoid if we are to break new philosophical ground." Here the crowd of astronomers made approving sounds, as if he were an advocate who had just made a telling point in court. "What is far more important, for everyday convenience and for the regulation of both public and agricultural life, is that the year start and end upon exactly the same day, and have exactly the same number of months as every other year, and that each month start and end on exactly the same days each year, with no variation."

"I suppose that is logical," I said, trying to get my mind around the concept of such a year. I, like everyone else, was used to the months wandering around a bit, and never knowing exactly how many days a month would have until the pontifexes announced the number.

"Very logical," he concurred. "To that end we have devised a solar calendar based upon this concept. It consists of seven months of thirty-one days each, four of thirty days each, and a single month of twenty-eight days."

I did some quick arithmetic in my head. "All right, that adds up to 365 days, but you still have that quarter day left at the end of each year."

Sosigenes beamed triumphantly. "That is where that short month comes in. It will be the only month that does not adhere to the rule that each month have the same number of days every year. Every fourth year, it will have an extra day added, making it a twenty-nine-day month for that year."

"And this structure will be stable, from year to year?" I asked him.

"Yes, with very slight discrepancies. That quarter day I spoke of is not precisely one-quarter of a day."

"So adjustment will be necessary, from time to time?"

"Yes, but not as frequently as now. In about a thousand years it will be a few days off and require correction."

"Oh. Well, let it be somebody else's problem, then."

"For the sake of convenience and respect for tradition, the twelve months will retain their customary names, even though some of these make little sense. Your most ancient calendar had only ten months, and those months named fifth through tenth are now the seventh through twelfth months."

"True, 'December' just means 'number ten,' but we've been using the names so long that they are just sounds to us. Nobody notices the illogic."

At that moment a slave summoned us to the midday meal, which was served on tables brought out from one of the temple buildings. We sat while one of the astronomers, who was a priest of Apollo, pronounced a simple invocation and poured a libation to that beneficent deity, and we launched into an austere meal of bread, cheese, and sliced fruit. The wine was, of course, heavily watered.

"Sosigenes," I said, "something strikes me as odd here."

"What might that be?" he asked.

"The fact that the year is arranged so haphazardly. Nothing seems to be very precise or consistent. There are the seemingly random numbers involved. Why 365 days, of all things? Why not a nice, even number easily divisible by a hundred? Then, why the disparity in the very length of the day, so that you end up with a partial day at the end of each year? We expect sloppy work from our fellow men. You'd think the gods would do better work."

"This is a topic much debated," Sosigenes admitted.

"There is some belief," said the old fellow named Demades, "that human convenience is not of great concern to the gods."

"Yet," said the pseudo-Babylonian, "the cosmos seems to work according to rules of great complexity and precision, if we can just discover what those rules are."

"That is the task of philosophers," said another.

"I thought," I put in, "that philosophers were primarily concerned with the correct way to live."

"That is one field," said Demades, "but from the earliest times, philosophers have delved into the workings of the universe. Even ancient Heraclitus speculated upon these things."

"And," said the would-be Babylonian, "even in that early time, philosophers concurred that the gods who created the universe are not the childish immortals of Homer, delighting in bloodshed and seducing mortal women and forever playing pranks upon each other. The true deity is far more majestic than that."

"'Deity'?" I said. "You mean there is only one? Yet our priest here just invoked Apollo."

"What Polasser means," said Sosigenes, "is that a great many philosophers maintain that there is a single divine principal, and that what we call the gods are the various aspects of that divinity. There is neither disrespect nor illogic in honoring these aspects in the convenient guise of superior persons who take human form. Thus is worship made far more simple for mere mortals. The true deity must be of a grandeur so vast that the puny efforts of mortals to communicate with him must seem futile."

"You're getting too deep for me," I told them, "but as long as you don't insult the gods of Rome, I won't protest."

"We would never insult anyone's gods," said Demades. "After all, it is likely that all peoples honor the same deity, just in differing forms."

To tell the truth, this sort of talk always made me uncomfortable. It isn't so much that I failed to recognize the childishness of certain of our myths. It was just that, knowing how difficult it can be to understand our fellow men, it seemed presumptuous to try to understand the nature of the gods, singular or plural, and we all know how angry the gods can get at presumption on the part of mortals.

"So," I asked, "when is this new calendar supposed to go into effect?"

"On the first day of January. Of course, Caesar in his capacity as pontifex maximus will proclaim exactly which day that will be."

"Any time soon?"

"In seven days."

I almost choked on a mouthful of bread. "Seven days!" I cried when I could speak. "But January is three months away!"

"Not any more. Surely you had noticed that we are well into winter, despite the name of the month, which customarily begins the season of autumn."

"Well, the calendar has gotten shamefully out of joint. Still, what is to happen to those three months?"

11

"They will just disappear," Sosigenes said. "Caesar has abolished them. Instead, the next year will have 445 days, with three extra months inserted as Caesar shall decree. This will be a unique year and all subsequent years shall be of 365 days as described."

"Unique is the word for it, all right. This is high-handed, even for Caesar," I mused. "Just to wave his hand and say three months are not to be. Adding an extra month is one thing: it's customary; but to eliminate one, not to mention three, seems unnatural. Then to compound it with an extended year containing not one but three extra months is, well, it's radical!"

That afternoon the astronomers drew up a small calendar for me and I took it to the sign painters who painted the news and government proclamations on whitewashed boards and posted them in the Forum. I directed them to make a very large sign, twenty feet long and eight feet high, with the whole calendar written on it, showing every day of every month, with the calends, ides, and nones of each month written in red paint. This was to be raised in the Forum on the Rostra so that the whole populace could see the new calendar and understand it.

The next morning, dressed in my best toga, accompanied by my freedman Hermes and a few clients, I went to the Forum and ascended the Rostra. A crowd had already gathered, gawking at the huge calendar and wondering what it might portend. I was inordinately pleased with the thing, and pleased with myself for conceiving of such a device. The painters had outdone themselves, not merely writing the name and days of each month, but adding small figures performing the labors associated with that time of year, to make the new order more easily comprehensible. Thus little painted farmers plowed in winter and sowed in spring and harvested in the fall. Others picked and trampled grapes, soldiers built a winter camp, grain ships set sail, and slaves feasted at Saturnalia.

I raised my hands for quiet and when I got it I addressed the citizenry.

"Romans! Your pontifex maximus, Caius Julius Caesar, is pleased to announce a gift to you! It is a new calendar to replace the one which has grown so out of date. It is to commence in six days' time. As you see, it has twelve months." I gestured grandly toward the great board. "Each month will have either thirty—"

"What about Saturnalia?" someone shouted.

Barely launched into my oration, I was caught aback. "What? Who said that?"

The man who spoke was an ordinary citizen. "What about Saturnalia? If the calends of January is to be in six days, what's happened to the month of December? How are we to celebrate Saturnalia this year with no December?"

"Good question," Hermes muttered from behind me. "You should have thought of it."

"Metellus!" shouted a man who was storming up the steps of the Rostra. I knew him vaguely, a senator named Roscius. "This is an outrage! For two years I have been planning the funeral games for my father! They are to be celebrated on the ides of December! I've bought lions! I have engaged fifteen pairs of gladiators! I've made arrangements for a public banquet! How am I to do all this if December is abolished?"

"Set another date," I suggested.

"The ides of December is specified in my father's will!" His face was scarlet with fury. "Besides, December is the traditional month for funeral games."

"Next year will have a December," I assured him. "Look," I said, pointing at the board, "it's right there in the lower right corner."

"And I am to feed those lions all next year? Do you have any idea how much it costs to feed lions?"

I knew exactly how much, having put on *munera* myself, but I wasn't feeling sympathetic. The crowd began to grumble, feeling they were being cheated of a good show and a banquet. Not to mention Saturnalia.

"Citizens," I shouted. "Your pontifex maximus, Caius Julius Caesar, will have answers to all your questions."

"We'd better hope so," Hermes muttered.

"Be still!" I muttered back. Then, in my orator's voice, "In the meantime, allow me to explain the many advantages of the new calendar. Some of the months will have thirty-one days, others thirty, and a single month will have twenty-eight."

"Hold up there," said another citizen. "I pay my rent by the month. Does this mean I'll pay as much for twenty-eight days as for thirty-one? That doesn't seem fair." There was much nodding and agreeing with this.

"Oh, shut up," I said intemperately. "You've never known exactly how many days any month might have until the pontifexes announced it. You thought that was fair enough."

"Fair!" bawled an enraged voice. "Nothing about this is fair! Senator, I own five *insulae* in this city, and more of them elsewhere in Italy. What is to become of three months' rent I am owed for this year if those three months are just abolished?" He was a fat, bald man in a dingy toga. Luckily, everybody hates landlords and he was quickly shouted down, but I foresaw great trouble from that quarter. Much of the great and powerful class of *equites* depended upon rents and they would all be furious.

"You'll have an extra three months next year!" I shouted.

"Who dreamed up this abomination?" demanded Senator Roscius. "And don't tell me it was Caesar! I know him well, and he could never have conceived of anything as—as *un-Roman* as this. This thing is the work of foreigners!"

"Actually," I said amid rising grumbles, "this fine and elegant calendar was created by the astronomers of the Museum of Alexandria, by—"

"You mean," someone shouted, "this thing is being foisted upon us by *Orientals*?"

"Not all of them are eastern," I maintained stoutly. "Oh, there's a turban or two and a fellow calls himself Polasser of Kish, but mostly they're Greeks. Alexandria is a Greek city, despite being located in Egypt." I thought I was being reasonable, but I had forgotten how much the lower classes despise the Greeks. The upper classes, too, for that matter. "The distinguished Sosigenes himself—"

"I don't care if he's Alexander the buggering Great!" bawled the landlord. "Romans can't let their calendar be dictated to them by foreigners!" The crowd growled agreement, temporarily forgetting that they hated landlords.

"This is the command of your dictator!" I yelled, getting desperate.

"This isn't our Caesar's doing!" shouted a man with the look of a centurion. "It's that foreign bitch Cleopatra! She's bewitched him! Next thing, she'll be annexing Rome as part of Egypt!" This raised a truly frightening outcry from the mob. Irrationality had taken hold, and that usually meant it was time to run.

"I should have seen it," I said to Hermes. "They'll never blame anything on Caesar. They love Caesar. It has to be foreigners. It has to be Cleopatra."

"You'd better hope so," Hermes said.

"What's that?" But the truth was already dawning.

"You're the one standing in front of them. You're the one who just announced the new calendar. Maybe they'll go storm Cleopatra's house instead of coming up here to tear us apart." Cleopatra had come to visit Rome and renew her liaison with Caesar, much to the annoyance of the Roman populace and that of Caesar's wife, Calpurnia.

"Good idea," I said. "Go to the other side of the mob and raise a cry to go kill Cleopatra."

"They might do it," he said.

"Then they have a long walk ahead of them. She's taking the waters at Cumae. Caesar told me so himself." This was much to Caesar's relief. He had paid ardent court to her in Alexandria, but she was an embarrassment in Rome, where nobody would regard her as anything but his Egyptian concubine.

"They'll set fire to her house and it could spread to the whole city."

"I suppose so," I said. Romans feared fire above all else, but they were all too ready to set them when they formed a mob, regardless of the inevitable consequences. They'd burned a good part of the Forum in the riots that followed the death of Clodius. "But she's living across the river on the Janiculum. By the time they get there they'll have forgotten what they're rioting about."

So Hermes left the Rostra and made his way around the crowd and found a few idlers to bribe and soon he had the rioters off down the Vicus Tuscus toward the Forum Boarium and the Aemilian Bridge across the river.

"SO WHAT HAPPENED THEN?" JU-lia asked me over dinner that evening.

"Well, nobody was really clear exactly where Cleopatra has been staying. Some went to the Janiculum, but others hared off into the Trans-Tiber, and you know how the people over there feel about City mobs intruding on their district. Well, pretty soon there were fights all over the place and the gladiators from the Statilian school came out to join the fun. By then I don't think anyone remembered that it was all about the new calendar. At least there were no fires or killings last I heard." I dipped a duck leg into some excellent garum.

"In a way it's unfortunate that Cleopatra wasn't home," Julia mused. "That woman is a menace."

"I thought you liked Cleopatra."

I do. She's wonderful company and better educated than any woman in Rome, by far, except for Callista, and she's a Greek. I can think of no one I'd rather be with when visiting Alexandria, but here in Rome she's a disruptive influence. She has ambitions for that boy of hers that bodes very ill for the future."

The boy in question was Caesarion, who she claimed to have been fathered by Caesar, and whom Caesar himself acknowledged, but I had my doubts. Caesar was famously infertile, having sired only one daughter who had lived, out of four marriages and innumerable liaisons. Yet Cleopatra had presented him with a son, the thing he most wanted, barely nine months after meeting him, at a time when it was tremendously in her interest to do just that. She regarded Caesar as a king and a god and she believed a son would unite Rome and Egypt under her descendants. It was entirely too convenient for my skeptical taste.

"I fear you're right. The people love Caesar almost unreservedly, the 'almost' part being his connection with Cleopatra. He should pack her and the boy back to Egypt, but he indulges her and I wonder why."

"It's so unfair to poor Calpurnia!" Julia said heatedly. This was perhaps the only subject upon which she was critical of her uncle.

"Since Cornelia, his marriages have been for the sake of political alliances," I noted. Cornelia was Caesar's first wife, the one he refused to divorce when Sulla had ordered him to. "I doubt that Calpurnia's feelings carry much weight with him." Calpurnia was the daughter of Calpurnius Piso, a man of great political importance at the time.

"It is not like him to be casually cruel to a wife, though," Julia insisted. "I think he must have some important reason for tolerating Cleopatra in Rome."

"Misdirection, perhaps," I said. "Caesar is the master of that. Look at the way he sent me out to take the blame for his silly calendar, which I now perceive will be the cause of endless trouble until people get used to it."

"Oh, you exaggerate. You always do when you're inconvenienced in some little way."

"A riot is not an inconvenience."

"It was just a little riot. And how does Cleopatra constitute misdirection?"

"To the crowd Cleopatra is just a foreign queen wielding a bad influence on their beloved Caesar. Do you know what the Senate thinks about her?"

"The Senate these days is nothing but toadies and treacherous false friends who plot behind Caesar's back."

"True enough, but it is also full of old-fashioned men who smell a would-be king anytime one of their number rises above the rest, as Caesar has. Crassus showed the world that great wealth buys armies, and what is the greatest source of wealth in the world?"

"Egypt, of course," she said uncomfortably.

"Precisely. We could have taken Egypt any time in the last hundred years, but no Roman would tolerate the possibility of another Roman getting his hands on all that wealth, so we kept hands off and supported the Ptolemys as our puppets. Cleopatra is for all practical purposes the last of that line, and she has declared herself body and soul for Caesar. How do you think that makes all those old-fashioned senators feel?"

18

"The last lot who opposed him are dead and they should be thinking of that."

"They are, believe me, but the holdouts aren't all dead. Sextus Pompey is still at large, for instance. Many are talking Caesar up as a Roman pharaoh. Quietly, of course."

"He would never try to make himself king, with or without Cleopatra's fortune!" Julia said hotly.

"As it occurs, I agree. That is what I meant by misdirection. He has the Senate focused on Cleopatra when they should be paying more attention to his other activities."

Her eyes narrowed. "What do you mean?"

"This calendar is only one of his reforms. He has a great many more to institute, and some of them are huge and radical. He is going to completely rebuild the city: new forums, expanded walls, vast public works, even a permanent stone amphitheater."

"So? Such changes are long overdue. Rome is the hub of a great empire and it is little more than an Italian city-state. That needs to change."

"That's the least of it. He wants to reform the Senate as well."

"I can't say that's a bad idea either."

"He plans to bring in provincials. Not just long-time provincials like those in northern Italy and southern Gaul, but Spaniards and Gauls from his newly conquered provinces. All of them his own clients, of course, because he is the one who got the citizenship for them."

That sobered her. "So soon? I knew he had plans for them, but I had thought in a generation, perhaps two, after they have had a chance to become fully Romanized, and then just the sons of chieftains who have been his allies. Does he really plan to extend the franchise to this generation?"

"Within the next year," I told her, "and the Germans won't be far behind. Who knows what plans he has for the Parthians." At that time Caesar was about to embark upon a war with Parthia, to recover the eagles lost by Crassus at Carrhae and retrieve Roman honor in that part of the world.

"It is radical," Julia agreed, "and it won't go down well with the remaining conservatives, the Brutii and their allies."

"It won't go down well with anyone in Rome," I said, "but Caesar thinks his position as dictator makes him unassailable. I know otherwise."

"I must speak with him."

"He doesn't listen to anyone any more, not even his favorite niece. Give it a try, by all means, but don't expect results. Caesar listens only to Caesar these days."

2

THE NEXT FEW DAYS I SPENT AR-
guing or fleeing as whole delegations of aggrieved citizens came to
protest about the new calendar. At first it was businessmen, whose
rents or other income were customarily calculated by the month,
concerned about the phantom months so blithely dismissed by Caesar. Furthermore, word got about with incredible swiftness and soon
the priests of a hundred temples descended upon Rome, furious that
festivals had to be delayed or eliminated altogether, and what was I
going to do about it? Then there were the officials of towns who depended upon the crowds of celebrants who came to town for those
same festivals every year and left a great deal of money in their
passing.

Like Roscius, there were many prominent men who had planned
munera for December to honor their deceased ancestors, that being
the traditional month for such obsequies, and the commons were furious at being cheated out of these shows, which had become as popular as any of the official games.

Then there were the heirs. The law was quite strict concerning the waiting time between the death of a propertied man and the day his heirs could claim their inheritance. A good many were supposed to lay their hands upon the old man's money and property during those three missing months, and their patrimonies and all bequests were now in a state of uncertainty. Naturally, they all blamed *me*.

From a position of great esteem, I had suddenly become the most unpopular man not just in Rome, but in the whole of Italy. Naturally, I took my distress to Caesar who, just as naturally, was highly unimpressed.

"They will grow used to it," he told me. "Just wait them out."

"They won't grow used to it anytime soon," I said. "And then it will be too late for me. I am being threatened with massive lawsuits by men who believe that I have cost them a fortune."

"They cannot sue. You have broken no law."

"Since when has that meant anything to rich men faced with the prospect of growing less rich? They want to hurl me from the Tarpeian Rock then drag me on a hook down the Tiber steps! There is no greater crime than costing rich men money!"

"They'll make it all back in the next year," Caesar insisted.

"They don't understand that! Our old calendar was unwieldy and difficult to understand, but it was customary and people were used to it. Now they have to learn something new. People hate to have to learn something new."

"All too true," Caesar sighed. "A new calendar, a new constitution, a new vision of Rome and the world, people balk at these things. They must be guided by those of us who have vision."

"You're getting philosophical again," I warned. "They don't want philosophy. They want their money and their amusements. Withhold these things from them and they withhold their favor, and that is something even a dictator must avoid."

He sighed. "Send the worst cases to me. I will somehow find

time to hear their complaints and satisfy them. I have truly momentous matters demanding my attention, but I suppose I must deal with these people, if you can't."

If this last was supposed to shame me, it was one of Caesar's rare failures. I didn't care in the least if he considered me incapable. The less work he saddled me with the better, as far as I was concerned. Of course, he'd just find something else for me to do.

Senators had little rest during Caesar's dictatorship. He thought an idle Senate was a breeding ground for plotters and that senators owed Rome service in return for their privileged status. In truth, the Senate had grown disgracefully lethargic in the previous years. Except for occasional military or governing duties, both of which were expected to be profitable, few senators felt inclined to bestir themselves on behalf of the state.

With Caesar in charge, we were allowed no such lassitude. Every man who wore the senator's stripe had to be ready at all times to undertake demanding duties and to travel to any part of our empire to perform them. From overseeing repair work on the roads of Italy to curbing the behavior of a client king to planning a giant banquet for the whole citizenry, we had to be ready to carry out his orders at once. The senators didn't like it, but they also disliked the prospect of being dead, which was a distinctly likely alternative.

So I continued to press the advantages of the new calendar upon a sullen public, and Caesar was able to placate or intimidate the worst complainers. I thought the worst was over when, on the first day of the new year and the new calendar, Hermes came to me with distressing news.

"There's been a murder," he said without preamble.

"I believe there is a court to handle just such cases."

"It's a dead foreigner."

"That narrows it. Let the *praetor peregrinus* handle it."

"A dead foreign astronomer," he told me.

I knew things were going too well. "Which one?"

"Demades."

I sighed mournfully. "Well, he's too old for it to be an aggrieved husband. I don't suppose he just wandered into the wrong alley and got his throat cut for whatever was in his purse?"

"I think we'd better go look," he said.

"It's the first day of the year," I told him. "I should go sacrifice at the Temple of Janus."

"You never bothered to before," he pointed out.

"That's irrelevant. Today I'd rather sacrifice than go see some old dead Greek."

"You want to wait until Caesar orders you to?"

He was right. Caesar held those astronomers in high esteem and would take the murder of one as a personal affront. "Oh, well. I suppose I must. Who brought the news?"

He called in a slave from the Temple of Aesculapius, identifiable by the little serpent-wound staff he carried as a sign that he had permission to leave the temple enclosure. I questioned him but the man knew only that Demades was dead and he had been sent to summon me. He insisted that there was no slave gossip about the matter. I sent him back with word that I would be there soon and turned to Hermes.

"How is it possible there's no slave gossip? Slaves gossip about everything."

"Either he's keeping quiet about it, or the body was somehow discovered before the slaves found out about it and the high priest has kept anyone from seeing anything."

"That's not good," I said. "I'm hoping for a simple, casual murder. I may be disappointed. Well, I'm often disappointed, I should be used to it. Come on, let's go have a look."

So we left the house and made our way through the City and across the Forum. This being the first of January, the new magistrates would be taking office. In ordinary years, this was a rather festive occasion, but since the new officeholders were for all practical purposes Caesar's appointees, there wasn't much excitement.

We went down the Vicus Tuscus toward the river and passed the Temple of Janus, god of beginnings and endings, busy with the usual sacrifices and ceremonies of the new year. I learned that the ceremonies were rather confused since the previous year had ended so abruptly and the priests had not even had time to conclude the year-end ceremonies. I decided that it would be a bad idea to present myself at the Temple of Janus that day after all.

Then we passed the City end of the Aemilian Bridge and through a vegetable market, all but empty at that time of year, and out the Flumentana Gate in the ancient wall and up the Vicus Aesculeti along the river bank to the Fabrician Bridge and across it to the Tiber Island. The high priest of the temple came to meet us, with Sosigenes right behind him.

"Senator," the priest began, "the sacred precincts of Aesculapius have been polluted by blood! I cannot express my outrage!"

"What's so outrageous?" I asked him. "Aesculapius is the god of healing. People bleed here all the time."

"But they are not attacked and killed here!" he cried, still in high dudgeon.

"Well, there's a first time for everything, isn't there? Anyway, it wasn't one of your priests or your staff who died, so I hear. It was a foreigner."

"There is some solace in that," he agreed.

"Senator," said Sosigenes, "my friend, Demades, whom you know, is the victim."

"So I understand. Please accept my condolences. Now, if you

would be so good, please lead me to the murder site. I wish to view the body."

So we walked down toward the "stern" of the island, where I had first met the astronomers in conclave. There we found a little group of men clustered around a recumbent body, which had been decently covered with a white sheet. Most of the men were astronomers, but I recognized some who were not, including a senator whose presence surprised me: Cassius Longinus.

"I didn't expect to find you here, Cassius," I said.

"Hello, Decius Caecilius," he said. "I take it Caesar has appointed you to investigate this matter?"

"I came before he had the chance." I had known Cassius for some time. We were on friendly terms, though we had never been close. He detested the dictatorship of Caesar and made no attempt to hide it. "What brings you here to the Island?" I asked him. "No illness in the family, I hope?"

"No, as a matter of fact I came here this morning to consult with Polasser of Kish." He nodded toward the man in Babylonian attire, who bowed back. "He is the most distinguished astrologer now in Rome and has been casting a horoscope for me." I caught the faint expression of derision on the face of Sosigenes. He considered the whole Babylonian astrology business to be fraudulent.

I squatted by the body. "A good thing Demades wasn't your astrologer. Has the purification been performed?"

"It has," Sosigenes said. "There are priests here qualified to purify the dead."

"Makes sense," I said. "People do tend to die here. Hermes, remove this shroud." He grimaced with distaste, but complied. For such a bloody-minded wretch, Hermes was finicky about touching the dead.

Poor old Demades was not looking his best, which is often true of the dead. He was all but unmarked, but his head lay at an odd angle. Somehow, his neck had been cleanly snapped. I could see no other wound, and he had the waxy pallor of one who has been dead for several hours.

"Hermes," I said, "go get Asklepiodes. He should be in town." Hermes hurried off, eager as always to visit the gladiatorial school where my old physician friend lived. There was something about that broken neck that bothered me.

"Might this have been an accident?" I said.

"A fall severe enough to have broken his neck should have left him badly bloodied." Cassius said. He gestured around us. "And there's no place to fall from around here. I suppose a strong wrestler could have done it easily enough." Although still young, Cassius had seen enough slaughter not to be disturbed by a common murder. He had seen an entire Roman army exterminated at Carrhae and had barely escaped with his life. "What do you think, Archelaus?" He addressed thus a man who stood near him, a tall, saturnine specimen whose dress and grooming were Roman despite his Greek name.

"I've seen necks broken that way with the edge of a shield, and once in Ephesus I saw a *pankration* where a man broke his opponent's neck with a blow from the edge of the hand." He spoke of the roughest of all the Greek unarmed combative sports, in which the fighters are permitted to kick, gouge, and bite.

"Decius," Cassius said, "this is Archelaus, a grandson of Nicomedes of Bithynia. He is here in Rome on a diplomatic mission on behalf of Parthia."

I took the man's hand. "Good luck. Caesar has every intention of resuming the war with Parthia." The man's status was clear to me now. He was a nobleman of a Roman province that had been an independent kingdom under his grandfather. The king of Parthia would not wish to send a deputation of his countrymen, who would be treated with hostility in Rome, so he sent a professional diplomat instead, one conversant with Roman customs. I had known others like him.

"I have every hope of effecting a reconciliation," he said, his expression belying his words. Rome did not forgive a military defeat, and a humiliation like Carrhae could not be wiped out with words and treaties. Rather than speak of this hopeless subject I turned back to Cassius.

"I wouldn't have taken you for a follower of the astrologers." Cassius was as old-fashioned a Roman as you could ask for, and among our class we believed the gods spoke in lightning and thunder and the flight of birds and the entrails of sacrificial animals. Astrology and other forms of fortune-telling were the province of bored, high-born ladies.

He looked sheepish, an oddity on his scarred, craggy face. "Actually, this is not for me. A certain high-placed Roman who must remain nameless sent me to consult with Polasser of Kish."

"Not—" but I knew better than to pronounce the name. It made a sort of sense. Caesar believed all sorts of odd things and he was obsessed by what he thought of as his destiny. He wanted to put Alexander in the shade and he wanted assurance of that from the gods. Sometimes, he came dangerously close to counting himself among their number.

"Why have you sent for this Asklepiodes?" Archelaus wanted to know.

"He is the foremost authority in the world on wounds," I told him. "I am hoping he can enlighten me on how this man met his death." I hadn't given up on the hope that it might prove to be an accident. It would make my life so much simpler. By now all the other astronomers had assembled around the corpse of their colleague and I addressed them. "Does anyone here know if Demades had an enemy or anyone with ill will toward him?"

To my surprise, the yellow-turbanned Indian cleared his throat. "I know of no one who bore him personal enmity, Senator," he said, speaking Greek in an odd, singsong accent, "but he was rather vehement in his denunciations of the astrologers, of whom there are a number here."

"This was a mere academic dispute," Sosigenes objected. "If scholars settled their arguments with violence there would be none left in the world. We argue endlessly about our own fields of study."

"I've known men to murder one another for the most trifling of reasons," I informed them. "I have been charged with this case and I may wish to question each of you separately or severally. Please do not be offended if I ask that you all stay where I can find you. I should take it very ill should anyone be seized with a need to visit Alexandria or Antioch. I should hate to have to dispatch a naval vessel to fetch you back at public expense."

"I assure you, Senator," said Sosigenes, "no one here has anything to hide."

"If only I had a denarius for every time I've heard that assurance," I muttered.

"Did you say something, Senator?" Sosigenes asked.

"Just that I am so glad to know that nobody here could be responsible."

"Decius," Cassius said, "I have other things to attend to. If I may borrow Polasser for a short while, I will leave you to your duties."

"By all means," I told him. The three men went off together and I returned my attention to the corpse. Shortly after this, Asklepiodes arrived on a litter accompanied as always by his silent Egyptian servants. Hermes walked behind the litter. The little Greek took me by the hands, smiling broadly.

"A lovely day for a murder, is it not?" he said. Over the years he had become increasingly morbid. I suppose his calling demanded it.

"But is it a murder?" I asked. "It is for this very reason I've asked for your help once more. I cannot for the life of me figure out how this man came by his death."

"Well, let's have a look at him." He examined the dead man for a while. "Poor Demades. I knew him slightly. We attended some of the same affairs and lectures." This came as no surprise. The members of Rome's small Greek intellectual community all knew each other.

"When you saw him did he mention enemies or any particular fears he might have had?" I asked.

"No. He scarcely spoke at all and when he did it was of astronomical matters. These people are very tightly focused and take little note of anything outside their particular field of study. He would take offense if someone asked him to cast a horoscope and complained that few understood the distinction between astronomy and astrology."

"Yes, I understand that to be the source of raging controversy hereabouts. Do you think he may have met with an accidental death?" I asked hopefully.

He gestured for his servants to turn the body over. He examined the back of the neck and felt the severed bones, frowning. At last he straightened. "I do not think it was an accident, but I must confess the nature of this injury has me mystified. I have never seen anything quite like it." This must have been a painful admission for Asklepiodes, who seemed to know everything about the human body and how it might be injured.

I told him of the speculations of Cassius and Archelaus. "Do you think there might be anything to that? Might the murderer be a professional lurking at the Statilian school?"

He shook his head. "A wrestler's hands would have left distinctive marks on the neck. Likewise, a shield edge would have marked the back of the neck. As to the blow with the edge of the hand"—he wafted his own hand in a gesture of uncertainty—"I think not. It is more plausible than the other two, but the displacement of the vertebrae in this case is of a different nature. Somehow the vertebrae just below the skull have been offset from right to left. These small marks"—he touched two roundish red marks above the break, and two identical marks below it—"I have never seen anything like them. I fear I must ponder this for a while."

"Please do. Caesar is going to be terribly vexed that someone has done away with one of his pet astronomers. Do you think there is anything further to be learned from the corpse?"

"The only evidence is the injury to the spinal cord, and now I have seen that, there is no further need for examination."

"Then I will turn him over to his companions." I turned to Sosigenes, who still stood by with a few of the Alexandrians and Greeks. "Will you undertake his rites?"

"Of course. He has no family here, so we will perform the ceremonies and cremation today. I shall have his ashes sent to his family in Alexandria."

"Very well then." I cast a last look at the late astronomer. "Why couldn't you have been killed in some routine fashion?" I asked him. Sensibly, he remained silent on the matter.

THAT EVENING I DESCRIBED THE day's events to Julia.

"It was probably a foreigner," she said.

"Why?"

"Romans kill each other all the time, but they use the simplest means: a sword or dagger, a club, something crude and basic. Women sometimes employ poison. You've investigated scores of murders. How often were you unable to understand how the victim had died?"

"Only a few times, and usually that was because I was overlooking something obvious. If an expert like Asklepiodes is stymied, what hope have I?"

"None," she said succinctly. "So for the moment you must forget about how and apply yourself to why. Why would someone want to kill a man like Demades, who from all appearances was a harmless astronomer?"

"That's exactly what I have been asking myself. By the way, there was another curious matter on the island this morning." I told her about Cassius and his odd errand and his diplomat friend.

"I do not understand why Caesar lets that man run around loose," she said. "He is rabidly anti-Caesarian and does not care who knows it." One of the few faults she would acknowledge in her uncle was his misplaced leniency.

"Maybe he'd rather have his enemies right where he can see them, not behind him professing friendship while they sharpen their knives for him."

"Perhaps so, but the men he has pardoned and called back from exile! Any other man would have had the lot of them executed."

"Maybe he wants a reputation for kinglike clemency."

"Now you're talking like them," Julia said ominously. "They're always saying Caesar wants to make himself king of Rome. They even interpret his mercy toward themselves as evidence of royal ambition."

"Well, I for one don't think he wants to be king," I assured her. "He's already dictator of Rome, and that makes him more powerful than any king in the world."

Even so, Caesar's power was not absolute. After conquering Gaul he had crushed his Roman enemies one after the other at Thapsus and Munda and many other, less famous fights. Nevertheless, there were still old Pompeians at large, some of them with considerable forces at their disposal.

"I think it strange that Caesar is so determined to prosecute this war with Parthia while so much is still unfinished at home," I said. "I know he wants to take back the eagles that were captured at Carrhae, but there is no rush about that. Yet when Caesar speaks of war he is always serious."

"Always," she acknowledged. "So what does this Archelaus hope to accomplish?"

"Maybe nothing," I said. "He is being paid to undertake this mission. Whether or not it succeeds, his pay is the same." I left unsaid my own suspicions about Caesar and his ambitions. The reputation of Alexander the Great had lain over the heads of ambitious military men for almost three hundred years. Each of them longed to surpass Alexander, and Alexander's conquests had been in the east, not the west. What was conquering Gaul compared to conquering Persia? And Parthia was the inheritor of the Persian Empire. If Caesar could conquer his way into India, then his empire would extend from the Pillars of Hercules to the Ganges and he would have outconquered Alexander the Great. His would be the new reputation for would-be conquerors to best.

Without a doubt, Caesar planned to establish a reputation at which rivals could only despair.

THE NEXT MORNING I CONFRONTED the man himself in his new Basilica Julia, which was to outshine all the other great buildings of Rome. Caesar looked an unlikely

Alexander that morning. The Macedonian boy-king had accomplished his feats while very young. The years of war had aged Caesar terribly, and he was not all that young to begin with. I suppose he was about fifty-five that year and he looked older than that. I had seen Crassus just before he set out for Parthia, and the old moneybags had looked half dead. Caesar had lost none of his energy nor any of his mental acumen, but I did not think him fit for the rigors of campaigning. Oh, well, Caesar had surprised us before. Maybe he could still do it, or perhaps he would sit sensibly in Antioch and leave the actual fighting to his fire-eating subordinates like Marcus Antonius. He could let Cleopatra levy troops for him, not that Egyptians are good for much. He intended to accomplish it all somehow.

"How was my astronomer killed, Decius?" he asked bluntly.

"And a gracious good morning to you, Caius Julius," I said, nettled. "I am working at that very question. He seemed a harmless old drudge, hardly worth killing, and his neck was broken in some mysterious fashion."

"Yes, Cassius mentioned it. I want to know who killed him, Decius, and why. I want to know all about this very soon."

"You seem to be taking it to heart," I noted.

"He was working on the new calendar. That is my project, Decius, and whoever killed him was indirectly attacking me."

How like Caesar. "You don't think it might have been personal, then?" I said. "Perhaps a jealous lover or husband?"

"Would it matter?" he said, and I suppose to him it did not. The slightest shadow cast upon the personal *dignitas* of Caesar, inadvertent or not, was not to be tolerated.

"That calendar is no more popular than it was a week ago," I told him.

"They will get used to it," he assured me. "Soon something else will come along to distract the public."

"Let us hope so." At that time, Caesar was rapt in admiration for his new building, and indeed it was magnificent. The vast, vaulted ceiling soared high overhead. I had never believed that an interior space could be so high. I had toured some of the immense buildings of Egypt but even in their mind-numbing hugeness they always felt cramped inside with their forests of squat columns and they were dark and gloomy. This building was spacious and bright, illuminated by its generous clerestory. Its walls were faced with colorful, costly marble, its metalwork was gilded, its entrances unprecedentedly wide, and its porches capacious. All this magnificence was his gift to the people of Rome for their public use. All he wanted in return was that they should worship him even more than they already did.

I went out into the City with only Hermes attending me. During my years of office holding, I had usually been accompanied by dozens or even hundreds of supporters, and I had never liked it. I much preferred to roam about by myself or with only one or two attendants. Julia thought this was very unworthy of me, that a Roman of importance should have a following. She never convinced me. Besides my personal convenience, it was not a good time to be showing off too much importance. Important men were dying in great numbers during those years. My years of public importance were behind me. I was a humble private citizen though a member of the Senate and that was how I liked it. I had salted away enough of a fortune to live comfortably and I needed no more: no more wealth, no more offices, no more honors.

I did, however, need to keep on Caesar's good side, so I set about my investigation with vigor. That is to say, I put Hermes to work.

"Go to the home of last year's *praetor peregrinus*," I instructed him. "Find his secretary and learn if Demades ever came before his court, or any of the other astronomers Caesar brought from Alexandria, in any capacity whatsoever."

"I'll give it a try," he said, "but don't get your hopes up. Last year the courts were pretty chaotic, what with praetors out of Italy commanding armies for or against Caesar. I doubt the *praetor peregrinus* spent more than a month or two in Rome."

"Still, it's a possibility. Maybe Demades had an argument with a citizen. I need to find some sort of motive in his death."

"What will you be doing?"

"I'm going to visit Callista."

"Will that sit well with Julia?" he said dubiously.

"Julia and Callista are great friends," I told him.

"What difference does that make?" he said.

"Run along and see what you can find out," I said, shutting off discussion.

I turned my own steps toward Callista's house in the trans-Tiber district. Callista was a teacher of philosophy and a leading light of Rome's Greek intellectual community. This made her a great curiosity in Rome where women were rarely teachers, though they were quite common in Alexandria. She was also one of the most beautiful women in Rome, which may have been why Hermes thought Julia might be suspicious. Of course, I was only answering the call of duty—and on behalf of her beloved uncle—so she had no cause for complaint.

The truth was, I seldom needed much of an excuse to call upon Callista. Besides her great beauty she was gracious and astoundingly intelligent. Though it pains me to say it, I had been involved with so many bad women that it was a great pleasure to have dealings with a good one.

Her beauteous housekeeper, Echo, led me inside the house, where Callista sat by her pool. When I was announced she looked up with genuine delight. Callista never faked her affections and would have considered such a thing philosophically unworthy. She lacked the capacity for any sort of deceit, a very un-Greek quality, in my estimation.

"Senator Metellus! This is a pleasure and an honor. You haven't called upon me in far too long!"

"The service of Rome has kept me too busy," I said pompously. "Besides, the intellectual quality of your company intimidates me. Cicero is more on your level."

"You are too modest. And how is Julia? I haven't seen her in at least a month."

"She is quite well and I am sure that she will call soon," I said. As soon as she found out that I had been here. They were friends, but there are limits.

"And how may I be of service?" She gestured me to a chair by a little table and she sat across from me while servants brought refreshments.

"I am investigating a murder at the particular behest of Caesar, and since the victim may have been among your circle of acquaintances, I thought you might be able to tell me something about him."

"A murder? And it was someone I know?" She was genuinely shocked.

"You may have known him. Demades, one of the astronomers who has been working with Sosigenes on the new calendar. Asklepiodes told me that he was sometimes to be seen at gatherings of the Greek philosophical community, so I immediately thought of your salon."

"Poor Demades! Yes, I knew him, although not very well, I confess. For a philosopher he was not very loquacious."

"Asklepiodes has attested to his reticence."

"And he was interested in little except astronomy."

"Again, exactly what Asklepiodes told me."

"Of course the subject of astronomy comes up from time to time at my gatherings, but there is far more discourse on other subjects. He took little part in those discussions."

"Could you tell me when you last saw him?"

"Let me see, it was the evening of the last day of the year just ended. He had more to say because the new calendar was about to go into effect. There were several of the astronomers present at that meeting."

"Do you recall which ones?"

"Sosigenes, of course. Some of them were foreigners, which surprised me. There was a pseudo-Babylonian who argued for the merits of astrology, and an Arab who knew a great many things about the stars unfamiliar to me, and a fascinating man from India who spoke for a long time on the transmigration of souls. Marcus Brutus found this enthralling, because he has been studying the philosophy of Pythagoras, whose theories involve just such metamorphoses."

"Brutus was there? He was here the first time I called upon you, years ago."

"Oh, yes. He has attended nearly every meeting since he returned to Rome."

Brutus was another of those enemies of Caesar who had been unaccountably recalled from exile. Caesar treated the whole thing as a boyish lapse of judgment. He always showed a great affection for Brutus, whom I only saw as a rather tedious drudge. Perhaps it was because of Caesar's old liaison with Servilia, Brutus's mother. There were even rumors that Caesar had fathered Brutus, but I never credited these. In any case, Brutus had philosophical pretensions and was often to be found at such gatherings.

"What other Romans were present?" I asked. "It might help to know with whom he mingled in his final days."

"Do you think this might be relevant?"

"One never knows. Sometimes a murder is casual, as when a thug stabs a victim to make it easier to lift his purse. Other times the murder is hired and a professional takes care of it. In neither case would my question be to the point, but I have found that in most cases the killer was someone known to the victim, very often a spouse or close relative. You see, there must be close emotional attachment for one to feel betrayal severely enough to kill. Or the killing is the result of a business dealing gone bad, or of someone impatient for an inheritance. In all those cases there is some close connection between murderer and victim. The idea is to discover what the nature of the connection might be."

Her eyes sparkled. "This is so fascinating! I have said before that you should organize your theories of detection into a study and write them down. You could found your own unique school of philosophy."

"'Detection'?" I asked. "It's a good word, but I fear that nobody else's mind works like mine. Such a study would be a dismal failure, and philosophers would consider the study of evil or aberrant behavior to be unworthy. They like to concentrate upon the sublime."

"I wouldn't be so sure. Nobody thought like any philosopher until the philosophers began to propound, and then they changed the ways people thought. And physicians study the illnesses and injuries of the body, so why not the workings of evil in the human mind and the behavior that results from it?"

Now that I think of it, I suppose that may be exactly what I have been doing these last few years as I idle away my time under the reign of the First Citizen. I have no gift for writing philosophical tracts, however, and instead inscribe these memoirs of my adventures during those dying years of the Republic.

"I shall consider it. Now, do you remember any other Romans present that evening?"

"Let me see. Brutus's wife, Porcia, was with him, still dressed in mourning for her father." Porcia was the daughter of Cato, who had committed suicide at Utica rather than endure the rule of Caesar. I never envied Cato anything save the manner and nobility of his death.

"Lucius Cinna was there, though I believe he came only because he was visiting with Brutus. He had never been here before and took little part in the discussion."

Cinna was another recalled exile. He was the brother of Caesar's first wife, Cornelia. That was another Caesarian connection, but could easily be a coincidence. Caesar had been married at least four times that I knew about, and had a whole horde of noble relatives. Almost any gathering of the senatorial class would have a few of them.

She named a few others, but they were persons of no consequence, just the usual equestrians who took up philosophy instead of politics. Then something struck her.

"Wait a moment. There was another Cinna there."

"One of Lucius's brothers or uncles? Which one?" The Cornelii were about the only patrician family that was very numerous. The others had dwindled and most had become extinct. Somehow the Cornelians retained their ancestral vigor.

"This wasn't a relative. He just had the same cognomen. Somebody remarked upon it."

I tried to remember other men of that name. "Was it Cinna the poet?" He had just taken office as Tribune of the Plebs, but in a dictatorship he was all but powerless.

"Yes! Brutus seems to think rather highly of him, but I confess that much of Latin poetry escapes me. I am well studied only in the Greek."

"He's a nobody as far as I know. Just another climber beginning a political career. He's not one of the patrician Cornelii. I don't even know his praenomen or nomen. Do you recall them?"

She shook her head. "He was introduced only as 'Cinna.'"

"Did he take much part in the talk?"

"We spoke of poetry for a while and he and Brutus expounded rather well upon the verses of Cato." She referred not to Cato the senator but Cato the poet of Verona, who taught the eminent poet Catullus, who in turn is not to be confused with the one-ell Catulus who was Caesar's colleague as consul. Sometimes I think half our problems are caused by our repetition of names.

"And when the astronomers began to argue over the relative merits of astronomy and astrology he weighed in vociferously in favor of astrology. He used some poetic metaphor to demonstrate that astrology is wonderfully poetic, whereas astronomy is coldly rational."

"Which do you favor?" I asked her for no good reason except that I loved to hear her talk and did not wish our interview to end.

"Would that I were learned in both. Most often I am inclined toward astronomy, because it is indeed coldly rational. Like your own specialty of detection, it is based upon observable phenomena. Philosophers like Sosigenes go out every clear night and make observations of the stars and planets. They track their movements, note their risings and settings and watch for the occasional spectacles such as meteors and comets. These they set in context and thereby seek natural explanations for their nature and behavior, eschewing the supernatural.

"Yet, I cannot deny the emotional appeal of astrology. It is in some strange fashion intensely satisfying, being able to read a human being's destiny in the arrangement of the stars at his birth and the movements of the planets and the moon through them in all subsequent life. It is irrational, but rationality is only a part of human existence. Philosophers must keep their minds open to all possibilities, so it may be that Sosigenes and the astronomers are wrong and the astrologers are right, or even that the truth lies between the two. The syllogism is a useful analytical tool, but it is a great mistake to take it for reality."

"You echo my very own thoughts on the matter," I said, wondering what in the world a syllogism might be. As if in response, Echo the housekeeper appeared. I almost made a witty remark upon this, but wisely held my tongue. I was in the presence of one to whom my sharpest wit would appear oafish.

I had never known Echo to be other than as dignified and gracious as her mistress, but her eyes sparkled and she seemed breathless, as if she had just come from a tryst with a lover, an unlikely thing so early in the day. "My lady, the dictator Caesar has come to call upon you." That explained it. Caesar had that effect on women of whatever station. That, and being the most powerful man in the world, could turn any slave woman's head. Free women too, for that matter.

Callista, imperturbable as always, acted as if this were an everyday occurrence. "Show him in, Echo, and see to the comfort of his lictors."

Caesar swept in and on his arm was none other than Servilia, mother of Marcus Brutus. I wondered if Caesar was reigniting their old flame. Servilia was a few years older than Caesar, but she looked many years younger, and still one of Rome's great beauties.

Callista stood, as did I. "Dictator, you do me too much honor. Lady Servilia, it has been too long."

Servilia embraced her lightly and they exchanged a social kiss on the cheek. "You must have had an interesting morning," Servilia said. "Here we find you with Rome's most eccentric senator." I wasn't sure how to take this. The Senate contained some genuine lunatics.

"Decius Caecilius is a remarkable investigator," Caesar said. "So what if his methods are unorthodox? He is looking into the death of a Greek scholar and I'll wager that is what brought him here." Very little escaped Caesar.

"I find that the senator has the most penetrating intellect in Rome," Callista said, "save only for your own." This was the highest possible praise, for Callista never stooped to flattery. Caesar acknowledged it with a slight inclination of his regal head. The gesture was made more impressive by the gilded laurel wreath he wore, to hide his baldness. He was not without his vanities.

"Decius Caecilius," Caesar said, "you have duties and I will not detain you."

I know when to take a hint. I took my leave of Callista and Servilia and Caesar and went outside. Caesar's twenty-four lictors crowded Callista's little courtyard sipping wine from small, tasteful cups, trying not to ogle the surpassingly beautiful girls who served them. Like Fausta, Fulvia, and Clodia, Callista had only beautiful servants, and all of Callista's were women or young girls. Whereas with the others it was a matter of sensuality, with Callista it was a matter of pure Greek aesthetics. She would not have ugliness around her. Despite this concentration of pulchritude, there had never been a hint of scandal or unseemly behavior from her household.

I went to a lictor named Flavius, who had been one of my own lictors during my praetorship. "What brings Caesar across the river?" I asked him.

"Now, Senator, you know we are forbidden to discuss our magistrate's affairs."

"Not even a bit of gossip?" I wheedled.

"It would mean my hide on the curia door if I talked," he said, taking a sip. "Not that there's anything to talk about," he amended hastily.

I gave it up for a bad job and left. I had a lot to think about.

3

HERMES FOUND ME AT THE TAV-
ern beside the old bathhouse just off the Forum, the one favored by
senators. The hour was still rather early, but a number of senators
were already fortifying themselves for their afternoon baths with
some of the tavern's excellent wine to accompany the specialty of
the house, fried squid with a sauce compounded of garum, pepper,
and mysterious ingredients known only to the old cook.

Hermes came in and sat and selected a neat, crisp-fried ring
from the great heap of them on my plate and dipped it in the bowl of
sauce and proceeded to chew ecstatically. The cook insisted that
the squid and sauce must be kept separate lest the former become
soggy and the flavor of the latter diluted. Any man, however highly
placed, who simply poured the sauce over the squid would quickly
find himself served sour wine and rancid fish.

"Do make sure you've had enough to eat before you render
your report," I said. "As always, your comfort is my highest goal."

He ignored my sarcasm, as usual. "The *praetor peregrinus* the last two months of last year was Aulus Sabinus. The first was Publius Hirtus but he was killed at Thapsus."

"On whose side?"

"Caesar's." He took another piece of squid and signaled the server for a cup. "Sabinus was appointed by Caesar personally."

"One of the advantages of being dictator," I noted, "is that you don't have to observe the niceties of formal elections."

He shrugged. "Rome needs praetors, and who would campaign for a praetorship of just two months?"

"It would have been at least five if Caesar hadn't dropped his new calendar on us. Anyway, what did you learn?"

"Only that there was never a shade of a chance of anyone bringing suit against any of those astronomers. I talked to Junius, the praetor's secretary last year. It seems that the astronomers are here as Caesar's personal guests and he stands in the position of *hospes* to them. That means that in court—"

"I know what their legal status means," I said, grabbing myself some squid while there was still any left. "In court, Caesar would be their personal representative. Imagine bringing suit against someone defended by a man who is not only one of Rome's greatest lawyers but dictator to boot."

"Your prospects would be pretty weak," he said, watching as a server filled his cup from the pitcher that stood on the table.

"Was there any court gossip about any difficulties concerning the foreigners?"

He frowned into his cup. "There was one man who wanted to sue one of them, but it wasn't Demades, it was Polasser of Kish, the fake Babylonian."

"Oh? What was the man's grievance?"

"He claimed that Polasser had sold him a fraudulent horoscope, one that encouraged him to invest heavily in grain futures.

Last year's harvest was huge despite the wars and Caesar got the Egyptian crop practically free from Cleopatra and the price of grain plummeted. The man lost a fortune. Sabinus told him who he was up against and said that he got off lightly, and he didn't want his court time wasted by a gullible fool. The man slunk off like a whipped dog. That was all I could find concerning the astronomers."

"Did you get the name of the man Polasser duped?" Hermes nodded. "Good. It's not much, but I may wish to talk with him."

"So what have you found out?" he asked. At one time this might have seemed presumptuous but I had long since learned that if he was to be of any use to me he had to know everything I did about an investigation we were working on together. I gave him an account of my talk with Callista.

"You didn't get much more than me," he said, "except that you got to enjoy Callista's company and sit in a house that contains some of the most beautiful women in Rome." He sipped and pondered, a habit he had learned from me. "I just can't see how the doings of a bunch of boring old philosophers can have anything to do with something serious, like murder."

"It's a puzzle," I admitted.

"It does seem that Caesar turns up everyplace."

"So he does, but he's involved in everything that goes on in Rome in a way that no other man is. He wants to be Caesar the Great but he may end up being remembered as Caesar the Ubiquitous. War, the law, religion, the calendar, huge building projects, he's into everything."

"Don't forget women," Hermes said. "Cleopatra, Servilia, there must be a dozen others. How can one old man be so busy?"

"He's not that much older than I am," I grumbled, "but then, I'm not trying to make myself the greatest man in history before I croak. That's the sort of thing that ages a man."

"Odd about the two Cinnas," he said, "and Cassius turned up at the murder scene."

I shrugged. "They're all part of Caesar's circle of close companions: Cinna, Cassius, Brutus, Servilia—it's not unlikely that where you find one you find them all. Cassius hinted that the horoscope was for Caesar."

"Why does Caesar make confidants of his enemies like Brutus and Cassius and Cinna when you've always been his friend and he treats you like an errand boy?"

"Julia had the same question. Right now, I'd just as soon not be a close friend of Caesar."

From the tavern, full of squid and our heads buzzing pleasantly with the wine, we went to the bathhouse. It was one of my favorites, though there were finer ones in Rome by that time. I did not pick it idly that day. It was a great favorite with the Senate generally, and I was looking for one senator in particular. He was seldom to be found at home. He spent most of his time prowling for inside information, useful intelligence, and gossip. I had little liking for him, but he was a fount of information on the doings of the highest people, the ranker the better. I was looking for Sallustius Crispus.

As I had expected, he was there, lolling in the hot bath. I undressed and joined him while Hermes went off to take the cold plunge in the *frigidarium*, an austerity I had never favored, but which gladiator lore insisted was essential for good muscle tone.

"Decius Caecilius!" Sallustius said with a broad, insinuating grin. He always managed to look like he knew all your guiltiest secrets. There was no doubt that he knew some of mine. A few years previously the censor Appius Claudius and his colleague had expelled Sallustius from the Senate for immorality in their general housecleaning. He was accused of a staggering list of transgressions and insisted that he was guilty of no more than half of them. He weaseled his way into Caesar's good graces and was soon back in the Senate.

"Good day, Sallustius," I said, settling into the water beside him.

"Aren't you looking into the death of that Greek?" he said. Naturally he knew about it.

"Among the other duties on my busy schedule. Speaking of which, what has Caesar got you doing?"

"I am to go to Africa as governor," he said. "It is perfect, because Catilina was governor there, and I'll be able to interview the people who knew him then." He fancied himself a historian and had been working for years on his history of the Catilinarian conspiracy. The thought of Sallustius governing a province was appalling, but he'd probably be no worse than Catilina.

"Congratulations. I'm sure you'll find your province both interesting and lucrative."

"So I hope. You rarely seek my company unless you're looking for information, Decius."

"What a coincidence. I've noticed the same thing about you."

He grinned again. "Trade?"

"First let's see if you have anything to trade." I told him most of what I knew already. There was little sense in trying to withhold information from Sallustius. The fact that I was asking would pique his interest and he would soon weasel out everything anyway. I even mentioned the fool who tried to bring suit against Polasser. He leaned back against the rim of the great pool and gazed at the ceiling. Around us other men, many senators, the rest mostly wealthy *equites*, relaxed or splashed about, gossiping and making business or political deals. They ignored us.

"I may have something for you," he said at length. "If you think my information valuable, I would like very much to know more about Caesar's doings back at the beginning of the war in Gaul, when you were his secretary."

"Actually, I was a cavalry commander," I informed him. "I only worked in the *praetorium* when I was being punished for insubordination and Caesar wanted to protect me from being killed by his other officers."

"Still, you've seen him at one of the most significant stages of his life at a proximity few can boast, and you were writing down his thoughts. You are what I call a valuable source."

"A new book?"

"I've finished my study of the Jugurthine War and I'm almost done with my Catilina. What greater subject can I have for my next book than the life of Rome's greatest man?"

"Greater than Scipio or Horatius or the first Brutus?" I asked.

"I meant the greatest man of our time, but I suspect that he will be greater than all of them together. Who else has accomplished as much?"

"There are many who dislike what he's accomplished," I noted.

"What of that? The resentments of lesser men are of no consequence. Do we remember those who resented Alexander or Philip? What of the enemies of Pericles? Only when peers struggle, as Achilles with Agamemnon, do we care. Otherwise, only greatness is worthy of notice."

"I suppose that is true; you're the historian. All right. If you can be of any help to me, I'll inform you about anything Caesar won't kill me for telling."

"Who can ask for more than that? Very well, then. Who would you think are Rome's most enthusiastic adherents of the cult of astrology?"

I thought about it for a while. "I know of few men who care for it. Most of those I have known who give it much credence are high-born women."

"Precisely. The wives of senators and great *equites* are almost uniformly bored and they are barred by custom from most male amusements like gladiator fights and politics. So they relieve their tedium by taking up foreign fads. If they involve religion or mysticism, so much the better. The great mystery cults such as the Eleusinian and the Delphic require foreign travel, but there are plenty of practitioners here in Rome to keep them amused. Astrology in particular has been all the rage in recent years."

"Has Polasser of Kish or any of Caesar's other pets been among their idols?"

"Let's draw back and look at this from a certain distance. We'll get down to details later."

I took a deep breath and settled down in the water. Sallustius had a habit of circuitous discourse, but he usually got to the point eventually, and when he did you realized that none of what had gone before was extraneous. He could be an infuriating person, but he had an incisive mind and a fine way of organizing information.

"This fad for astrology has been active in Rome for some time. There have been many practitioners hustling among our bored ladies. What is required to unite these women into something resembling a cult is a really highborn woman who is a part of their circle and has a wonderful knowledge of the subject."

I ran the list through my mind and came up with nothing. Sallustius was watching me, smirking knowingly and then I realized I was wrong in considering only Roman women. "Cleopatra!"

His eyebrows went up. "You are quick, I confess it. Yes, despite their resentments of her foreignness and her seductive wiles, Rome's women are fascinated with the Queen of Egypt. The common rabble think she is a native Egyptian, but of course she is actually Greek, and well-born Greeks are respectable."

"Actually she's Macedonian, but that's close enough. I hadn't considered it. For such an intelligent and educated woman, she is crazed by every form of mysticism imaginable. And I've visited that temple in Egypt that has the zodiac set into the ceiling. Astrology made its way from Babylonia to Egypt centuries ago."

"So for many months now Cleopatra and her Roman friends have been having stargazing parties at her house out on the Janiculum. Her astrologers are always on hand to deliver nebulous pronouncements, advise the ladies on their love lives and their husbands' careers, and what the future holds for their children."

"And are some of these astrologers among the calendar crowd on the island?"

"Ah, here is my boy Apollo with some refreshment!" His "boy" Apollo was perhaps the ugliest old man in Rome, a lifelong retainer of the Sallustius family who, according to long rumor, had as a youth been incredibly handsome, hence his name. Whatever his history, he carried wine not in a skin, but in an enormous bottle of green glass that was worth a fortune. The cups he carried were of fine hammered gold and he poured us each a cup. It was wonderful Caecuban.

"Sallustius, with your love of fine things, why do you have that ugly old man dogging your steps?"

"Decius, there are some things better even than beauty. Loyalty is one of them."

"Profoundly true. You were about to tell me about those astrologers."

"No, I was about to ask you a question."

"I was afraid of that, but for the sake of wine this good, I'll be patient."

"Every social circle has a leader at its center. Which Roman lady do you think has been the most enthusiastic about astrology and who first broke the ice and took her friends to Cleopatra despite their initial resentment of that exotic queen?"

"You're not going to tell me that it was Calpurnia, are you?"

"I am a historian, not a fabulist. Who is the second most unlikely?" It was just his annoying Socratic method.

It struck me. "Not Servilia!"

"Servilia, indeed. Back several years ago, when she was trying to win back Caesar's affections, she consulted with every crackpot, lunatic, fraudulent witch, fortune-teller, and mystic in Rome. As you know well, Rome abounds with such people. If I were one inclined to gossip," he assumed a look of comical innocence, "I might tell you that she engaged in some practices with these people that might lay her open to some very severe punishments, were they to come to light."

I examined the fine gold cup and speculated about the sources of Sallustius's wealth, but said nothing.

"So she was able to set aside her understandable resentment toward the latest lady to acquire the ever-migrating affections of the great man?"

"So it would seem. It might have been calculation but I prefer to attribute it to greatness of soul."

"Who could doubt it? Now, I will grant you I doubt that Demades was involved in these convivial explorations of the gods' plans. He was, after all, of the anti-astrology party, if I may so term it. Were any of the pro-astrology party present? Polasser, for instance, or the Arab or the Indian?"

"Oh, but you are wrong. Demades was there at many of the meetings. As to the others, I confess ignorance."

"Why would the rationalist Demades take part in these mystic gatherings, when he evinced great hostility toward such things?"

"My friend Decius," he said, grinning, "I can only present you with the facts available to me. It is your special art to make sense of these things."

"And so I shall, in time," I assured him, rising to go.

"But wait. You agreed to an exchange of information," he protested.

"I agreed on the proviso that your information should prove useful to my investigation. That is yet to be proven. Should I decide in the affirmative, rest assured that you shall have your interview concerning Caesar in Gaul."

"You are a legalistic hair-splitter, Decius," he said.

"It's my heritage," I told him. "We Metelli are all great lawyers."

Outside I found Hermes and told him what I had learned. I was unsure about the value of Sallustius's information. The presence of Servilia had come as a jolt, but I probably would have discovered it eventually as Cleopatra was among the persons I had intended to interrogate. The astronomers were, after all, her own gift to Caesar, for his calendar project. Unfortunately she was out of Rome and one didn't summon a queen to come back to the City to answer the questions of a lowly senator. And I wasn't about to demand that Caesar call her back.

"Who next, then?" Hermes asked me.

I thought about this for a while. Then it came to me. "You know, I have a source very close to home. We are talking about great patrician ladies here. I think I'll wander home and talk to Julia."

"But she'll learn that you went to visit Callista without her."

I sighed. "She'll find out anyway. She probably knows already."

Indeed, I detected a certain frostiness in Julia the moment I crossed my threshold.

"You've been to see Callista," she said, coolly. She didn't fool me.

"Indeed I have, and at the instructions of your uncle the dictator. In fact, I ran into him at Callista's."

For once Julia was thrown off-balance. "Just a moment. Caesar ordered you to go there?"

"As good as. Who better to ask concerning a Greek philosopher, eh?"

"And Caesar went with you?"

"Actually, I was already there when he arrived with Servilia."

"Servilia?" She put a hand to her brow and held the other up for silence. "I know you are trying to confuse me. Come sit down and just tell me what you've been up to."

This was what I was hoping for. As long as I could lay out the facts in an orderly fashion, she would have to acknowledge that I had behaved in a logical and blameless fashion. At least, I hoped so. And, as I had also hoped, the mention of Servilia appearing on Caesar's arm distracted her from all lesser matters.

"Servilia! This sounds ominous."

"How so?" I asked. "It's bad news for Calpurnia, but when has Caesar ever worried about the sentiments of his wives? Except for Cornelia, that is. He does seem to have had a certain affection for her."

"It could mean that he intends to adopt Brutus as his heir."

This hadn't occurred to me. "Well, he must adopt soon, I suppose. He's never had a son that lived except for Caesarion, and no Roman is going to accept the son of an Egyptian queen as Caesar's heir."

"Certainly not. Caesarion is a charming boy, but a bit of a mongrel. Brutus is at least a patrician. Of course, there is Caius Octavius, Caesar's great-nephew. He shows promise but he is awfully young."

"I think we make too much of this patrician business," I said.

"You would, being plebeian," she said. "But at least your family is one of the noblest of the old plebeian names. I think half of my uncle's cronies are men who hope to be his adopted heir, or want it for their sons."

"Like Servilia," I said.

"Like Servilia."

"And speaking of those great ladies, Egyptian and Roman, let me tell you what I learned from Sallustius." So I gave her that story. "You are far more conversant with the great ladies of Rome than I. Have you heard about any of this?"

She sat quietly for a while, marshaling her thoughts and memories. It was a process I knew better than to interrupt. "A good many of the ladies of my circle are interested in astrology. I am myself, but a few are besotted with the subject and constantly consult with supposed experts concerning the most trivial aspects of their lives. I believe most of these practitioners to be frauds, but some are true scholars. And who is more likely to be a true scholar than one who practices at the Museum in Alexandria?"

"But Demades was not a believer, yet he was present at several of the affairs attended by Servilia and her crowd at the house of Cleopatra. Any thoughts about that?"

"Not just yet, but I can see that it's been far too long since I called on Servilia. Now that things seem to be warming between her and Caesar, what could be more natural than a visit?"

"Excellent idea. What do you know of Brutus? I know him only slightly. I see him in the Senate and I occasionally run into him at dinners, but he has never appealed to me as a companion."

"Too philosophical?"

"That, partly. I've heard he's a bit of a money grubber. Not a very patrician quality, is it?"

"I only know what I've heard. A few years ago he is supposed to have lent a vast sum to the island of Cyprus so they could settle their tax debt, and they couldn't pay on time."

"Hardly surprising at, what was it? Two hundred percent interest or something of the sort?"

"I don't think it was that bad, but pretty steep."

"I also heard he used a Roman army to collect. I call that misuse of a public resource."

"What set you thinking along these lines?" she asked.

"I'm just trying to picture what sort of person he would be as Caesar's heir. Yes, by all means do pay a call upon Servilia. Make sure you get everything she knows about the astronomers, not just Polasser and the astrologers, but all of them."

"I shall do exactly that," she said, "and I'll call on Callista, too."

I knew that was coming.

The next day I went to the Tiber Island and sought out Sosigenes. I found him in his study, doing some sort of calculation on papyrus with dividers and instruments so arcane I didn't want to ask him about them.

"Old friend," I said, "we need to talk."

"By all means," he said. We went out to a little terrace off his study and he sent servants for refreshments. We sat for a while and I enjoyed the vista. From this spot we had a fine view of the low, massive bulk of the Circus Maximus just across the Forum Boarium, and towering above it the magnificent Temple of Ceres. The refreshments came, we sipped and nibbled, then I got down to business.

"Sosigenes, I've learned that some of your astronomers are very popular with the fashionable ladies of Rome."

He sighed. "You already know my opinion of astrology. Unfortunately, far too few Romans share my skepticism. This is especially true of the ladies."

"So I've learned. The most prominent among these are now intimates of your queen."

He nodded. "I have never been able to persuade her majesty that she is wasting her time, but it is at worst harmless, I suppose."

"Far from it," I told him.

"Eh? What do you mean?" Like so many great scholars, Sosigenes dwelled in a world other than our own, a world of knowledge and scholarship that he thought to be above the petty affairs of men. In Alexandria he lived in the middle of a palace complex and did not realize what evil places they can be.

"Nothing that involves the highborn people of Rome can be termed harmless," I informed him. "And that goes for the women. This is a place where politics is played for the highest stakes. At any gathering of great Roman ladies, you will find a number who will happily kill to advance the fortunes of their husbands or sons."

"But, how can this concern us?"

"Did you know that, periodically, the aediles or censors expel all fortune-tellers from Rome?"

"I was unaware of this. Why?"

"Because they can influence politics here in Rome. It isn't just bored noblewomen. The common people of Rome are passionately devoted to all sorts of fortune-telling. They are easy prey for any kind of fraud and if one of those persons predicts a particular outcome to an election or prophesies when a great person is going to die, it can affect public matters in unpredictable ways."

"Yet you have your official augurs and haruspices. You take the omens for every sort of official business."

"Precisely. Our augurs are public officials, but they, and the haruspices, emphatically do not predict the future. All they can pronounce upon is the will of the gods at *that particular moment*. The gods, of course, are free to change their minds. That calls for further omen taking. That's the way we like it, with supernatural matters under competent official control. We don't like unpredictable factors, like fortune-tellers, even if they are learned stargazers from Alexandria."

"You are telling me that some of my colleagues may have embroiled themselves, however innocently, in Rome's political intrigues?"

"I knew that a man of your acumen would understand. I am still puzzled by the role of Demades in all this because he was of the rationalist faction."

"I wish I could help you there but I am just as puzzled as you. Polasser or Gupta or the Arab (he used the unpronounceable name), certainly. This is their art. But Demades was as unlikely as I to take part in these affairs. We were colleagues, but not confidants."

"Sosigenes," I said, "as much as I esteem you and your company, I think that it would be best if you and your friends were to leave Rome. Caesar may seem to have things under control, but that is far from the truth. There are all manner of intrigues and plots under way, and should you get entangled in them you will have little hope, being foreigners. The calendar is done. Why not just take your leave and return to the far more congenial milieu of the Museum?"

He sighed and made a Greek gesture of the hands and shoulders. "Personally, I would be most happy to go, but the choice is not mine. It lies with my queen and Caesar. We are here at their behest, and we will go only with their leave."

"Why are they keeping you around?" I asked him.

"I do not know. At the moment we are continuing projects begun in Egypt, where the conditions for observing are better than here. We give lectures, or, a few of us, indulge in the activities that you have described."

It seemed to make little sense, yet the great people of Rome tended to behave in senseless ways sometimes. I knew men who bought tremendously expensive and skilled architects, and then never built anything. Many owned impressively skilled slaves and never made use of them. It was a way of showing off their wealth and importance, that they could waste money in such an extravagant fashion. I supposed that keeping a gaggle of philosophers around doing nothing of importance was the same sort of foolishness.

"Well, you—" at that point we were distracted by a high-pitched shriek from somewhere toward the southern tip of the island. Moments later the high priest came running.

"Senator! There has been another murder! I will stand for no more of this!"

I got to my feet. "Yes, the serenity of your sanctuary has been taking a bit of a beating lately, hasn't it? Who's dead? Oh, well, let's just go look. I like surprises."

The Tiber Island has many little terraces like the one where Sosigenes and I had been enjoying the view before the rude interruption. On one of these, just below the temple on the City side, not far from the bridge, we found another corpse, seemingly fresh this time and not decently covered. Most of the little crowd staring down at it were astronomers. The Arab was there, and Gupta the Indian, turban off and long hair streaming, and quite a number of Greeks.

"Where's Polasser?" I asked. "Oh, that's him there on the ground, isn't it?" Indeed it was the fake Babylonian, lying peacefully if somewhat grotesquely with his neck broken. "What a pity."

"You sound saddened, Senator," said the high priest.

"This eliminates him as a suspect in the murder of Demades, and he was the one I thought the most likely. Oh, well, I should have known better than to think this job would be easy. Who found him?"

"My chamber is just over there," Gupta said, pointing to a row of doorways a few dozen steps away set into the base of the temple.

He babbled nervously, his Greek almost incoherent. "I was meditating, as I always do at this hour. I heard a strangled cry that seemed unnatural and I threw on a robe to come see what it was." Strangely, he blushed. "I fear I am not decent." He took a long, yellow band from inside his robe and with incredible swiftness and efficiency would it around his head, completely covering his long hair.

"Men of Gupta's sect are forbidden to cut their hair," Sosigenes explained. "When meditating, they remove their turbans, robes, and sandals and wear only white cotton loincloths. They think it indecent to go out in public with their hair uncovered."

"Well, I know of stranger customs. How did everybody get here so fast?"

"Most of us, great lord," said the Arab, "have quarters nearby. But in fact Polasser sent a servant to summon us here, saying that he had news of import that concerned us all. Some of us were already on our way."

"Well, he's not going to deliver this news. Where is the servant?" They looked around, then at each other. There was much shrugging. "Had anyone seen this servant before?" More shrugs.

"Why was I not sent for?" Sosigenes demanded.

"Maybe he was going to say bad things about you," I hazarded. "I want a search made for this servant." I turned to the priest. "Can you take care of that? Get a description from these gentlemen, but round up any servant-looking person on the island who cannot be accounted for."

"I will do so, Senator," he said with ill grace, but of course, an hour later no such person had been found.

Before noon I was in front of Caesar in the *Domus Publica*, his residence in the Forum in his capacity as pontifex maximus. "Things are getting out of hand. At this rate you'll be completely out of astronomers soon."

"They do seem to suffer a high mortality rate. Have you any suspects?"

"My best one is dead. I have a few leads I am following."

"What sort of leads?"

I knew better than to mention Servilia and her coterie of star enthusiasts. There were some matters one did not bring up to Caesar without a pile of corroborating evidence. He was a sensitive man about some things, things touching his personal life being high on the list.

"I hesitate to bring them up without further investigation," I told him.

"Well, I have little time for suppositions and wild guesses. Come back when you have evidence worthy of a trial. And make sure that it is soon."

I took my leave of Caesar with great relief. He was an uncomfortable man to be around in those days and it was a bad idea to displease him. I wandered out into the Forum and amused myself for a while looking at the many monuments to the old heroes. There were Romulus and Numa, Severus, Horatius, Cincinattus and Curtius and Marcellus and Regulus. It seemed to me that they had lived in better, simpler times when choices were plain and simple.

This is probably an idle conceit, doubtless their lives seemed as complex and frustrating to them as my own did to me. They must have engaged in plots and intrigues as devious as any practiced in the time of Caesar. I had known nothing all my life but the greed and grasping of great men who wished to be greater than they already were. No doubt it had been the same in the time of Rome's old heroes.

Before long Hermes found me with news.

"Cleopatra's back in Rome. She moved back into her house last night."

I smiled. "Let's call upon the lady, then."

4

Since the first citizen took absolute power by defeating Cleopatra and Antonius at Actium, it has been fashionable for his flatterers to blacken her reputation. It is always safe to portray Cleopatra as a heartless Oriental temptress who seduced Antonius into rebellion against Rome. But I have no interest in flattering the First Citizen, and now I am too old to care what he thinks.

In truth, Cleopatra was no worse than other rulers of the time and a good deal better than most of them. If she was ruthless, all rulers have to be. It is an inescapable fact of history that the worst rulers are not the cruel ones but the weak ones. The former may oppress some of their subjects, but the latter bring disaster to all. Cleopatra was firm, but I never knew her to be needlessly cruel. In her liaisons, first with Caesar and later with Antonius, she always tried to make the best possible deal she could arrange for Egypt, not just for herself and her family. She was a realist and she knew that Rome was the future. Egypt's only hope lay in a favorable treaty with Rome.

Her house in the Trans-Tiber district was a sprawling mansion of no particular floor plan that had once housed the Egyptian embassy. Years before it had been home to a wonderful old degenerate named Lisas, who had thrown the finest parties Rome had ever seen. Alas, Lisas had made the classic error of getting involved in local politics, including a few ill-advised murders, and he had been forced to commit suicide. The fat old pervert had been a good friend for all that and I missed him.

Cleopatra kept considerable estate in her Roman residence, since she made it her policy to entertain the highest society. Invitations to her affairs were sought-after, especially among the *equites*, but she was too alien ever to become truly popular. She had expanded the already lavish pile of architecture and had imported statues from Egypt. She had widened and deepened the crocodile pool and stocked it with hippos, the first ever seen in Rome. In this she miscalculated. She should have played up her Greek ancestry and culture instead of Egyptian exoticism, but she truly believed that in this way she could make Egyptian customs seem less foreign to Rome.

A guard of black spearmen and Libyans armed with enormous swords stood before her door and bowed as we went inside. In the courtyard a chorus of beautiful boys and girls sang us a welcome apparently composed for visiting senators. Slave girls armed with sprigs of hyssop dipped them in bowls of perfumed water and sprinkled us with fragrant drops. More slaves washed our hands and feet and as we went into the house yet more servants flocked to us with trays of delicacies and cups of astoundingly fine wine. I decided I would have to come here more often.

Cleopatra received us in what can best be described as a throne room, although no such facility would have been tolerated in Rome. Nonetheless, it was a very large room with a very large chair elevated on a lavish dais. Cleopatra sat in the sumptuous chair in a suspiciously pharaonic pose, lacking only the crown, crook, and flail. When she saw us she smiled brightly and skipped down from the dais. She seemed genuinely delighted.

"Senator Metellus!" she cried. "Why haven't you been to see me sooner?" I had known Cleopatra at various stages of her career as a little girl, a headstrong young woman, a desperate fugitive, and a fearsome queen. In all of them she outshone her contemporaries the way Caesar outshone his peers.

"Caesar keeps me too busy to get away from the City very often," I told her.

"My husband is a demanding man, I fear." She always referred to Caesar as her husband, despite the fact that he had a wife in Rome. In Egypt, Caesar did not disdain the title, but she was something of an embarrassment at home.

"I wish this were a social call," I told her, "but something very serious has happened and I need to speak to you about it."

"Is Caesar safe?" she said, concerned.

"Healthy as a Thracian," I told her. "No, there have been murders on the Tiber Island. Two of your astronomers have been killed."

"Not Sosigenes?" she said. The old man was one of her favorites.

"No, Demades and Polasser."

"Oh." She sounded relieved. "I knew them, but not very well." She made no false pretence of sorrow. She had seen so many killed, including her own siblings, that it took the death of someone truly close to move her to mourning. "Please come with me. We can talk more comfortably by the pool."

"Not the one with the hippos in it?" I asked. The huge, boisterous beasts sprayed water and less savory fluids everywhere.

"Oh, no. I have far more tranquil pools. This one is perfect for intimate conversation."

She led us to a pool that could have floated a trireme, surrounded by a veritable forest of palms, myrrh shrubs and other exotic vegetation. Among the bushes, tiny black people of a type unfamiliar to me rushed about, shooting miniature arrows at hares. In the water beautiful naked nymphs swam about, singing hymns to obscure river gods while on the island a handsome youth attired as Orpheus played upon the lyre.

"The very soul of intimacy, indeed," I commended. She reclined on the cushions of a sort of half couch, a type I had seen in Alexandria, similar to a dining couch but made for only one person. Hermes and I sat in more conventional chairs. Slaves armed with fly whisks kept us free of vermin.

Cleopatra was about twenty-five years old at this time, and at the height of her beauty, which was not all that great. She could not compare with the great beauties of Rome, such as Fausta and Fulvia, but what she lacked in symmetry of feature she made up for in the sort of radiance that seems to come naturally to people who have a special relationship with the gods. In Egypt she *was* a god, but that is just a sort of political formality in some barbarian countries. Kings and queens in those places get old and die just like other mortals.

"Your majesty," I began formally, "in recent days Demades and Polasser were found with their necks broken in a singular fashion—"

"What was singular about it?" she asked.

"It is an injury so odd that even the distinguished Asklepiodes cannot figure out how it was done, and I thought he knew every possible way to kill somebody."

"How interesting," she said. "Far be it from me to be morbid, but it is pleasing to know that somebody has brought a little originality to something as commonplace as murder."

"Ah, yes, I daresay. Anyway, Caesar is understandably upset.

These men were in Rome at his invitation, working on a project very dear to him. He is taking this matter personally."

"Well that's bad news for somebody. Look at what happens to people who cross my husband."

"Precisely. So I am trying to settle this matter as expeditiously as possible. Now, we have two victims. Both were astronomers but aside from that they were opposites. One was a Greek rationalist, the other a pseudo-oriental mystic. For whatever reason, Polasser chose a Babylonian persona, probably because gullible persons consider the Babylonians to be masters of the astrological arts."

"They are," she said.

"How would you rate Polasser as an astrologer?" I asked her. It had not been a question much on my mind, but it struck me now. There had seemed to me to be something distinctly *off* about the man. It was not just that I considered starry forecasts to be fraudulent any-way, or that his foreign pose was absurd. I had known many perfectly agreeable frauds in my life, some of them delightful persons.

She considered it for a while. "Let me put it this way: He was a competent astronomer, or he would not have been in the company of Sosigenes and the others, employed upon a project as important as the new calendar. He could perform observations and calcula-tions as well as anyone. But astrology is different. Calculations are only a part of it. A truly great astrologer must have inspiration. His art partakes of prophecy."

"And how deeply did Polasser partake?" I asked.

"He was what I would term a social astrologer. His art was cast-ing horoscopes for wealthy people and trimming them to reveal what his patrons wanted to hear."

"Yet you give credence to this art," I pointed out.

"Certainly. The success of a fraudulent practitioner does not invalidate the art. During my years as a princess with my future always uncertain and precarious, I consulted with many astrologers; Egyptians, Greeks, even a few genuine Babylonians. Some were like Polasser, interested in ingratiating themselves with me or, more often, with my father or my brother or sisters, all of whom were far more powerful and with better prospects than I. But there were others whose calculations were careful, who did not deal in flattery and who predicted for me much sorrow, tragedy, and an early death."

"Surely you don't believe that last part," I said.

"Oh, but I do. It is only to be expected. I have already outlived the rest of my family. It is unworthy of a queen to desire more years than the gods have decreed for her."

"Admirably philosophic," I told her. "Now, I have heard that you have held parties in this house for many of the great ladies of Rome."

"As many as I could get to come," she said.

"And that both victims attended some of these get-togethers."

She frowned slightly. "They may have. I confess I don't remember. There are often more than a hundred guests at my parties and they bring along their servants and so these are very crowded affairs. Since my guests are of widely varying tastes, I bring in many sorts of people to entertain them, from philosophers to actors. I have poets, charioteers, dancers, even funeral-fighters. I usually invite Sosigenes and the others since there are so many who are curious about the stars."

"So while they may have been here, they were not the reason for any of your social occasions?"

"What do you mean?"

"I've heard that the great lady Servilia has been—" at that moment a tiny arrow whizzed by, just before my eyes, nicking the tip of my nose in passing. I jerked my head around and saw one of the tiny black men looking wide-eyed. Then he disappeared in the brush.

Cleopatra leapt from her couch. "You! Come back here!" She grabbed a whip from a slave who was standing by, apparently just in case his mistress should need a whip. She dashed after the little hunter, flailing away with the whip, making leaves fly. In an instant she was lost to sight but we could hear sounds of vigorous pursuit and her choked shouts of rage.

"Your nose is bleeding," Hermes said.

"Of course it's bleeding. That little bugger almost shot it off with an arrow." I dabbed at the wound with a napkin and came away with a sizable bloodstain. Within seconds a physician came hustling, followed by slaves who carried his instruments, medications, and bandages. He blotted at my nose with a stinging astringent and soon the blood stopped, although I felt as if my nose had been stung by a hornet.

Cleopatra came back sweating, her hair in disarray and tangled with leaves and bits of vine. "The little wretch got away. I'll have him crucified as soon as I catch him."

"Nothing that serious," I said. "My barber cuts me more severely with great frequency, and I usually don't even have him flogged."

"He might have killed you! How would that have looked, a senator murdered in my house? And with an arrow?" A flock of girls busied themselves with restoring her appearance, straightening her clothes, brushing her hair, repairing her cosmetics.

"Creative homicide is enjoying something of a revival here in Rome these days," I said. "What are those people, some sort of pygmies?" The race of tiny men were long rumored to live somewhere near the headwaters of the Nile, where they fought battles with cranes and other large birds. At least, that was what they did on wall paintings.

"I think so. A dealer came down the river a few years ago with more than a hundred of them. It became fashionable to provide them with a little forest to hunt in. I never thought they might endanger my guests. I do apologize."

"Think nothing of it. So many people have tried to kill me that it's a pleasure to be attacked by someone so exotic. He was probably shooting at a bird or a monkey and failed to pay attention to what else was in the way."

Her maid Charmian came into the courtyard. "My queen, the ambassador of King Hyrcanus of Judea has come to call."

"That scoundrel," she said. "Hyrcanus, I mean, not the ambassador, who is more agreeable than most diplomats. Senator, I fear I must take my leave. I do hope that arrow wasn't poisoned."

"I hope so even more fervently," I assured her. "I will need to come back and continue our conversation."

"Please do. I always enjoy your company."

As we left through the atrium I saw the ambassador and his entourage waiting. With them was Archelaus, the ambassador from Parthia. I nodded to them in passing.

"That's one time too many we've seen that man," I said to Hermes as we left the house. I touched my nose gingerly. The small wound had scabbed over.

"Ambassadors are always in one another's company," Hermes said. "It's probably just a coincidence."

"Maybe I'm just being overly suspicious. Getting shot by a pygmy is enough to unnerve a man."

"That was Cleopatra's doing," Hermes said.

"What!" I all but shouted, turning to face him. "What do you mean?"

"That one was lurking close by the whole time you were talking, not running around with the others. Cleopatra gave him a hand-sign"—he moved his hand from the wrist, waving his fingers subtly,—"and he shot."

I couldn't believe it, but I knew better than to think that Hermes would speak idly. He had been a slave, and slaves learn early how to read their master's little unspoken signals. If he had seen Cleopatra make that gesture, then she had made it.

"Well, obviously she didn't want me killed," I said.

"Unless the arrow really was poisoned. How are you feeling?"

"She just wanted to distract me. What were we talking about?" The incident had come as such a shock that I had actually forgotten.

"You'd just brought up Servilia's name."

"So that's what she doesn't want to talk about. It could be for a number of reasons. For one, if Caesar really has taken back up with Servilia, it could be a very sore point with Cleopatra." I rubbed my nose again. "Still, this seems a bit extreme, just to avoid an unpleasant subject."

"She may be planning to kill Servilia."

"That would be a good reason to want to avoid talking about her," I agreed. "Or maybe the two of them are up to something together." We walked toward the Sublician Bridge and the City proper. "I wish Caesar wasn't so addicted to dangerous women."

"It's a fault you've shown from time to time," he pointed out.

"Don't remind me."

Before reaching the bridge we called at the Statilian *ludus*, where some of Italy's best gladiators trained. Some claimed that the Campanian schools were better, and they certainly had a longer history, but the old Statilian school turned out fighters as fine as any I ever saw. We went to the hospital and found Asklepiodes standing behind a seated trainee.

"Ah, Senator, come in," he said. "Look at this." We stepped close and I saw that he had drawn little circles on the back of the young man's neck corresponding to the red marks we had seen on the backs of the two victims' necks. "Observe, we have two marks

71

to the left of the spinal column, two corresponding marks some-what lower to the right side. Now look." He placed the two first knuckles of each hand against the circles. The correspondence was perfect.

"Were their necks broken with a two-fisted punch?" I asked him. "I've never seen such a blow."

"I think not. It would be a stunning blow, but it would just knock the man forward. I cannot see how it could apply enough le-verage to make the vertebrae shear and dislocate in such a way. I've had the pugilism instructors here and questioned them about it. They say the same thing. Such a blow could break a neck only un-der freakish circumstances, and your murderer accomplished the feat twice in a row. No, we are dealing here with a deadly art of which I was utterly unaware."

"Perhaps when we've solved this business you'll get a good philosophical paper out of it."

"I intend to," the little Greek said. "It will make me the envy of many of my colleagues. We so seldom come across something new in the methodology of killing."

"There are others like you?" I asked.

"Oh, certainly. Just as some physicians specialize in particu-lar diseases and conditions, there are a few of us who specialize in deadly violence and its effects upon the human body. Polygonus of Caria, for instance, and Timonides the Paphlagonian. We are a small but enthusiastic body of scholars."

"And I thank the gods that we have you," I assured him.

"There must have been some means of applying leverage," he said.

"Eh? What do you mean?"

"There must have been something to immobilize the neck while pressure was brought to bear from the rear. It is the only thing that makes any sense. I would suspect a garotte, but there were no ligature marks on their necks."

"It is a puzzle," I agreed. "Keep working on it. Oh, I wished to ask you about something. You may have noticed the somewhat damaged condition of my nose."

"I had taken note of your disfigurement, but thought it indiscreet to inquire."

"Well, nothing particularly embarrassing about it. But it was caused by an arrow."

"We don't see many such injuries here in Rome," he said.

"Indeed. I was just wondering, is there any way to tell if an arrow was poisoned?"

"Surely. If it was poisoned you will die a lingering and horribly painful death."

"But short of that?" I asked.

"I would not worry about it. Arrows are rarely poisoned, though everybody seems to think they always are. Poison would cause immediate inflammation and I see none in your majestic proboscis."

"Excellent," I said, relieved.

Of course, it was the first thing Julia noticed when I got home. "You've been fighting again!" she accused as we walked in.

"Nothing of the sort. I am the victim this time." I threw off my toga and a servant caught it expertly.

"So what happened?"

"A pygmy shot me in the nose with an arrow."

She glared for a while. "Please show me enough respect to make up a better lie than that." So I had to give her the whole story and she was mollified. She never apologized for naming me a liar, though. We went to the triclinium and reclined while dinner was laid out. Hermes went off on some errand of his own.

A slave brought in the family *lares* and I performed a perfunctory libation. Then I took a cup, tore off a hunk of bread, dipped it in garlic-flavored oil and talked between bites and swallows. "Did you pay a visit to Servilia?"

"Oh, yes. She acted as if she had been expecting me. You'd think she was suspicious."

"She has reason to be. How did it go?"

"To begin with, I was far from the only lady there. A woman as prominent as Servilia has flocks of callers."

"Were there any notable names among them?" I asked, grabbing a handful of oil-cured olives.

"Fulvia was there, loaded with scandalous gossip."

"Well, she's the one to have it, being more than a bit scandalous herself." The flamboyant Fulvia had been married to my old enemy Clodius, who was killed by my friend Milo, then she married Curio who had died fighting for Caesar in Africa. Recently she had married Marcus Antonius and was pushing his career as fiercely as she had those of her first two husbands. Julia named a few other prominent women.

"That sounds promising," I said. "What was all the talk about?"

"The usual things. We had to listen to Servilia praising her son Brutus as the very paragon of Roman virtue. Fulvia described Antonius's endowments in embarrassing detail. Several complained of the inconvenience the new calendar is causing them. They blame you."

"Naturally. Anything germane to my investigation?" I pulled a plate of baked fish closer.

"Not at first, but then I am more subtle than you. I don't reveal my intentions by diving straight into my subject of inquiry."

"Very sensible," I said, "and when in your circuitous fashion you finally got around to that subject, what did you learn?"

"You are trying to rush me," she said, plucking grapes and

popping them into her mouth one by one. "I dislike it when you rush me."

It was going to be one of those times. "At your own speed, then."

"That's better." She pushed the heap of grapes aside and picked up a dish of cherries and cream. Julia adored cherries and had a slave whose principal work was to remove their pits, a tedious and exacting task. She began to eat them with a golden spoon that had been a gift from Caesar.

"Atia arrived after the morning sacrifice at the Temple of Venus Genetrix. She had young Octavius with her. The air grew noticeably frosty. Servilia considers Octavius a rival for Caesar's inheritance, of course."

"Either way it's a stretch," I observed. "Octavius is a great-nephew, Brutus barely a relation at all. There's no real reason he should adopt either of them. He could as well adopt me." I caught her look. "Don't even think it."

She sighed. "It would never happen. For one thing, you aren't ambitious. Caesar will adopt only someone ambitious. Brutus is ambitious, or at least Servilia is ambitious for him. Octavius is quiet but very deep. He's spent a lot of time with Caesar lately."

I barely knew Octavius and had only seen him a few times, from a distance. He was just another young man beginning his career and there were hundreds like him. I couldn't keep track of them all. "Why was Atia there, since the two women detest one another?"

She ate another spoonful of cherries. "I'd thought you would have guessed by now."

"You're being—" then the light dawned. "Atia wants a horoscope cast for Octavius?"

"And who better to go to for advice than Servilia?"

"What is to stop Servilia from giving her bad advice?" I asked.

"She wouldn't dare in front of all those women of their circle.

Someone would be sure to tattle to Atia. That would put the tattler in a good position should Octavius prove to be the heir." These women had a system of politics as complicated and cutthroat as that of the Senate.

"So there were two women at the gathering, each hoping to be in possession of Caesar's heir."

"Three," she corrected. "Don't forget Fulvia."

"Ah, yes. How could I forget?" Marcus Antonius was yet another with eyes on the glorious inheritance. In Gaul, he had been Caesar's right-hand man, supplanting the formidable Titus Labienus, who had turned against Caesar in the civil war. When Caesar was made dictator he named Antonius his Master of Horse, second in command and enforcer. In Roman public life of the day, Antonius was a character out of Plautus: a soldier-buffoon who had himself carried about in a lavish litter while slaves carried his golden drinking vessels before him on purple pillows like holy cult objects. Caesar had forced him to give up his foolishness for a while, but he kept lapsing. Despite his many faults it was almost impossible to dislike Antonius. He was the eternal boy-man. We loved the boy and feared the man.

"I heard Antonius and Caesar have fallen out lately," I said. "Caesar won't be taking him to Parthia."

"They've fallen out before, but they always patch it up," Julia observed, having finally finished the bowl of cherries. "I don't know why Caesar keeps him around. The Antonii are a family of hereditary criminals."

"That describes most of the senatorial class," I reminded her. "The Claudii, for instance."

"Yes, but the Antonii are truly egregious. They've done everything but loot the treasury and rape all the Vestals."

"I don't have much hope for the treasury once Caesar leaves Rome," I told her. "I've heard Antonius is to be prefect of the city."

She rolled her eyes upward in a dramatic gesture. "We should move all our goods out of Rome. Once he's run through the treasury he'll start looting the best houses. The lifestyle he and Fulvia favor requires vast wealth."

"Oh, I don't know. I've always got on well with Antonius. I've helped him out of a few scrapes from time to time."

"I have a feeling any loyalty of which he is capable will fade as his money dwindles. He'll suddenly remember he has an old grudge against you."

"Well, he's done nothing yet and Caesar probably won't leave the city until next year. A lot can happen between now and then. They may have a more serious disagreement and Caesar could exile Antonius. Or Antonius may die, or Caesar may die, or some German king we've never heard of could forge a grand alliance of the tribes and invade Italy. That's for the future. My problem exists in the present. So what sort of advice, good or bad, did Servilia give Fulvia?"

"You know, it might not be such a bad idea to get your horoscope done, dear. You have a future, and it always pays to be prepared."

"Eh?" I said brightly.

"Well, Servilia said that now that Polasser of Kish is dead, the one to consult is a woman called Ashthuva."

"I never heard such a name. Where is she from?"

"Nobody is certain, but it's someplace far to the east."

"Naturally. You never look westward for one of these stargazers. She's probably some Greek freedwoman who's adopted an exotic persona, just like Polasser. I still don't see why—" I am not totally dense, and it came to me. "You invited yourself along, didn't you? You're going to accompany Atia to see this Artooshvula person."

"It's Ashthuva. And yes, I am going. So is Servilia. She is to make the introductions."

"I don't like it, but you may learn something. Anyone else going with you? Fulvia, perchance?"

"I would never go anywhere with Fulvia," she said. "She's scandalous. Servilia is merely ruthless and Atia is as respectable as you could wish."

"Why should I wish her to be respectable? Respectable women are boring, for the most part."

"Anyway, I think I'll take Callista along. She's quite respectable, for a foreigner."

I considered this. "Not a bad idea at all. She should be able to read this fraudulent Ashtabulus—"

"Ashthuva. You can pronounce it perfectly well. You're just trying to be annoying and are succeeding."

"Anyway, Callista is an excellent choice as a companion. Have you gone to see her yet?"

"I plan to call on her tomorrow morning. We are supposed to go see Ashthuva tomorrow evening, after the sacrifice at the Temple of Vesta."

"Take some of the men," I advised. "I don't like the idea of you wandering around the city at night. It's far from safe, despite what our dictator would like us to think."

"I'll take a couple of torch boys," she said. "Servilia has a veritable private army and Atia always has some of Caesar's veterans as a bodyguard."

"There was a time when Romans didn't go around in fear of their fellow citizens," I grumbled.

Julia smiled at me fondly. "There was a time when the gods came down from Olympus to sort out people's problems, too."

5

CAESAR WAS GETTING IMPATIENT. There was a meeting of the Senate that morning, as there was almost every morning since he had assumed power. As dictator he could even set aside days that were *nefasti*, when official business was forbidden. Before his time, meetings had been irregular, usually called by a sitting consul or some other very prominent senator or one of the highest priests. However, Caesar had much to accomplish and he wanted his senators to attend upon him like a court before an oriental king, another of his regal habits that so many found so annoying.

On that morning, after assigning duties to a number of senators he surprised us by announcing the reception of an envoy. "Conscript Fathers," he said, stealing one of Cicero's favorite turns of phrase, "today we receive Archelaus, the envoy of King Phraates of Parthia."

"But, Caesar," said a very old senator, "by ancient custom we receive envoys in a temple, not in the Curia."

"This is Pompey's theater," Caesar pointed out. "I can't think of a better place to receive a representative of a country like Parthia or a king like Phraates. If any of you are too traditional for that, remember that up at the top of the auditorium is the Temple of Venus. That's close enough. Call him in."

A lictor went out and returned a minute later with Archelaus, accompanied by a few colleagues. All of them, like Archelaus himself, appeared to be Greeks. I saw not a single one who looked like a Parthian. They stopped before Caesar's curule chair and bowed low in the eastern fashion.

"Parthia salutes great Caesar," Archelaus intoned.

"Would that Parthia had come personally," Caesar said, fiddling with a ring and gazing off at a carving somewhere on the ceiling. It was behavior very unlike Caesar and I wondered what it might signify. "Your king presumes much, sending ambassadors when it is clear that a state of war exists between our nations, as it must until the stain of Carrhae is blotted from history, the death of my friend Marcus Crassus and that of his son avenged, the Roman captives freed, and the Roman dead given the proper rites, which shall be performed by me, their pontifex maximus."

He spoke this in a very quick, clipped, and rather agitated voice. I looked around and saw many faces that looked bemused, puzzled, or dismayed. The mobile, expressive face of Cicero in particular was a mask of alarm. Brutus looked concerned. Marcus Antonius seemed amused and mildly bored, but then he often looked that way at Senate meetings.

"Great Caesar," Archelaus began, "there is no cause for such enmity between Rome and Parthia. No cause for war ever existed between our nations. The campaign of Marcus Crassus was the military adventure of a lone man. The Senate of Rome never condoned it. The people of Rome, through their tribunes, expressed their anger at the temerity of Crassus." This was all quite true, but Caesar was unmoved.

"Marcus Crassus was my friend," he reiterated. "A Roman army was massacred at Carrhae. Eagles were captured. Those eagles are the tutelary gods of our legions, sacred to every Roman soldier. Until those standards are returned to the Temple of Saturn," here he pointed in the direction of that temple, "then the hand of every true Roman is raised against every Parthian, sword drawn."

"Caesar," Archelaus said, this time omitting the "great" part, "the return of your eagles is a point for negotiation. It need not involve a resumption of hostilities."

"Rome does not bargain like some merchant for possession of her gods. What was taken from us at sword's point we will recover with sword in hand. Inform your king of this."

Now the Senate looked truly appalled. This was high-handed behavior even for a dictator. Ordinarily, war was debated at great length in the Senate and the Assemblies. When it came to war, the Senate usually had the upper hand of all our plethora of public bodies, although the *comitia tributa* and *consilium plebis* apportioned the commands. For Caesar to address a foreign ambassador in this way, without even the pretense of consulting the Senate, was more than the act of a tyrant. It was a deep, personal insult to the Senate as a body. Had he simply briefed us on his plans, motives, and goals, we would have stood behind him to a man, even his enemies. We always do that in time of war. He was dictator, but there are limits. I wondered if Caesar was becoming unhinged.

"Mighty Caesar," now Archelaus's tone was somewhat less than respectful, "it pains me to remind you that you speak these vaunting words to a king whose army, although smaller than that of Crassus, smashed those legions as utterly as Hannibal ever did." There was a collective gasp from all around. To speak that name in such a fashion, to the very Senate of Rome, was unprecedented. Then he went on, in a more moderate tone. "But it ill behooves statesmen to harangue one another like schoolboys. We have deliberative bodies," here he turned and gave the Senate a slight bow, "and exchange ambassadors between nations, so that we may behave as mature men."

"I do not speak as a statesman," Caesar said, his hand working on the ivory baton that he usually carried when presiding over the Senate. "I speak as the commander in chief of all Rome's armies, the dictator, with total imperium." As if anyone needed reminding of this, Caesar was seated as usual with a golden wreath, dressed in his *triumphator*'s purple robe and scarlet boots, his twenty-four lictors arrayed before him.

"Caesar, I am my king's ambassador, but even I—"

"You are no ambassador," Caesar interrupted rudely. "You are some sort of diplomatic mercenary in the pay of a sovereign who is not your own. Go and report my words to him. Now get out of my sight."

This was a rare spectacle even for the Senate of Rome. Archelaus and his entourage left with flaming faces, at which no one could be surprised. I noticed a number of senators giving them looks and gestures of sympathy. I had only the slightest acquaintance with Archelaus, but I felt his humiliation keenly.

Caesar rose from his curule chair and I saw a slight lurch, the faintest loss of balance, when he did so. I had always known him as a man of superb physical address. This slight lapse was as disturbing to me as anything that had happened that day. "Senators!" he said. "I now call a recess of this meeting. Go refresh yourselves. I shall wish to see some of you in one hour." He called off several names and mine was among them. Then he went out by way of the door to the rear of the dais, just behind the statue of Pompey the Great.

The meeting broke up in confusion, as might be suspected. Little knots of senators formed to talk over the extraordinary events that had just transpired. The pro-Caesar and anti-Caesar factions were well represented, naturally. I went outside and found the group I wanted to join, standing in the shade of the portico. They were gathered around Cicero. Brutus was among them, along with Cassius Longinus, Calpurnius Piso, and other distinguished men. Cicero smiled when he saw me approach. He took my hands courteously. "Well, Decius Caecilius, what do you make of all this?" I was no longer of any great political importance since the destruction of my family, but Cicero acted as if my name still meant something.

"It's the most remarkable performance I've ever seen him put on," I said. "I saw him receive deputations of German barbarians in Gaul with greater respect."

"But," sputtered a conservative old senator, "did you hear how that man threw the name of Hannibal right into our faces?" There were mutters of agreement.

"Personally, I don't blame the man," said Brutus, surprising everyone. "He was provoked beyond endurance. So what if he is a Greek professional? Such persons have been employed for centuries when feelings between two nations are too intense for rational discourse. They are always to be accorded the courtesies due to ambassadors just as if they were fellow nationals of the powers that employ them."

"That is very correct, Marcus Junius," Cicero said. "What we just saw in there was something unprecedented. As dictator, Caesar has the constitutional right to act according to his own judgment, without having to consult the Senate or anyone else. But we have always chosen dictators who are men of sound principles, dedicated to the welfare of Rome."

"That was when dictators were chosen by the Senate," Cassius said. "Let us make no mistake about it, this dictatorship is unconstitutional, just like the dictatorship of Sulla. It is no more than a military coup. At least Sulla had the decency to step down from office once he had the constitution reordered to his liking. I do not foresee Caesar doing any such thing."

"Not likely," Cicero agreed, shaking his head sadly. "He has publicly declared Sulla's abdication of office the act of a political moron."

"What shall we do about this?" said a senator I now recognized as Cornelius Cinna, formerly Caesar's brother-in-law.

"Do?" I said. "What can anyone do about a dictator? They are above the law and their powers override the constitution. Nobody has ever unseated a dictator."

"But this situation cannot continue," Cassius said. "I was at Carrhae and I want those eagles back as much as any man, but it must be done by a Roman army under constitutional command. We've had enough of one-man adventures in that part of the world."

"I cannot accept even a dictator setting foreign policy that will last far beyond his own dictatorship," Cicero said. "This has never been our way."

With a sour feeling I saw in them the futility of the Senate, and the very reason Caesar had made himself dictator. The Senate, once the most remarkable body of men in the world, had degenerated into a pack of greedy, self-seeking politicians who had put their own narrow, selfish interests ahead of the common good of Rome. Even the ones like this lot, who were better than most, could only look back to some sort of idealized past with a vague notion of restoring the good old days.

Caesar was a man with a different vision. He saw the Senate

as a futile body, so he ignored it or made use of it as he saw fit. He saw that the day of the old Republic was over and he replaced it with one-man rule. Since he was well aware that he was the best man in Rome, he saw no reason why he should not be that ruler.

"Here's Antonius," somebody muttered. The seditious talk silenced. That is how serious these men were. The great Antonius swaggered up to us, his toga draped carelessly. He only wore one to formal occasions like a Senate meeting, preferring to go about in a tunic that was briefer than most, the better to show off his magnificent physique. He had a wonderful build and a great many battle scars, and was inordinately proud of both, as well as of that endowment of which Fulvia had spoken.

"Well, it looks official now," Antonius said without greeting anyone formally. "No turning back from this war now that Caesar's dressed that Greekling down so publicly."

"You didn't find it rude?" Cicero said dryly.

"Rude? You can't be rude to an enemy. You can speak forcefully, though."

"On a basis of forcefulness, then," Cicero said, "I cannot find fault with the proceedings."

"I think Caesar should have beheaded the lot," Antonius said, "then pickled the heads in brine and send them to Phraates. That's the sort of language a Parthian understands."

"Or an Antonius," Cicero said, "but, as a wise dispensation of our ancestors would have it, Rome can have only one dictator at a time."

"Of course there can be only one dictator," Antonius said. "What use would it be to have two?"

"What, indeed?" said Cicero, with the air of a man hurling catapult stones at a rabbit. The others suppressed grins, but I watched

Antonius and did not like what I saw. His own little smile of amusement was confident. He was far shrewder than his enemies guessed and his show of genial boneheadedness was a pose.

"Will he take you with him, Marcus?" I asked.

His expression soured. "No, it's still the city prefecture. Calpurnius and Cassius are to go, though."

"You'll have your chance," Calpurnius Piso said. "Once Caesar has added Parthia to the empire, he may want to take India."

"That would be something," Antonius said, brightening. "Awful long march, though."

In time we went off in search of lunch. A great many taverns had sprung up all around Pompey's theater complex. I joined a couple of senators of no great reputation at a table beneath an awning and ordered heated, spiced wine. The day was cool but clear, the air free of the many stenches that pervade Rome in the summer. Hermes found me there just as a heaping platter of sausages arrived. He had spent the morning exercising at the Statilian school and upon arrival he sat, snatched up a sausage and bit it in two all in a single motion.

"Did you speak with Asklepiodes?" I asked him.

He swallowed. "I did. The old boy's at his wits' end. He can't stand it that somebody's found a way to kill people that he can't understand. He keeps wailing that he needs to find something he calls the fulcrum. Half the boys have sore necks because he's been experimenting on them."

"It's good to have a dedicated researcher," I remarked.

"What's all this, Metellus?" asked one of the senators, so I had to give them a shortened version of my problem.

"Why does Caesar care so much about it?" said the other senator. "They were just foreigners."

"He has a way of taking things personally," I told them.

After lunch I went back to the Senate chamber Pompey had built into his theater complex. Several senators were seated on the bench once occupied by the tribunes of the people, unoccupied since the dictatorship usurped their power of veto.

"You look like a pack of schoolboys about to be disciplined by the master," I observed.

"I expect he plans to assign us parts of Parthia to govern, as soon as he's conquered the place," said Caius Aquilius, an acerbic man.

"I'd rather have Egypt," said Sextus Numerius, "but it'll probably go to his brat, Caesarion, when the boy's older. A Roman general has never fathered a king of Egypt before, but Caesar has no respect for precedent."

These men belonged to a generation that never hesitated to speak out about their leaders. Even a common Forum idler would berate a consul to his face. All that is gone now.

"Decius Caecilius!" came Caesar's voice from within. I left the others and found Caesar seated by Pompey's statue, a couple of folding desks nearby, piled with papers, scrolls, and wax tablets. Two of his secretaries stood by with writing kits. He could wear out whole relays of secretaries with his dictation of speeches, endless letters, and dispatches. Still, he found time to write poems and plays. The latter were not distinguished, though. Caesar's gift was for the prose narrative, at which he was peerless.

"Caesar wishes?" I said.

"Caesar wishes you would find this killer so Caesar can execute him. Caesar would also like very much to know what all this is about." No, he was not in a good mood.

"I fear my investigation is not complete, but I have isolated some factors that keep turning up too often for coincidence."

"Factors such as?"

"Such as astronomers as opposed to astrologers and their manifold differences, native Romans and foreigners and even pseudo-foreigners, certain great ladies and their social circles—"

"Great ladies?" he said in a leaden tone that told me to tread carefully.

"Exactly. Including one whose name I rather expect you will prefer not to hear."

"Just tell me Calpurnia is not involved." I supposed that he was still going by that absurd Caesar's-wife-must-be-above-suspicion nonsense.

"Her name has not come up in any capacity. Actually, I have no real proof that any of these people were involved in the murders, only that they keep appearing in my investigation so I suspect that I may have reason to look into them more closely."

"Do whatever is necessary," he said.

"It might be best if you send the astronomers back to Alexandria while some of them are still alive. Their work on the calendar is done. You don't need them here anymore."

"That might have been a good idea a few days ago, before the killings started. But one of them may be the killer, though I can't imagine why."

"I can't either, but that signifies nothing. People kill one another for a great number of reasons, it isn't always for world-shaking stakes or simple, understandable jealousy or points of honor. I've known people to kill for reasons that seem perfectly adequate to themselves but defy all understanding by anyone else."

"Quite true," Caesar said, already sounding bored. "Very well, get on with it, but bring me some results soon. I am hard-pressed for time these days and I want all business, major and minor, concluded before I depart for Parthia." He did not indicate whether my investigation was a major or a minor affair.

So I departed. Ordinarily, this was the hour for going to the baths, but that was going to have to wait. I gathered up Hermes and we walked a few streets to Rome's great grain market. Here was a huge square almost the size of the Forum itself, surrounded by granaries and the offices of grain merchants and speculators. The granaries were giant warehouses where every day of the harvest season wagons came in from the countryside to discharge loads of wheat and barley. It would buzz with activity again when the barges came up the river to unload the Egyptian harvest.

In its center was a spectacular statue and shrine of Apollo. There was also a more modest shrine to Demeter, goddess of the harvest, but Apollo had pride of place. He might seem an eccentric choice as patron of grain merchants and protector of granaries, but in very ancient times, farmers sacrificed to Apollo to protect their granaries from mice, and some learned persons claim that Apollo was originally a mouse-demon from Thrace before the Greeks promoted him to his current glorious status as a solar deity, patron of music, culture, and enlightenment.

Grain is the most volatile commodity on any market. People absolutely must have it to live, and you never know how much of it there will be in any given year. This meant that there were vast fortunes to be made from the stuff and much collusion went into artificially inflating prices.

A few years previously Pompey, as proconsul, had been given an extraordinary five-year oversight of Italy's grain supply. Part of his task had been to eradicate this sort of business. He had had some success, but it seems to be especially difficult to root out such harmful practices when they are so long established. It didn't help that so many senators got rich out of it. Senators were not supposed to engage in business, but the fact that it was grain meant that it was actually a part of agriculture, which was honorable. Besides, they always had stewards and freedmen and foreign partners to act as fronts.

We were looking for the offices of one Publius Balesus, grain merchant. I have long thought that life would be greatly simplified by having some sort of system of identifying where persons live and businesses are located. Unfortunately, so far the only way to keep things under control is to concentrate certain trades in a particular district. Then you go to that district and keep asking questions until you've found what you are looking for. This we did, and soon found our man. His office was located on the second floor of one of the huge granaries, opening off a balcony overlooking the plaza. The rich, pleasant smell of grain permeated everything.

I did not think much of my chances here, but this case was so devoid of solid leads that I thought it was worth a try. The man, who looked up from his desk as we came in, was a big, bald-headed specimen who looked as if he had done his time in the legions. His face and right arm were scarred and he had blunt, peasant features that had the cast of southern Latium.

"Yes?" he said, looking slightly annoyed, a busy man interrupted at his work.

"Publius Balesus?" I said.

"That's me." The accent matched the face. He was from somewhere south of Rome.

"I am Senator Decius Caecilius Metellus, and I need to ask you a few questions."

He looked a little more accommodating, but still suspicious. "I remember when you were aedile. Those were fine games. How can I help you, Senator?"

"You may have heard that the foreign astronomer who called himself Polasser of Kish was murdered a few days ago."

He nodded. "I heard the rogue was dead. Good riddance, I say. The man was a fraud and a cheat."

"The *praetor peregrinus* of last year, Aulus Sabinus, says that you tried to bring suit against Polasser, but he wouldn't hear it."

"Probably got a whopping bribe from Polasser, if you ask me."

"Let's not get into that," I said, knowing that it was all too likely. "In what way did Polasser cheat you?"

"First off, he's supposed to be able to see your future, right?" He began to fume. "All these eastern star-men are supposed to be good at it. Well, he told me to buy heavy, that the coming year should be a good one for speculating in grain. It made sense, didn't it? Civil war, everyone nervous, everyone hoarding. So I followed his advice. Well, you know what happened to the grain market last year, don't you? You're a senator, you have estates."

"The market was flooded first with a good harvest here and then with cheap grain from Egypt."

"Exactly," he said disgustedly. "I know what your kind think of mine. You think we're schemers who batten on the misfortune of others, Well, it's business, isn't it? It's a hard world. And when things turn out good for others, nobody sheds tears because it's a disaster for us."

"I'm not passing judgment on you," I assured him. "I know plenty of senators who are in your business, at one remove or another."

"Buggering right," he said. A man came into the office.

"Master, some wagons just came in from Apuleia."

"Good," Balesus said. Then, to us, "I bought this lot before it was planted. See what a risky business it is? Let's go look at it. I'll show you some things."

"Lead the way," I said. Hermes raised his eyebrows at me but

I ignored him. We went out onto the balcony and down some stairs to a yard behind the building. Eight or ten wagons stood there, loaded with big leather bags.

"Late harvest in Apuleia this year, and these wagons were a long time on the road. Now the first thing you do is this." He went to the third wagon and selected a bag apparently at random, opening its top. He reached in and took out a handful of grain. He held it up close to his eyes. They were fine, fat grains as far as I could see.

"Looks good so far," he said. "No mold, properly dried, no mouse dung in it. Now this is the next thing you do." He thrust his hand down into the grain until his arm was buried past the elbow. He withdrew another fistful of grain from deep within and examined it. "The same stuff. We'll go through some other bags before I'll take it, but it looks like I'm not being cheated. Now I'll show you something else. Come along."

So we followed him across the plaza to a rather splendid building decorated with reliefs of wheat sheaves, harvest implements, and various gods of field and storehouse. It was the guildhall of the grain merchants. He led us to a room where a bored clerk sat with a pair of scales and a number of weights.

"I want to show the senator those bags the thief from Neapolis brought here last month," Balesus said.

"Help yourself," the clerk said, indicating a number of the big leather sacks that leaned against a wall nearby. "It's not needed as evidence anymore, the man's been sentenced. I was going to throw it out and sell the sacks."

"Then we're just in time." Balesus hauled out a sack and set it before me and opened it. "Here, Senator. Give it a try."

I took a handful of grain from the top and looked at it in the light that streamed in through a window. These looked like healthy grains to my eye. "Looks fine."

"Now dig deep, like I just did," he said, grinning.

I stuck my hand down in as far as it would go and closed my fingers around a fistful and drew it out. This I examined as well. The grains were shriveled, showed signs of mold, and were laced with unpleasant black flakes. They even smelled foul.

"You see? You have to be careful in this business. The man should have known better than to try this trick in Rome, but he did. Tried to sell it out there in the great market at the peak of the harvest, thinking buyers wouldn't look close when they had so many tons to move. Well, he was wrong. We hauled him before the curule aedile but he can only levy fines and judged this too serious and passed it to the praetor's court. The man's property was confiscated and he was sold as a slave. I hope he works shoveling other people's grain for the rest of his miserable life."

We went back outside and walked back toward his office. "You seem to know your business." I said.

"That I do. Well, these star-men have their own schemes, and I wish I knew as much about them as I do about the grain business."

"What do you mean?" I asked him.

"I didn't try to take Polasser to court just because he'd gulled me with a false horoscope. I'd just look like a fool then, wouldn't I? I learned he'd advised half a dozen other merchants, and probably others who wouldn't admit it. Some he told to buy, like he told me. Others he told to sell. Any way it came out, he'd have a string of merchants who thought he'd given them a proper fortune. What do you want to bet he'd charge more for his services the next year?"

"Very clever," I said. "Why didn't the other men you mentioned join you in pressing for this suit?"

He snorted. "Not buggering likely, not after I told them who his patron was. Nobody'd touch it then."

Hermes was bursting to say something, and he'd held his silence long enough, so I nodded to him

"Who recommended Polasser to you?"

"A patrician lady who was selling off the produce from her dead husband's estate last year. Name was Fulvia."

I had been very afraid that he was about to speak another name. This was bad enough, but it still came as a relief. "Did she advise the others as well?"

He shrugged. "I suppose so. They must've found out about the fraud from somewhere."

"Well, I thank you, you've been very helpful. And now I know what to do when somebody tries to sell me grain in bulk."

"Anything for the Senate and people. And, Senator?"

I was turning to go but turned back. "Yes?"

"There was nothing wrong with our old calendar. Why did you have to saddle us with this new one? It's caused me no end of trouble. Contracts have dates on them, you know."

We made our way back toward the Forum. "Fulvia, eh?" Hermes said.

"Well, I knew she was part of Servilia's little group. So what has this told us? It could be nothing. She must have wanted to sell off the produce from Curio's estates before his other relatives could lay hands on them. I don't know what the disposition of those estates has been, now that she's married to Antonius." Curio had been a remarkable man, at first a conservative, then an adherent of Caesar and a tribune of the people, and very successful in every role. He'd had a brilliant future ahead of him and had married Fulvia, who always furthered her husbands' careers to the best of her ability, which was saying something. Then he had gone to Africa in Caesar's cause and had been killed in some obscure skirmish, a sad end for such a man.

"It could be nothing," I said. "She may have been besotted with these astrologers and babbled about them to anyone who would listen. I've known others like that."

"And Polasser may have looked at how the grain business works and decided that there was a killing to be made. Still, Balesus seems like a hard-headed man, not likely to be taken in by such a fraud."

"You never can tell. I've known many men to be sensible and no-nonsense in their own line of work, but gullible fools when out of their depth. A fraud artist I once knew said that a self-made man was often the easiest victim."

"Why should that be?" Hermes wanted to know.

"He said it's because they think they know everything. Starting with nothing they build great fortunes and they think they have perfect judgment. They won't consult with more knowledgeable people because they think they've made it where they are by always knowing exactly what they are doing. In fact, they often succeeded because they were lucky, or just hard-working or shrewd in a very narrow field. So they will trust a transparent fraud when a five-minute conversation with someone like Cicero or Sosigenes or Callista would show them the error of their ways. They have too much confidence in themselves."

"Like the ones who come out from Rome and think they're great natural military leaders because they're born into famous families?" He was remembering some bad experiences we'd had in Gaul.

I shuddered. "Exactly. The world is full of people who have perfect confidence in themselves for all the wrong reasons. They cause no end of trouble."

Still, this was another name that had come up more than once in all this business: Fulvia. I had known her slightly for a long time and avoided closer acquaintance. She was one of those bad women to whom Hermes had hinted I was too attracted. The first time I had seen her she was in the house of Clodia. In Clodia's bed, in fact. She'd been no more than fifteen and even then had struck me as some sort of anthropophagous creature. We had had a few encounters in the years since, none hostile but always tricky. Fulvia plus Antonius made a combination I was particularly anxious to avoid, especially now that I no longer had the protection of a family of enormous political importance. I had not realized what an advantage I had had being a Caecilius Metellus until the family fortunes had collapsed in the civil war.

We went among the throng of afternoon frequenters in the Forum, taking hands and trading political gossip in the immemorial Roman fashion. All the time I was pondering what I had learned and how it all fitted together. Surely Polasser had not just hit upon his grain scheme in a fit of inspiration. I ran through my mind a list of Roman rogues, villains, and lowlifes I numbered among my acquaintance, and I found depressingly many.

"Hermes," I said at last, "I think we need to call on Felix the Wise."

"Him?" Hermes said, unbelieving. "I'm all for it. I hear he holds court at the Labyrinth these days."

"Then let's go there. Julia will be attending the evening sacrifice at the Temple of Vesta, then going on her mysterious errand with Servilia. So we have the evening all to ourselves. Let's go to the Labyrinth."

The establishment thus named was at that time Rome's largest, most fabulous, and most successful brothel. It was located in the trans-Tiber, which gave it both more space and less oversight from the aediles. People visiting Rome for the first time always made it a point to visit the Labyrinth. It attracted more of them than the Temple of Capitoline Jupiter.

We made the long, leisurely walk across town and across the river into the trans-Tiber and got to the Labyrinth just as the sun was going down. The building towered five stories high and was as large as any of the apartment blocks in Rome. Before it stood its infamous sign, a larger than life-sized sculpture of Pasiphae and the bull rendered in excruciating anatomical detail. The queen was depicted as splayed quadrupedally, the cow disguise devised by Daedalus merely hinted at with hoofed boots and gloves. The bull was well endowed even for a bull.

We went through the long corridor that led from the entrance to the vast courtyard within. There were about a hundred long tables inside beneath a canopy worthy of the Circus where people feasted and watched the entertainment. I was recognized instantly, being a well-known public figure, of course. The madam, an immensely tall woman who emphasized her height by wearing an actor's buskins and a towering wig, greeted me with a resounding kiss on the cheek.

"Senator Metellus!" she said in a voice that echoed off the walls, "you haven't honored us with your presence in far too long!" Heads turned from all directions to gape at me. There was a good deal of laughter.

"Ah, yes. Well, as it occurs I'm here on official business. I need to consult with Felix the Wise. Is he here tonight?"

She hooted a great laugh. "Business! Oh, that's a good one, Senator! Business! Well, all right, I'll go along with it. Felix usually comes here later in the night. Come along, let's find you a table and get you something to eat." We followed her elaborately swaying bottom to a small table near one wall, beneath a fine plane-tree that was hung with colored lanterns made of parchment. Its centerpiece was a wonderfully obscene statuette depicting Ganymede and the eagle.

The madam clapped her hands and servants laid the table

with a remarkably fine dinner and a pitcher of first-rate wine. "Senator, can't you convince Caesar to pay us a visit? It would do me ever so much good with the patrons and it would convince the aediles to accept smaller bribes to leave me alone."

"Doesn't he ever come here?" I asked her.

"Never once. Nor to any other lupanar that I ever heard of. Not that I blame him for avoiding them, they're pigsties. But the Labyrinth is the most illustrious lupanar in the world. Do you suppose those stories about him and old King Nicomedes are true? Well that's no matter, I have boys of every race and age if that's to his taste. Or does he just prefer that his whores have patrician pedigrees?" Once again she threw her head back and hooted out her great laugh. "Now Sulla was a proper dictator. Practically lived in the whorehouses and chummed around with actors and entertainers, so my grandmother told me. She was running the Palace of Delight across the river back then." She sighed. "Those must have been great times." Another Roman pining for the good old days.

"Perhaps the good times will come again," I told her. "In the meantime, you'll just have to be content with being the most stunningly successful madam in the history of Rome."

"Oh, you're too kind, Senator. Well, I must toddle off. I'll send word when Felix gets here. Business, indeed!" She swayed off, laughing and snorting.

So with nothing better to do we set teeth to our dinner, which was better than most great houses could provide. Granted, it was a menu she reserved for her highest ranking guests, but even the ordinary fare was better than you could get at any tavern.

"Rack of venison in wine sauce," Hermes marveled. "Roast duck stuffed with quail eggs, octopus cooked in ink, poached pears—we must come here more often."

"She's buying favor," I told him. "In case I should be praetor again, or city prefect, or have any of the new titles Caesar is busy inventing. She wants to be safe."

"What of it?" he said, stuffing his mouth. "We rarely get to eat like this. I don't anyway. You sometimes get to eat at Caesar's table."

"And there I dine miserably," I informed him. "Caesar cares nothing whatever about food or wine. I don't think he can even taste them. I've seen him pour rancid oil over his eggs and never notice it." I tore off a rib of venison and it was superb.

"He doesn't care about food and his only use for women is their pedigrees," he mused. "What's wrong with Caesar?"

"Some men care only about power. That's Caesar. He wants to accomplish things and he has to have power to do so, so he has pursued power with a single-mindedness such as I've never seen. It makes him uncomfortable to be around. I prefer a brute sensualist like Antonius. He wants power, but that's just so he can accumulate more wealth and more women and wine and food and houses. Power to him means things he can taste and feel. To Caesar"—I shrugged— "to Caesar I don't know what it means. I can't fathom him."

By the time we finished dinner the evening's entertainment had begun: a troupe of actors who played Atellan farces with great energy. Then there were singers and Spanish dancers and tumblers and mimes. Wrestlers and pugilists from the nearby Statilian school put on an exhibition and while these were performing, the madam sent a dwarf to inform us that Felix had arrived. The dwarf dressed in a stylized burlesque of a gladiator's outfit, with the addition of a huge stuffed leather phallus protruding in front, painted scarlet and gold.

We rose a bit unsteadily and made our way to the alcove where Felix lorded it over his minions. In Rome proper he would have come to me, but this was his little kingdom so I called upon him.

The alcove was lined with huge cushions on which Felix and the others sat with little Arabian tables in front of them.

Felix the Wise was Rome's premier gambler, handicapper, and tout. Whether it was fights, athletic competitions, or races Felix would bet on it or advise you how to bet, for a percentage. He knew intimately every racehorse in every stable in Rome and for many miles around. He took a percentage from every gambling establishment and his strongarm boys acted as his collectors and enforcers. His gang prospered when all the others were crushed because unlike them he avoided politics as others avoid noxious disease. Gambling was his only interest and passion and it had served him well.

"Well, this is an honor, Senator. Have a seat." Some men moved aside and Hermes and I sat. Felix was a small, white-haired old man with sharp features and he always carried a faint scent of the stables, since he spent the better part of every day in them. He poured us cups ceremoniously and waited until we had tasted the wine, then said, "What will it be, a tip on the upcoming races?"

"Perhaps later," I told him, "but right now I've run into a puzzling operation and I'm wondering if you could enlighten me."

"Anything to be of service to the Senate and People." His bright old eyes glittered. I told him what I knew of the game Polasser had been playing.

"Have you ever run into anything like it?"

He nodded a while, stroking his chin. "I've never heard of an astrologer doing it, but it's an old handicapper's dodge."

"How so?" I was surprised that he had recognized it so quickly.

"It works like this. You have four racing companies, right? The Reds, Greens, Blues, and Whites. Now everybody backs one faction or another and claims to bet only their own color, but there are plenty of people who prefer to bet on whoever they think will win. So you select, say one hundred men you know are gamblers. When the next big races come up, say the first race of the Plebeian Games, you tell twenty-five of them the Reds will win, twenty-five the Greens will win and so on. After the race, you eliminate the seventy-five you gave a bad tip to. The twenty-five you gave the good tip to, you do the same. Here's why: You have to wait until you've got a few left that you've steered right in three straight races, then you start charging big money for your tips. In time you'll have a fool who's won at least four or five straight races and thinks you're infallible. Then you take him for everything he has. With luck, he'll steer some friends your way and you can make extra off of them. Of course, you can't pull this one too often. It's a good idea to keep traveling to towns that have big circuses."

"Amazing. It's so simple, absolutely elegant. Is there anyone here who's known for that sort of dodge?"

"They don't work in Rome once I learn about them," he said grimly. "Oh, I'm not against a bit of chicanery now and again. The gods send us these fools so they can be fleeced, and it angers the gods when you turn down their gifts. But a big job like that can give us all a bad name, especially when the fool is rich and well connected. That's the sort of thing that brings the aediles down on all of us."

"Who has tried it most recently?" I asked him.

"Let me see—there was a man called Postumius, a freedman who worked for a while at the headquarters of the Reds. See, having that position, it was easy to convince people that he had all sorts of inside information, when he was nothing but a clerk. I gave him a warning—just broke his arm and told him I'd cut out his tongue if he tried that trick again in Rome."

"Admirable forbearance. Do you know if he's still in Rome?"

"He is. I've seen him around these last few months. He took

my advice and traveled Italy and Sicily for a while, but the problem with a habit like his is that it makes you real unwelcome quick, so you have to keep traveling. He just couldn't stay away from the Great Circus for long, I guess. But I'd know if he was up to his old tricks."

"Have you any idea where he might be found?"

"Well, Senator, last I heard he was clerking at the Temple of Aesculapius, on the Tiber Island."

6

I̲T WAS MOST ENTHRALLING,"
Julia told me the next morning. "Callista met us right after the
ceremony—she's a foreigner so of course she couldn't take part—
Servilia was there, with a sizable bodyguard, and Atia, with an
equal number."

I was being shaved, always a delicate procedure with my rather
battered and scarred face. "Did Callista hint at what business Caesar and Servilia had with her the day I visited?"

"She and Servilia were both being intriguingly discreet about
it. They just barely acknowledged knowing one another. Anyway, we
all got into Servilia's litter—it's a rather large one, you know."

"I've seen it."

"Callista is very unaccustomed to traveling in a litter, would
you believe it? She says she always walks. It's some sort of philosopher's austerity, I think. I can hardly imagine walking everywhere in
Alexandria, but if she lives at the Museum like so many of the pro-
fessors she doesn't really need to go much of anywhere, I suppose."

"And this marvelous conveyance took you where?" I prodded.

"You're trying to rush me again, dear. Don't do that."

"Sorry."

"So the four of us were carried across the river into the Trans-Tiber and up the slope of the Janiculum almost to the top, where the flag flies. There are hardly any dwellings up there, it's mostly just the ruins of the old fort, but there are a few new houses since even the Trans-Tiber is getting crowded these days. We stopped at a beautiful little house surrounded by an exquisite garden full of fruit trees and flowering shrubs. At least they will be flowering in the spring. They're rather bare right now but the proportions of the garden are beautiful."

I relaxed in my chair. She would get around to what I wanted to hear in her own good time.

"So," she went on, "we went inside and were greeted at the door by the most amazing woman."

"Amazing how?" I asked.

"To begin with, she wore a gown that seemed to be made of a single long strip of fabric wound several times around her. It fit very closely, but was really quite modest and incredibly graceful. It was made of a very thin cotton dyed in bright colors. The lady herself was rather dark but quite beautiful in an exotic fashion, with huge black eyes. Her hair was black, too, parted in the middle and gathered behind and very long, almost to her heels. Her hands were painted with henna in very intricate patterns. She had dots and stripes painted on her face in red and blue."

"I think I will recognize her in a crowd now."

"Don't be facetious. She bowed in the most charming manner—used her hands and arms, feet, head, all moving at once. I've never seen anything like it."

"What else? Was she tall, short, plump?"

"She was quite, well, quite feminine. Very small, but formed like some extremely ancient concept of Aphrodite. Rather full breasts and hips but with a waist I think my hands could have spanned. All this was very obvious because her gown was so tight. Oh, and it left her navel exposed."

"Anything unusual about her navel?"

"She had a huge ruby or garnet in it. Wherever she comes from, they must artificially stretch a girl's navel, the way some people stretch the earlobes or lips to wear jewelry."

"So it's safe to say that she's not some runaway Greek slave woman. I suppose that would have been too simple."

"Servilia introduced us and told her what we wanted. Ashthuva led us into a quite spacious room lit by what seemed hundreds of lamps and candles. Its walls and ceiling were painted all over with constellations, marvelous to see."

"What was the style of painting?" I asked her.

"That's an odd question. Well, the treatment of the familiar figures, the lion, the Capricorn, and so forth, looked rather Greek."

"Were these paintings new or had they been there for a while?"

She thought about it. "Now that you mention it they looked rather fresh. I could still smell the paint, and the ceiling wasn't smudged with lamp soot. But then the whole house looked new, as well as the plantings in the garden."

"Very good. What next?"

"On one wall she had a bookcase. It was in the honeycomb style, but much larger than usual because it held star charts instead of ordinary scrolls. She asked us the birth dates of those whose horoscopes we wanted cast, and she went to the case and drew out several of the charts and took them to a broad table. She unrolled some of them and weighted their corners with little linen sandbags."

I started to say something but she hurried on. "And before you ask, the charts gave every appearance of being quite ancient. They weren't made of papyrus or parchment, and they were in a style that was not Greek or Roman or Egyptian. In fact, they resembled no style of art I have ever seen. And the writing was utterly incomprehensible, just tiny squiggles attached to long, straight lines. Yet the constellations were perfectly recognizable, once you understood the stylization of the art."

"Who went first?"

"Atia. She gave Ashthuva young Octavius's birth date and time and Ashthuva went over a sheet that seemed to be some sort of conversion table. I could make out a column that listed the Roman consuls of the past fifty or so years, and next to it a list in Greek of the Olympiads and the successive archons of Athens and next to that a column of writing in that odd language from the charts. It was pretty clear that this was her way of translating Roman and Greek dates into her own system. It was not ancient like the charts and it was written on very fine parchment."

"Quite clear," I commended. "There was no nonsense with braziers and arcane things burning? No purification ritual or mysterious libations?"

"None of that, and what if there were? We have plenty of those things in our own religion."

"Yes, but it seems to make more sense when we do it."

"Anyway, astrology is not a religion. How could it be? It makes no provision for the will of the gods, nor of their mutability. It involves no sacrifices or appeals to higher powers. It simply deals with human destiny as it is determined by the positions of the stars and planets at the moment of birth and their relations and juxtapositions as they change throughout life."

"You sound very taken with this business," I noted with more than a bit of alarm.

"I find something very satisfying in it. It is as rigorous as the study of Sosigenes, it merely applies these things to human life, while the astronomers simply study celestial phenomena without regard to the doings of humanity, as if the stars were above such things."

"I suppose so. Still, it seems unnatural. No taking of omens, no sacrifices, no prayers. Why are these stars telling us about our destiny when we're doing nothing for them?"

She rolled her eyes upward in a long-suffering gesture. "Why do I bother?" She took a deep breath. "To continue, and please try not to interrupt unless you have a truly pertinent question."

"I promise."

"Ashthuva told us that what she would do that night constituted only a preliminary casting, that each horoscope would require much longer study and detailed analysis."

And cost more, I thought without saying it.

"She explained how the sign of Octavius's birth was affected by the planets of that moment, which was ascendant, which was actually within the sign, how the phase of the moon affected all these things. It was quite fascinating."

I hoped the woman foretold an early death for the brat, but I was disappointed.

"She said that Octavius had a most remarkable congregation of signs at his birth, that he would rise unprecedentedly high in the world and would be served by the best and most loyal people." She caught my expression. "All right, go ahead."

"How can she go wrong predicting a bright future for a high-born woman's only son? It's what any fortune-teller would have done."

"You are such a Cynic. She told Atia she would have a much more detailed horoscope prepared for her in a few days. Then she did yours."

I felt a slight shiver. I always hated this sort of thing. I have always been content to meet my bad fortune as it comes, without having to anticipate it. What good fortune I have enjoyed has always come as an agreeable surprise. "Go on."

"Well, first of all, she predicted no future greatness for you."

"It would be a stretch, at my age. If I were going to achieve greatness I'd have done it long before now."

"But she did say that you would live a very long life, full of incident and adventure. She said you would die very old and very sad."

"If I achieve great age I suppose I can anticipate great sadness at the end of it, though I think relief would be more in order. Anything else?"

"She asked Callista, but Callista said she was just there to observe, and that inquiring about the future would violate her philosophical principles."

"How did that sit with Ashthuva?"

"She seemed to accept it with great serenity. In fact, if I had to choose a word to describe her other than 'exotic' it would be 'serene.'"

"Servilia asked nothing?"

"No. It was clear that she had been consulting with Ashthuva for some time. We will be going back to have our own horoscopes cast in a few days."

The barber patted my face dry and I got up. "Well, my dear, your expedition has been extremely informative and helpful. Keep close to these women and let me know what you learn. I'm off to the Tiber Island. I need to check out some information I picked up last night."

"Picked up where?" she wanted to know.

"Oh, well, you know how it is. I had to interrogate one of Rome's shadier characters so I had to go to a low place to find him."

"Public service is so demanding," she said sweetly. This boded ill.

If only it were public service, I wanted to say. It was Caesar's personal service. I've never liked being someone's flunky, though I've had to play the role often enough in my life.

I rounded up Hermes and we made our way to the island. There was no Senate meeting that morning, for a welcome change. Caesar was overseeing the layout of the huge new Forum he was planning. It was to be an expansion of our ancient Forum. He planned to condemn and level an area of several blocks of land adjacent to the Forum and build an ambitious new facility with a vast open space surrounded by multistoried terraces to be used for business, government, religion, and even entertainment. It would be roomy and orderly and rational, unlike our cramped, irregular, monument-studded, old Forum.

I suspected that it would prove to be just as unpopular as his new calendar, with its impeccable rationality. We Romans *like* some things to be chaotic and disorderly. As a people we have always been martial and disciplined in war and government and sternly observant in religion. So it pleases us to leave some things in their naturally irregular state, especially if we are used to them that way.

At the Tiber Island I asked for the high priest and he arrived with his usual show of impatience. "Yes, Senator?"

"I won't take up much of your time. Do you employ a clerk here named Postumius?"

He looked puzzled. "We did, but I have not seen him in several days. I assumed he had sought more congenial employment elsewhere. Is it important?"

"I believe so. Where did he work?"

"In the accounting department, where we catalogue donations to the temple. The overseer is Telemachus."

"I'll trouble you no further. Where may I find Telemachus?"

The accounting department turned out to be a cavernous room

at the north end of the island, stuffed with dedications and dona-tions of every imaginable sort, from fine sculpture to good old-fashioned sacks of money. Several clerks worked there under the watchful eye of an old man who had spent his life at the temple, first as a slave, now as a freedman.

"Postumius?" he said to my question. "Certainly, Senator. He showed up early last year seeking employment. You will recall that after the great flood during your aedileship, there was terrible sick-ness in Rome. We lost a few of our clerks and their replacements had not all been satisfactory. This man demonstrated that he was very good with numbers so I took him on."

"And was he satisfactory?"

"He would have been had he applied himself to the work, but he proved to love chariot races more than accounting."

As he talked we walked around in the vast, dim room. I saw, besides the usual statues, pieces of obsolete armor, farm imple-ments, stones carved with archaic lettering, documents, a few char-iots, a sundial, bags of fragrant substances, potted plants long dead, even what appeared to be the spar and sail of a ship. It looked like an auctioneer's yard after the breakup of a very old estate.

"It is the bane of all temples," Telemachus said. "Donations of money are one thing, but dedications are quite another. People think they are honoring the gods by dedicating these things, but sometimes I wonder whether the gods truly appreciate it all. Once a thing has been dedicated to a god, it cannot be sold or thrown away. They ac-cumulate and clutter the temple precincts. Some years ago, the Tem-ple of Apollo at Delphi became so crammed with armor dedicated by the Greeks after a few centuries' worth of victories that they hit upon the idea of using it for landfill at the building of a new stadium. Since the stadium was also dedicated to the god, it was adjudged not to be impious."

"I know the problem," I said, commiserating. "I worked in the Temple of Saturn when I was quaestor. It looked like the hoard of a pack of thieves down in the crypt."

"Precisely. Perhaps you could apply to Caesar. As pontifex maximus perhaps he could provide us with a solution that would be satisfactory to both the god and the temple."

Everybody thought Caesar could solve their problems.

"I'll mention it to him. Maybe he can excavate a new storeroom below this one. That would keep it within the temple precincts."

"An excellent idea. You will have my gratitude."

"Now, about Postumius?" I prodded.

"The man was always sneaking out to go to the Circus and the stables. He was constantly trying to get the other clerks to engage in bets on horse races. It was affecting the work here, which was unsatisfactory enough to begin with. I had to dismiss him. Slaves are much better than free-born citizens or freedmen for this sort of work. They can be confined, and there is an array of punishments available to correct their behavior. Had it not been for the shortage of skilled accountants I never would have hired him."

"It is a great bother," I agreed. "When did you dismiss him?"

"About a month ago."

"Did he seem greatly distressed at losing his position?"

"Not at all. He was quite insolent about it, in fact. He hinted that he no longer needed to do any such work and was moving on to something better."

"I thank you, Telemachus. You have been of great help to my investigation."

"Investigation? Is this something to do with the killings?"

"I have every confidence that it is," I told him.

Hermes and I went outside and made our way to the area where the astronomers lived. Its fine terrace, recently the site of

Polasser's murder, had an excellent view of the north end of the Circus Maximus, the end where fine statues of four-horse chariots stand above the gates through which the racing chariots enter the field.

"Picture yourself standing here," I said.

"Why?" Hermes wanted to know. "I *am* standing here."

"Picture yourself," I said again, "standing here looking out at this view and you are in congenial company. What do you talk about?"

"The races," he said without hesitation. He was a true Roman.

"Exactly. You speak of your mutual interest in racing and, no doubt, gambling. Then, with this common interest established, you go on to other things, such as your work."

"So Postumius strikes up a conversation with Polasser about racing," Hermes said. "Then he learns from Polasser about astrology, most particularly about how highborn Romans, especially women, are enthusiastic about it."

"There you are. And if there is one thing my life and experience have taught me, it is that one rogue will always recognize another. I will wager that not too many conversations occurred before Polasser learned that Postumius was a professional gambler and not an honest one, and Postumius learned that Polasser concocted favorable horoscopes for anyone who would pay him."

"So it wasn't long before they devised the fraud to profit from trading in grain futures. It must have been mainly Postumius's doing. Polasser was an amateur fraud. Postumius was a real professional."

"That is my thinking. Come, let's talk with Sosigenes."

We found him on the observation terrace with its arcane instruments, alone for a change. After the usual greetings we sat at a table and got down to the business of the day.

"How well did you know Polasser?" I asked first.

"Not terribly well. He was highly recommended by Danaos of Halicarnassus, who was a very distinguished astronomer."

"'Was?'" I queried.

"Yes, he died about three years ago. It must have been just after he recommended Polasser, because the news of his death reached Alexandria about the time Polasser came to the Museum."

Hermes raised his eyebrows and cut a look at me but I made a signal to say nothing. "And what did you think of him once he arrived?"

"He knew his astronomy quite well and was keen to work. His observations were always reliable. That was one reason I brought him here with the others."

"Did his devotion to astrology ever get in the way of the work he was doing for you?"

"I would have preferred that he not use our time and instruments for that purpose, but his transgressions were not sufficient to secure his dismissal. I had no cause for complaint with the work he did on the calendar. He said that the new calendar would actually make the work of astrologers much easier since it will establish everyone's birth date with precision."

"But it's only Rome's calendar," I pointed out.

"Caesar seems determined to make it the whole world's calendar," Sosigenes said.

"I can't argue with you there. What do you think of Polasser's Babylonian pose?"

"Well, I suppose it isn't impossible that he was from Kish. There are Greeks everywhere."

"I thought Kish was just a heap of ruins somewhere on the banks of the Tigris."

"The Euphrates, I believe," Sosigenes said.

"Oh. Well, I always get those two rivers confused."

"At least it is still a place. There may still be a village there. It is near Babylon. His choice of dress is a bit harder to explain, except perhaps for his enthusiasm for the ancient Babylonian art. You have been to the Museum, Senator. You know that a good many—eccentric persons live and work there."

"Loony a pack as I've ever run across," I agreed. "What did Polasser do when he wasn't looking at stars and drawing up horoscopes? Did he have any daytime activities?"

"He was very fond of the Hippodrome. Overfond, I thought." The Hippodrome is Alexandria's equivalent to the Circus Maximus, and a much finer building, though not quite as large.

"How do you mean, overfond?" I asked.

"Such diversion is suitable upon occasion, and every Greek is enthusiastic about athletic competition, some passionately so. Polasser took, shall we say, more than a philosopher's interest in the chariot races. He was difficult to find on any day devoted to the races, both in Alexandria and here in Rome."

"I see. You are aware that here in Rome everyone proclaims allegiance to one of the racing factions? And that these factions are distinguished by colors: Green, Blue, White, and Red?" He nodded. "Did Polasser seem to care greatly which of these factions won?"

"He never spoke to me about it if he did," Sosigenes said. "It would be unlike a Greek anyway. As I understand it you Romans are practically born into your chariot factions. A Greek, on the other hand, supports the competitor from his own city or community. But in Alexandria the horses and drivers come from everywhere and people take sides according to a number of causes, and some just gamble."

"Was Polasser often short of money and did he borrow heavily?" He looked surprised. "If he was not interested in the colors, then his interest in the races was that of a gambler. It has been my experience that men who gamble a great deal lose a great deal. I myself am a fine judge of horses and charioteers, yet even I lose occasionally." Hermes made a strangled noise which I ignored.

"He never came to me for money, perhaps from a sense of decency, but I overheard some of the others advising each other not to loan Polasser money because he could never repay. It was all distressingly unphilosophic."

"I suppose sometimes even philosophers give way to their base instincts. Did he owe Demades money? Or was there any other source of enmity between the two?"

"They barely tolerated one another," Sosigenes said. "I cannot imagine Demades loaning money to Polasser, or Polasser asking."

We talked a while longer but learned nothing more of value. I thanked Sosigenes for his aid and took my leave of him. As we crossed the terrace where Polasser had died Hermes saw something on the pavement, stooped and picked it up to examine.

"What have you found?" I asked.

"Have a look." He tossed it to me and I turned it over in my hand. It was a brass coin larger than a silver denarius and twice as thick, stamped with odd writing on both sides. "Where do you think it came from?"

"I don't know," I admitted. "People come here from all over the world and make offerings. It could be from Sogdiana, for all I know." Naming one of the remotest countries of my sketchy knowledge, I knew only that Alexander had passed through there. I tucked it into the purse I carried in a fold of my tunic. You never know when something may prove to be of value.

"What do we know now?" Hermes said. "It is pretty certain that this Danaos of Halicarnassus was probably already dead when Polasser wrote himself a glowing recommendation and put Danaos's name to it. Maybe he killed him. We know that Polasser and

Postumius were in together on the scheme to fleece grain speculators. That gives a number of people a reason to want Polasser dead. Postumius may have run to avoid the same fate."

"A Roman would have simply stabbed Polasser, or bashed his head in with a brick."

"We don't know that he restricted himself to defrauding Romans," Hermes pointed out.

"True. Yet Demades was killed the same way. What was the connection?"

Hermes thought for a while. "Perhaps the aggrieved party killed Demades by mistake, then came back the next day to get the right man."

"That's a possibility. It does seem unlikely that a man in Greek dress could be mistaken for one dressed like a Babylonian, but if it was dark enough it's possible. And the killer may have been a hired foreigner. But somehow I think not."

"Why?"

"Polasser had access to some of Rome's richest, highest-born people, and some of her most foolish. A man like Postumius must have drooled at the thought of fleecing them. I think the two of them must have had something else going. The grain speculators were just practice. Maybe they just didn't understand that those wealthy people are also some of the most murderous in Rome."

My next call was upon Callista. Echo showed us to the courtyard where we found Callista going over a great pile of scrolls with the assistance of a secretary. She looked up at us and smiled. "I regret not bringing my whole library from Alexandria. I always tell myself that I am going to send for it, but then I tell myself, why bother since I am going to return soon? Of course, I always put off going back. I've been in Rome almost ten years. Please be seated."

We did as bidden and a girl brought wine and snacks. "Why

do you stay here, Callista?" I asked between bites. "Personally, I hope you never leave, but I've been to Alexandria and it's a wonderful place. For a philosopher, Rome must seem a dreadful backwater to one accustomed to the Museum."

She thought a while. "Rome is many things. I have never seen grandeur and slums in such proximity and extremity anywhere else. It is an intensely vulgar emporium for every sort of money-grubbing and the amusements of the people are profoundly trivial. The ruling classes are not merely bloody-minded and grasping but they practice their power games on a scale, to the best of my knowledge that is the greatest in all of history."

"Well," I said, taken somewhat aback, "it's not all that bad, is it?"

She smiled brightly. "You don't understand. This is what I *like* about Rome. It is the most exciting place in the world to be at this moment. There is more going on in any one day in Rome than transpires in a century in most cities. In many ways Alexandria is enthralling, almost magical, but the atmosphere is also stultifying. The king or queen is a god and all pay them obeisance. Even the greatest people are little more than slaves. The only political life is palace intrigue, in which every petty noble fancies himself to deserve a throne."

"There are the street riots," I reminded her. "Don't forget the street riots." I had been in a few of those myself. I'd been the cause of two of them.

"Yes. It is a pity that the closest the people ever get to political life is rioting. As a Greek this saddens me. We Greeks have always taken a lively part in the political life of our cities. Not always wisely, but with passion."

"I thought philosophers were supposed to be above such things," I said. "Philosophical detachment and all that."

"I have never been as detached as that," she said, "and I think it is a mistake to divorce oneself from the common experience. A philosopher is not defiled by association with people who have to live their lives in the real world, as far too many of my colleagues profess to believe."

"I'll give you no argument there," I said. "What is all this?" I gestured to the pile of writings on the table.

"I am trying to identify the writing I saw on that woman's astrological charts last night. I'm sure I have seen it before, but I cannot remember where. That means I must have seen it when I was a child. Clearly it is from the east, but where in the east I cannot say. That is why I wish I had my whole library. I might have a sample of that writing somewhere."

"So you couldn't make out her nationality?"

She shook her head. "I have never seen anyone quite like her. She is quite dark, as I suppose Julia told you, but very different from a Nubian or Ethiopian. Her features are very small and fine, and her hair very straight. She has an elaborate vocabulary of bodily gestures, but they are unlike any I know. Her accent is very peculiar."

"What about her astrological procedure?" I asked.

"Quite conventional. I would have expected from her appearance that she might have some unique interpretation of the signs, but it was just as it has been for centuries since the art came out of Babylon."

"What do you make of that?"

"Either she learned the art since coming from her homeland, or the art spread from Babylon in all directions and is practiced identically in lands we have never heard of."

"Did she strike you as being credible? I ask this because I am investigating a fraudulent scheme that involves falsified horoscopes."

"Oh? You must tell me all about that, but as for the woman,

I confess that I am not sure. I spoke of her odd gestures. It is amazing how much we interpret from the language of gestures. Here in the west we share the greater part of our vocabulary of gestures. A Greek, a Roman, a Spaniard, or a Gaul can converse and share a large amount of their unspoken communication. We recognize things like passion or untruthfulness as much through interpretation of these signs as through the words we hear. There will be differences between peoples, of course, but we share more than we differ."

"I think I understand," I told her. "When I have been speaking with a Gaul for some time, I am pretty confident whether he is lying to me, or angling for favors, or is afraid of me. Germans are much harder to read. They are more alien to us than Gauls."

"You have it exactly," she said. "I have seen the same thing in Alexandria, where black slaves are brought from the interior. When they are newly arrived their habitual gestures are as strange as anything else about them. A nod may mean dismay rather than agreement. Where we look for hands folded together they wave to the side instead. A shrug of the shoulders may denote happiness, and fear may be expressed by slapping the chest with the palms. That is how it was with Ashthuva. I observed her closely, but when she spoke everything was just enough off-key to prevent me from making a confident evaluation of her truthfulness or motivation."

Echo appeared and announced the arrival of a group of people whose names I recognized vaguely as being among Rome's intellectual elite, which is to say people without political significance. I rose to go and she apologized for having discovered so little.

"Callista, I cannot imagine anyone I would rather have studying this matter. Your knowledge is matched only by your breadth of insight."

"You are far too kind. Oh, I must clarify something. In this unspoken language of gesture, which includes things like posture, physical address, attitude, and so forth, there is one exception to the cultural division."

"And what is that?" I asked.

"The language of sexual allure and seduction. Ashthuva was using it last night."

"But you were a group of women except for the escort—not Julia?" I was aghast, but she laughed almost girlishly.

"Oh, no, Senator, have no fear on that account. Ashthuva was trying to seduce me."

7

I HAVE ALWAYS BEEN ABLE TO summon up some courage when it was absolutely necessary, as it was now. I have dealt with unpredictable Gauls and Britons, fearsome Germans, ferocious Spaniards, treacherous Syrians and Egyptians, and even a dangerous Greek or two, although those were really Macedonians, which is not quite the same thing. Now it was time to dredge up that courage once more. I was about to call on Servilia.

This was an age of dangerous women, and Servilia was more dangerous than most because she was more subtle than most. I knew she was ambitious because she was trying to win Caesar and you couldn't get more ambitious than that. Calpurnia stood in her way, but I doubt that she ever let a mere wife thwart her plans. There was also Cleopatra, but she was a foreigner whom Caesar would never marry. Servilia on the other hand was a patrician and eminently suitable, could she but convince him.

Their relationship was one of long standing, dating from a time when Caesar was nothing but a debt-ridden young politician whom nobody credited with much of a future. Yet Servilia saw something in him, or perhaps he was just a formidable lover. Caesar's dalliances were legendary, and almost all of his conquests were wives of senators. When news of his affair with Cleopatra reached Rome certain Forum wags proposed a day of thanksgiving to Venus that this didn't mean yet another senatorial cuckold.

That morning I sent Hermes off to his practice at the *ludus* and walked alone to Servilia's house on the Palatine. Hermes was useful and he was ordinarily good company, but I sometimes enjoyed being by myself. Julia thought this was terribly undignified, but I have never been perfectly conventional. I made my way, stopping from time to time to chat with shopkeepers and idlers. In a street lined with the stalls of cutlers, I found a dealer in luxury weapons and bought a new dagger, its ivory handle carved in the form of a Thracian gladiator. I decided that Julia would not upbraid me for extravagance because I wouldn't tell her about it.

Whatever her plotting and scheming, Servilia maintained an exceedingly correct household, probably because she thought it was a fit setting for her beloved Brutus. The major-domo who greeted me at the door was a Greek of immense dignity, and educated Greek slaves were esteemed to be in the highest of taste. In fact, there was a notable absence of beautiful girls, which may have been because Servilia considered them a bad influence or because she didn't want to be compared unfavorably with them. The Greek led me to the courtyard with its beautiful pool, and I admired the fine statuary around it, all of it original, from the Greek islands. The wall paintings were similarly tasteful.

"Senator Metellus!" Servilia swept in swathed in a saffron-colored gown of Coan cloth, layered to avoid the scandalous transparency for which that fabric was famous and for which it was frequently banned by the censors, to no effect. "Your dear wife visits me for the first time in ages, and now here you are. Can this be coincidence?" Servilia was nearing sixty, but her face was unlined and the years had served only to refine her loveliness, bringing out the fine bone structure that is the basis of true beauty. Admiring her, I had to remind myself that Medusa had been a beautiful maiden who turned out rather badly.

"As a matter of fact, it was something you said to Julia that brings me here today," I said.

"Oh? What might that have been?"

"You are aware of the investigation Caesar has me working on?"

"About the murdered astronomers? Surely. How may I help?" While we spoke slaves hustled in and arranged chairs and a table. It was early in the day so they set out bread and sliced fruit and a pitcher of water instead of wine. This was more respectability than I cared for.

"According to Julia, when she inquired about a reputable astrologer, you told her that since Polasser of Kish was dead, the best to consult would be this foreign woman. I take this to mean that you had consulted with Polasser?"

"Why, yes, I did," she answered coolly, offering no further information.

"When would this have been?"

"Several times in the last half-year."

"Not to pry, but, what did you consult with him about?"

"You *are* prying."

"And I apologize humbly, but I am trying to frame an impression of what this man was doing. Whoever killed him had a reason and that reason may have had something to do with his clients."

"Why should that be? Demades was murdered as well. Why not inquire about him?"

"Demades was more of a cipher. Polasser was more colorful and, to be blunt, he was the sort of man to attract enemies."

"I can see that he might be more enjoyable to investigate, but I certainly wasn't one of his enemies."

"I would never suspect that you were." That was a laugh. "But did anyone of your acquaintance perhaps make remarks indicative of a certain hostility toward the late astrologer?"

"Let me see—" she seemed to go into a reverie, doubtless studying the mental scroll of all her acquaintances together with whatever they might have said. I found this somehow unlikely. Servilia would remember instantly anything pertinent that had been said, who had said it, exactly when, and probably the phase of the moon on that date. For whatever personal reason, she was stalling me. Finally she returned to the world we all know, shaking her head. "No, I can think of nothing."

"That is unfortunate," I said. "Caesar will be very unhappy if I do not soon find the man's killer." I expected this to strike home considering she wanted to link Caesar's fortunes to her own, but I was disappointed.

"Caesar," she said, "will rather quickly get over the death of a foreign astronomer. He has had to cope with a great many deaths, and some of those were persons of importance." Servilia, patrician to the core, had a fine appreciation of the relative value of people's lives. To her, Roman patricians were of utmost significance and no one else, Roman or foreign, counted for much at all. I myself, being a Caecilian and a plebeian, was one of those persons of little importance. My wife Julia, who was not only a patrician but a Caesar, was another matter entirely. I could see that I had made a mistake. I should have sent Julia to pump Servilia for more information.

"Nonetheless, I have been charged with this investigation," I said.

"Which I am sure you will fulfill to everyone's greatest satisfaction," she said.

"What's this?" The voice came from the direction of the atrium and a moment later I saw Brutus emerge from the dimness of the colonnade. He was a dreadfully serious-looking man who always seemed to have deep matters on his mind, although I suspected he spent more time thinking of ways to collect on his outstanding loans than on philosophical matters.

"Decius Caecilius is looking into the deaths of those two astronomers on the Tiber Island, dear," Servilia said.

"Oh, yes. Terrible business. I shall miss Demades."

"You knew him?" I said.

"Yes, and I wish I had known him better. He was marvelous when he spoke of his astronomical observations. He could make you feel the excitement of discovery, which can seldom be conveyed on the written page."

This was new. "I think I know what you mean," I told him. "The first time I met Sosigenes at the Museum several years ago he almost managed to convey some of the excitement of his work, and I am usually immune to the charms of philosophy. I think it was the enthusiasm he brought to the subject."

"Yes, that is it exactly. I truly enjoyed talking with him."

"I marvel to hear you say so," I said. "Others I have spoken to considered him a dull sort, a drudge."

"Then you have been speaking with the astrologers and their followers. I prefer philosophy unpolluted with superstition, so I esteemed the company of Sosigenes and Demades and the true astronomers."

"Now, Brutus," his mother said through tight lips. To my amazement, Brutus was entirely uncowed.

"Mother, you and your crowd pursue those fraudulent mountebanks like children chasing after the crossroads magicians who make doves appear from empty purses and extract denarii from their ears."

"That will be quite enough," she all but hissed, but somehow her son had grown a spine.

"I've studied too much philosophy and come to appreciate the truth in it, Mother. I've put aside all that childish nonsense about the gods taking a personal hand in the affairs of men and placing the stars in the heavens to tell us whether it's a good day to arrange an advantageous marriage for a daughter or begin building a house. The gods are far too majestic for such sordid matters."

She unwound to her feet like a cobra rising and spreading its hood. "That's not how you talked when your horoscope predicted the highest of destinies for you! And you have forgotten how to treat your mother with respect before strangers."

"Oh, Decius Caecilius is hardly a stranger, Mother. We've known him for rather a long time, haven't we?"

She turned to me and I confess I flinched back. "Senator, I fear I must be rude and take my leave. I hope my son will be able to help your investigation." With this she whirled and stalked off, radiating anger in an almost visible miasma.

"She isn't going to forgive me for witnessing this little scene," I sighed.

Brutus put a friendly hand on my shoulder, another unexpected gesture. "Pay no heed. Servilia's day is done. She is an old woman trying to be a young one."

"She seems to have regained Caesar's favor," I said. "I saw him squiring her about just a few days ago."

"Caesar is the greatest man in the world at this moment," Brutus said ponderously. "He can have any woman he wants. He already

126

has Cleopatra and even an incredibly rich queen of Egypt is not enough for him. No, he retains a fond memory of his former connection with my mother, that is all."

"Well, it's none of my business anyway," I said. "What *is* my business is these murders and I would greatly appreciate any help you could give me. I had not known you were acquainted with Demades, much less fond of him."

He frowned at the pitcher of water and turned to a slave. "Bring the senator something more suitable to drink. The Campanian, from the estate at Baiae." For once I found myself actually liking Brutus.

"How did you come to meet Demades?" I asked him.

"It was at one of Callista's salons, shortly after the astronomers arrived from Alexandria. Callista made sure that they were introduced to Rome's scholarly community. I met Sosigenes and the others at the same time. After that, I saw him from time to time at various gatherings of the philosophical set."

"You found that they appealed to you?"

"The true astronomers, not the fortune-tellers. As you may have gathered I learned to regard the latter with some distaste. I have studied philosophy for much of my life, but the astronomers struck me as the men of purest thought, matched only by the mathematicians."

"You mean like the Pythagoreans?" I asked. "I've known a few of those." The slave returned with the wine and it was excellent.

Brutus snorted. "Pythagoreans are to real mathematicians what astrologers are to true astronomers. They are just mystics who cloak their mummery in some of the trappings of philosophy. They propound absurd doctrines of transmigration of souls and commerce with spirits and ridiculous dietary practices and try to justify it all with some basic geometry and progressions of musical notes."

"I always thought it was rather silly," I said.

"Men like Demades and Sosigenes are the farthest thing from all that trash. They draw their theories and conclusions only from observable phenomena, eschewing all mysticism and supernatural explanations. If their observable data cannot explain a thing, they look for more data instead of resorting to the supernatural."

"Admirable," I murmured.

"Exactly."

"But where does that put our auguries?" I asked him. "Where does it put most of our religious practice, for that matter?"

"I would never suggest that the gods do not exist," he said, "but as I told my mother, they are not petty creatures that take an interest in the affairs of individual mortals. They are not Homer's Olympians. It may be that they take an interest in the fates of entire nations, though I rather doubt the efficacy of discerning their will in the flights of birds, or in thunder and flashes of lightning. These are the beliefs of our primitive ancestors." He'd been hanging around those Greeks on the island, all right. "At least," he went on, "the augurs are more dignified than the haruspices, with their examinations of the entrails of sacrificial animals."

"I've never liked that business either," I agreed.

"The people must have religion and they must see that their leaders are suitably pious. This is essential to social order. One of the wisest provisions of our constitution was to make the priesthoods a part of official office. Thus we have always avoided the dangers of religious fanaticism, and of hereditary priesthoods contending for power with legitimate government. You have been in places where these things prevail, have you not?"

"I have. Things can get quite awful. Egypt, Gaul, Judea, the list goes on."

"Yes, religion has a place, but it must be a clearly restricted, controlled place. And I feel that the childishness of fortune-telling, divining, astrology, and so forth have no place at all. If I were censor I would drive them all from Rome, and from Roman territory."

"They'd just come back," I told him. "They always do. I've seen the mountebanks and the mystery cults expelled from Rome three or four times in my lifetime. I would say that right now they are more numerous than ever."

"You are correct, of course. Something stronger than expulsion is called for. Caesar was rather thorough in cleansing Gaul of Druids."

Caesar had considered the Druids' habit of mass human sacrifices distasteful, but it was their political influence he could not countenance. Kings followed their counsel and they were a uniting force among the very disunited Gallic tribes. Caesar had solved the problem by slaughtering them all. I wondered whether that was the fate Brutus had planned for the fortune-tellers. I didn't like them myself, but it seemed a bit drastic. I decided it was time for a change of subject.

"Did Demades have other admirers? Conversely, did he have enemies? I already know that he disputed with Polasser, but they are both dead, which pretty much clears Polasser of the charge."

"Why so? Demades was killed first, wasn't he? Perhaps Polasser killed him, then someone else killed Polasser."

"That would be a consideration, were it not for the fact that they were killed identically and in a fashion so strange that even Asklepiodes, who knows all about killing people, is having a hard time figuring out how it was done."

"Really? That is intriguing. What is so unique about it?"

I saw no harm in explaining about the broken necks and the odd marks flanking the vertebrae. Like many other aristocrats Brutus fancied himself an expert amateur wrestler, though he couldn't have gone a single fall with an expert like Marcus Antonius. With his hands he pantomimed various grips and agreed that it didn't seem possible with the hands alone. "And the garotte is ruled out, you say? I've known some Sicilians who are excellent with the garotte."

"Asklepiodes says it would leave unmistakable marks."

"I am sure that I heard Demades mention a person or persons with whom he was in dispute, but it doesn't stick in my memory because I was far more interested in his teachings and discoveries than in his conflicts, which I assumed to be of an academic nature, not something that might cause his murder."

"Some people take academic matters seriously," I said, "but I agree that the killer was proficient in more than the studies of Archimedes and the lectures of Plato."

"Actually, Plato was better known for his dialogues."

"Well, whatever it was those philosophical buggers did. I think the killer was more likely a professional assassin."

"Probably hired, then. He would be the most dangerous sort of assassin, too."

"How do you mean?" I asked.

"You can't disarm such a man by searching him for weapons, can you? It looks as if he doesn't use any. He could get close to his victims unsuspected. If I were a person of power who feared for his life, it would make me most uncomfortable to know such an assassin was at large."

"That is an excellent point," I conceded. "I am not certain that it is germane to this particular case, but I would think that a man like this could be very unsettling, indeed. Of course, killing your victim is only half the job. Getting away alive presents special challenges if you've just killed a king."

"Be sure to let me know when you have this man in custody,"

Brutus said. "If you don't find it necessary to kill him upon apprehension, I would like to interview him. I think he must be a very interesting sort of person."

"I will be most happy to gratify your wish, should he survive. Should I survive, for that matter. Killers often object to being taken into custody, in my experience."

"Well, take care. I can lend you a few good bullies should you require a little muscle power."

"Thank you. I have some of my own. Everyone needs them from time to time." I rose. "Do send word should you remember any names Demades might have mentioned that I might find interesting."

He stood and took my hand. "I shall be sure to do so. Good luck, and I wish I could be more helpful. And I do apologize for my mother's behavior. She hasn't been the same since Caesar returned."

"None of us have, I fear."

Back out on the street I tossed some new thoughts around in my mind as I made my leisurely way toward the Forum. Now I had yet another factor to consider: a professional killer loose in Rome who was far more dangerous than the usual, common murderer. He had a way of killing that was unknown in Rome and could foil most precautions taken by those who had reason to fear assassination.

We Romans of the political classes had always disdained extraordinary precautions against attack. It smacked of unmanliness. We are a martial people and a grown Roman was expected to be able to take care of himself. You were a poor prospect for the legions if you couldn't. Bodyguards weren't considered a sign of timidity. It just meant that an attempt on your life would mean a street fight and we always enjoyed street fights.

Assassination of the sort that we associated with the Orient was a different matter. We have always had a horror of poisoning, which is associated in Roman law with witchcraft. We reserve some of our most savage punishments for poisoners, who are usually women who wish to eliminate rivals or objectionable husbands. The idea of a professional with an exotic means of killing was repugnant to the Roman mentality.

The question of the dead Greeks was almost driven from my mind by this new possibility. Maybe this assassin was in Rome for something far different. Maybe the astronomers were a ruse. Maybe this man had been brought to Rome to hunt far bigger game. There was only one victim I could imagine being important enough for such a plot.

I FOUND HIM IN HIS NEW BASILICA, going over some huge drawings spread on a table. "Ah, Decius Caecilius, come here and tell me what you think."

"Caesar, I—"

"In a moment. First take a look at this."

I went to the table and studied the drawings. They seemed to be the plan of a city, one with broad avenues and generous open spaces. It was on a river and I saw the unmistakable outline of the Circus Maximus. "Surely this can't be Rome!"

"Why not?" Caesar said. "This is Rome as it ought to be, not the overgrown, overcrowded, chaotic village we inhabit. I am going to rebuild the city with streets as wide as Alexandria's and temples worthy of our gods. It will no longer be subject to disastrous fires and will be a much more healthful place to live."

"But what will you do with the Rome that is already here?" I asked him.

"Much of it will have to be demolished, of course. I am sure there will be objections at first."

"I can promise you that. Everyone will have to be relocated. It will be like being transported to an alien city."

"But a much finer city."

"That will not matter. Romans love the Rome they know, filthy and chaotic firetrap that she is."

"They will get used to it," he maintained imperturbably. "Now, you had something for me?"

"Caius Julius, I think there is an assassin in the city who has come here with the intention of murdering you."

"Is that all?" He did not look up from his plan, to which he was adding notes and sketches with a reed pen.

"Isn't it enough?"

"People have been trying to kill me for a long time. None has succeeded."

"But this man is subtle. He is the one who murdered the astronomers and he is skilled at killing swiftly and without weapons. Guards will turn up nothing by searching him."

"I have never had anyone searched before coming into my presence, you know that. I am going to widen the open area around the Temple of Vesta and plant a grove there."

"Very pleasing, I'm sure, but I think you are in serious danger."

"When the gods decree that I shall die, then I shall die. In the meantime I have much to accomplish."

"Now you sound like Cleopatra," I said.

"The queen of Egypt and I have much in common. A sense of personal destiny is one of them. It ill behooves us to fret over things like danger and death. The best thing to do with this assassin is to catch him first. I was rather hoping you could take care of that."

"I am striving to do so. It is just that I had thought his crimes to be more limited in scope, and I thought you should know about it."

"I am touched by your concern, Decius. Now be about your duties."

I walked away fuming. The man just didn't appreciate either his own danger or my value. He dismissed first-class investigative work as if it were some sort of clerk's function. I was about ready to join the crowd of anti-Caesarians, but then I reminded myself where the real power lay and what a pack of second-raters they all were. I could swallow a little pride if I had to.

Once again I checked my roster of criminals and lowlifes. Who in Rome might have an idea of where I could find a foreign assassin? Back when my friend Titus Milo was the most prominent gang-leader in Rome he could have turned the man up for me within hours. But Milo was long dead and my own influence was lamentably low these days. Then I remembered Ariston. I headed toward the river port.

Ariston was an ex-pirate who had been of great help to me a few years before, when I was playing admiral and putting down a resurgence by some of his former colleagues. When Pompey had suppressed the pirates in his great campaign, those who wanted to live had surrendered and vowed to move inland and never go to sea again. Ariston had violated this agreement by taking up the sailor's life once more and had been liable to execution, but with Pompey dead I had secured his pardon. Now he was a more or less a legitimate importer and occasional merchant captain. I hoped he was in his place of business and not sailing to Trapezus or some such faraway place.

The port was always a bustling, smelly place where you could hear every language in the world and see some very odd people indeed. The wharfs were stacked with bales and amphorae and ingots of metal. That day an endless string of barges were being unloaded, their cargo nothing but fabulous marble for Caesar's endless building projects.

Ariston was in his warehouse, a long, rambling building that fronted on the river with a tile roof and no wall on the river side. He was a big man with a scarred and battered face. He was burned dark brown from constant exposure, which made his blond hair and bright blue eyes even more striking. He grinned when he saw me.

"Senator! You don't come down here very often. I haven't seen your accountant lately. Has this new calendar affected our agreement?" As his patron I naturally received a small percentage of his profits every year.

"Not at all. I came to consult with you." I took his hand.

"Any way I can help. Are you planning a voyage?"

I shuddered. "No, for which I thank all the gods. . . . It's a rather sensitive matter. . . . I'm starving. Let's find a tavern and get something to eat."

"I know just the place." He gave some orders to his slaves and we went a block cityward and into a low-ceilinged dive that had a distinctively smoky aroma. We sat at a table and a server brought the usual bread and oil along with a bowl of roasted and salted peas and another of tiny smoked fish and smoked sausages. That explained the smell of the place. They had big, brick smokers in the back. I took a handful of the crunchy, salted peas, then a few of the fish. The rough red wine common to such places was the perfect accompaniment. "This is excellent," I told him. "Is the cook a Spaniard?"

"The cook, the owner, his wife, and most of the servers. They brought their smoking process from Cartago Nova."

I tore off a piece of the tough brown bread and dipped it in oil. "Ariston, I am trying to find a foreigner. He is very dangerous. He's already killed two men I know about, and I suspect he is not done. Within the last few days he murdered two of the Alexandrian astronomers who have been staying on the Tiber Island."

"Why do you think it's a foreigner?"

135

I told him about the distinctive method of homicide. "Have you ever heard of anything like that?"

He shook his head. "I've known men who could break necks bare handed, but it wouldn't leave marks like that. It may be something oriental, maybe Egyptian. Those people would rather kill a man in some complicated fashion than step right up and stab him, like we would. I'll ask around. If he's a professional far from home, he'll probably be offering his services for pay. You don't do that right out in the Forum. You go the taverns and brothels and drop a few hints. Sooner or later someone will find you and make an offer."

"Do that. You'll do very well out of it if you can help me find him." I reached into my purse to pay for our lunch and came out with the strange brass coin. I handed it to Ariston. "Have you ever seen anything like this?"

He glanced at both sides. "You see them all the time in the Red Sea trade. They're from India." He tossed it back, and I caught it and tucked it back.

"Oh," I said, disappointed. "I found it near the quarters of the Indian astronomer. He must have dropped it. I was hoping it might be something significant. What do the Indians trade for?"

"Spices, dyestuffs, but mainly frankincense. It's as important in their temples and ceremonies as ours. Speaking of which, I have a line on a cargo that includes some chests of the white Ethiopian frankincense, the most valuable kind. I can get you some cheap."

"Cheap because it was smuggled or cheap because it was pirated?" I asked.

"Now, Senator," he chided, "there are some questions you don't ask."

"I'll pass. If you get this cargo, please don't tell me about it. Sometimes the less I know the better."

He grinned again. "As you like it, Senator. Your wife wouldn't mind a gift of white frankincense next Saturnalia though, would she?"

"I don't see why she should," I said. There is such a thing as carrying incorruptibility too far, after all.

I left him and trudged back toward the Forum. His remark about Egyptians had set me to thinking. It would not be unlike Cleopatra to have an assassin in her employ. In many quarters, such a specialist is considered merely a tool of statecraft, but she was the one person in Rome I could not suspect of plotting Caesar's death. What reason would she have for killing her own astronomers? Of course, an Egyptian assassin living at the old embassy could well hire himself out secretly, just to keep in practice. I also had not forgotten that I had almost lost my nose to a pygmy's arrow in Cleopatra's house.

Still, there were other easterners in Rome, and among them there was the envoy sent by King Phraates of Parthia. The envoy Caesar had so publicly humiliated just days before.

8

THE FIRST TIME I HAD SEEN
Archelaus he had been with Cassius. The second time he was in the
company of Hyrcanus's ambassador. I had no idea where he lived.
Unlike Egypt, Parthia had never maintained a permanent residence
for its embassy. The Parthians sent embassies whenever there was
something to discuss or settle with Rome.

Hyrcanus's ambassador had a house on the Germalus, just a
few doors up the Clivus Victoriae from the house where Clodius and
his sisters had once lived. It was a very fashionable neighborhood,
unlike the Subura, where I lived. The Subura was full of the poorest
Romans and many foreigners, but I preferred it.

Some years before, there had been a dispute between princes
over succession to the throne of Judea, a not uncommon occurrence
in that part of the world. One of the brothers, Hyrcanus, had appealed to Pompey for aid that Pompey had supplied gladly. He was
always looking to enlarge his *clientela* and loved to boast that he
had kings among his clients. Now Pompey was dead and Hyrcanus
had transferred his allegiance to Caesar. Hyrcanus was a weak

man and the real power was his chief advisor, a man named Antipater.

I knew Herod, son of Antipater, from the time of Caesar's eastern campaigns. The family was of Idumaean Arab origin, and they wore their Jewish religion lightly. Antipater was an enlightened man who selected the best aspects of Hellenistic culture and managed to reconcile them with the beliefs of Hyrcanus's always recalcitrant and often violently reactionary subjects.

Herod was a man very different from his father. He shared many characteristics with Sulla. He was brilliant and fierce. He combined great personal beauty with a ruthlessness that chilled the hardest of men.

Like Cleopatra, Antipater saw clearly that Rome was the future, and Caesar was the man of the hour, and he guided Hyrcanus wisely. Naturally, he and Cleopatra hated one another with a blind passion.

I had gotten along well with Herod and had ridden with him on bandit-hunting expeditions, which he practiced with the fervor that most eastern monarchs devote to hunting beasts. He and Antonius had become great friends as well.

The ambassador at that time was a Hellenized Jew named Isaac bar Isaac. He was a courtly man and he received me with great courtesy. His hair, beard and clothing were Greek. His Latin was excellent, with only the slightest accent.

"Senator, what a pleasure this is. Do you bring requests from Caesar? Caesar knows that my king is his friend and wishes to put his kingdom at Caesar's disposal."

This took me a bit off guard. "Eh? Why, no, I come on another matter entirely. Were you expecting requests from Caesar?"

"Certainly. Caesar will go to war with Parthia. It is only natural that he will wish aid from his ally, King Hyrcanus, in the form of ships, supplies, troops, and so forth, all of which my king is most anxious to provide."

"Yes, it's good to have friends like Hyrcanus," I said. "I take it that he approves of this war?"

He made an eloquent gesture of hands and shoulders. "How not? Parthia is an expanding power and casts envious eyes on Judea. Phraates would very much like to have our fertile lands, our city of Jerusalem and especially our seaports."

This was news to me but it sounded likely enough. I never heard of a king who thought he had enough land, and since all land is claimed, the only way to get it is to take it from your neighbors. We Romans have taken quite a bit of it that way, though we usually had a good excuse.

"I am sure that Caesar appreciates King Hyrcanus's manifest friendship with Rome."

"Excellent. Now, how may I be of help to you?"

"A few days ago I saw Archelaus, the envoy from Phraates, in your company at the house of Queen Cleopatra."

"Ah, yes," he sighed. "Both Egypt and Judea are allies of Rome, and Archelaus had hopes of convincing us to intercede with Caesar and avert the war that must come. The queen was most tactful, but she made it plain that Caesar's will was her own, and that it was futile to expect Egypt to take a separate course."

"At least she and King Hyrcanus have one thing in common," I said.

He sighed again. "I do wish that this enmity did not lie between the two monarchs. Yet I must represent my king, and he refuses to recognize the legitimacy of Cleopatra's claim to the throne of Egypt."

"Caesar may wish to have a few words with your king concerning that matter." I had some vague memory that Hyrcanus had supported the claim of one of Cleopatra's sisters and the sister's husband to the throne of Ptolemy, but I did not care to get entangled in the affairs of the benighted land of Egypt and its equally benighted neighbors. They might resent it, but most people were far better off just doing as Rome told them rather than trying to manage their own affairs.

"I was wondering," I said, "if you might be able to tell me where Archelaus is staying here in Rome."

"But of course. He has taken a house not far from here, just off the Forum Boarium, on the street called Harness Makers."

I thanked him and took my leave. Like everyone else I had interviewed, Isaac had given me a lot to think about. The politics of the east had always been complicated, which was unsurprising since the place was full of easterners. Its great wealth was always a temptation to our greedy and overambitious politicians. Whatever turmoil was going on in Syria or Bithynia or Pontus or Egypt or Judea had a way of poisoning life in Rome as well.

I had a feeling that Caesar's one-man rule was all that kept our more warlike senators from falling into civil war over who was to have Egypt or Parthia. The day was long past when Roman statesmen put the good of Rome as a whole ahead of personal gain. What might happen should Caesar die? Much as I disliked dictatorship, I shuddered at the thought of the anarchy that must follow its demise.

Harness Makers Street lay near the Temple of Janus. So near the Circus Maximus it was natural that the many crafts that served the races were concentrated in the district. There were builders of chariots, wheelwrights, makers of axle grease, brewers of horse liniment, artisans who made the souvenir figurines that race fans bought by the ton and, of course, harness makers.

Tanneries smell so foul that they are banned from the city, so working only fully tanned leather is permitted. Thus the street smelled wonderfully of that most fragrant of substances, and I found myself inhaling deeply as I passed the many shops where tanned hides were cunningly carved into long strips, then stitched and riveted into the many kinds of reins, control lines, breast bands, and cruppers required by the specialized sport of chariot racing.

The two outer horses on a four-horse team are not yoked and must be controlled by the complicated strapping system alone, a tremendously demanding skill and only the finest leather work will do. Newly dyed harness hung from tall drying-racks after being given the colors of the four racing factions.

Still other workers applied the gleaming brass ornamentation to the finished harnesses. In one shop I saw chariots that were little more than skeletons having the webwork of leather strips that form the front, sides, and floor applied to them. Racing chariots are kept as light as possible and are little more than a pair of wheels and an axle with a tiny platform for the charioteer to stand on. The front of the chariot comes no higher than the driver's knees. To look at them, they seem so flimsy one wonders why they do not fly apart under the stresses of racing.

Yet I had seen Britons go into battle in chariots little more substantial, though they carried two men rather than one. In fact I never saw a chariot without feeling a twinge in my leg. I was once run over by a British chariot and had almost lost that leg. The fact that I still had it was due to the skills and exertions of Caesar's personal surgeon, a man whose mastery was as great as that of Asklepiodes.

A few questions led me to a three-storied house with a façade painted a vivid yellow, which was a sensible precaution in this part of town. To paint your house red, blue, white, or green would be to declare allegiance to one of the factions and could lead to its being attacked in one of the occasional riots that erupted between the supporters of one color and another. Nonetheless, the ground floor wall was decorated with paintings of the races, not an uncommon motif in the area.

The doorkeeper announced me and soon the tall, saturnine Archelaus appeared. "Senator, welcome to my house." He took my hands as if no enmity at all lay between our nations. Or, rather, between Rome and Parthia, since he was not of that nation himself. "Please, come with me." Instead of going to the usual poolside, he led me up three flights of stairs to the roof of the house, which had been turned into a garden with flower boxes, planters, and small trees growing in big clay pots. The arbors overhead were bare, but it was a warm day for the time of year and it was a delightful place to converse. It had a fine view of the imposing northern face of the Circus.

We took chairs beautifully woven from wicker and paused while the usual delicacies were laid out and then did not talk of important things while we ate. He was a Roman citizen from a long-Hellenized part of the east, but I knew that he would follow the eastern practice of eschewing business until a guest has eaten. This was not a difficult habit to gratify, because he laid a table that was a combination of modesty and sumptuousness. Nothing was so bulky as to suggest a full meal, which would have its own set of rituals, but the ingredients of the small dishes were all of the highest quality. The hard-boiled eggs had been halved and the yolks combined with a paste of anchovies, olives, and vinegar and the broiled quail were stuffed with pine-nuts.

Replete, I produced an appreciative belch and set to business. "First, Archelaus, let me express my sympathy for your plight. That scene in the Senate the other day was uncalled for. It was also very unlike Caesar."

"A number of your colleagues have called upon me and have

expressed the same thing. I will not take it as characteristic of the Senate of Rome as a whole."

"Nor of the Roman people," I said. "They love Caesar but few Romans are keen on another war with Parthia. They loathed the expedition of Crassus and think he got what he deserved at Carrhae. It was a great shame that so many good Romans died there as well, but it is to be expected when a fool is in charge. I, too, would like to get our eagles back through negotiation."

"That is understood. Do you bring me a private message from Caesar?"

Everybody expected me to be Caesar's messenger. I suppose it was a logical assumption. "I'm afraid not. Actually, I come on a matter concerning my investigation of the murdered astronomers."

"I was wondering how that was progressing. Poor Demades. And he was soon followed by Polasser of Kish, I hear."

"That is the case. You recall that the neck of Demades was broken in a most singular manner?"

"Vividly."

"Polasser died in an identical manner. I have reason to believe that both were murdered by a professional assassin who hails from the eastern parts of the world."

He considered this. "And I, although a Roman citizen, am from the east, but why would I want two astronomers killed?"

"Oh, please don't misunderstand. I do not suspect you of any complicity. I think this killer is most probably a freelancer who has hired himself out, probably to a Roman employer. You have recently arrived from the east. You represent a great monarch, so I assume you traveled with an entourage befitting your station?"

"The king wanted me to have a much larger one," he said, "but I urged upon him that in the west embassies are expected to be modest. However, he insisted that I take what he considered an absolutely minimal escort of guards and servants. I managed to avoid the entertainers and huntsmen and dog handlers."

"Are any of those men with you here in Rome?"

"Just one or two here in the house. The rest are in quarters across the river, on the via Aurelia."

"I will wish to go out there and have a look at them," I told him.

"Assuredly. I shall send instructions that you are to receive fullest cooperation. Do you wish to inspect the household staff?"

"I hate to put you to the trouble, but I must. Only those who came with you from the east. Not your personal staff, but those pressed on you by Phraates."

"No trouble at all." He summoned his steward and ordered the staff be assembled. He did this with the greatest graciousness, but that was because he was a professional diplomat. Personally, I would have been offended by such a request, but my duties overrode personal feelings.

A short time later the steward reappeared, followed by a small group of men and women who wore puzzled expressions. Some of them had markedly eastern features. I dismissed the women. I had known a number of women to commit murder, usually by poisoning, a few who killed their victims with daggers, even one strangler, but I could not imagine a woman as a neck-breaker. It's difficult enough for a man to do.

Of the men one was clearly too old so I dismissed him. The three who remained looked young enough and strong enough for the task. One in particular struck me as suspicious. He was a short but burly man with a scarred, pockmarked face and a massive beak of a nose. He wore a long eastern robe and he had the look of a man handy with weapons. Across his forehead lay a pale welt, such as is caused by wearing a helmet for many years.

"Where are you from?" I asked him.

He bowed and touched his spread fingertips to his breast. "I am from Arabia, my lord, but I have served in the army of King Phraates for many years."

"Were you at Carrhae?" I asked him.

"No, my lord. I rode in the desert patrol until I was assigned to the bodyguard of Ambassador Archelaus."

"What is the nature of your duty here in the City?"

"When my master must go out at night, I accompany him as a bodyguard, my lord."

"Show me your hands."

Mystified, he complied, displaying his hands palm-up. I took them in mine and examined them visually and by touch. They were callused from long practice with sword, spear, and shield, but they lacked the marks common to a wrestler's hands, and the base between the wrist and the smallest finger was not hardened as on the hand of a pankratist.

"Your people do not practice unarmed fighting, do they?"

"No, Senator. Forgive me, but we consider such brawling beneath the dignity of a warrior."

"I was afraid of that. All right, Archelaus, you may dismiss these to their duties."

He saw me to the door. "I am sorry I could not be of more help."

"Oh, one never knows what may turn out to be helpful. I thank you."

"When will you wish to see my people on the via Aurelia?"

"Oh, I shall find time soon. Do not concern yourself." Of course I did not wish him sending word ahead that I was coming. I had little suspicion of him or his people, but it always pays to be cautious.

By now the afternoon was well advanced. On most days I would have made my way to the baths and idled away the rest of the day with ease and gossip, but needed something more active. I felt that my waistline was going soft, and that I was getting slow. That would not do. Murder investigations can often be fraught with the danger of personal violence. Ordinary daily life in Rome at that time presented even more such danger. And, as Julia never tired of pointing out, Caesar might at any time put me in command of an army and send me off to fight Sextus Pompey or conquer Ethiopia or something of the sort. As a propraetorian I was supposedly qualified for such martial distinction, but I felt that merely having held the requisite offices did not make anyone a competent general, however hallowed with antiquity the custom might be. Still, the choice would not be mine to make.

There were exercise facilities at the baths, of course, but I needed something livelier, so I crossed the river and went to the *ludus*. Hermes was still there, and for once I wasn't displeased. He was supposed to be attending upon me by noon, even if I didn't want him with me but he would spend his life at the *ludus* if I let him. Since I had imprudently given him his freedom, he abused his new status shamefully.

Just then I needed a sparring partner and the gladiators were seldom satisfactory for this purpose. Either they were overawed by my senatorial status and wouldn't give me a good fight or they were vicious brutes who would beat me bloody for the fun of it. Hermes had long experience of both my abilities and my temper.

When I entered the training yard the head trainer strode up to me. "Are you here to see the doctor, Senator? I'm afraid he went off somewhere this morning and he's not back yet." This man, like all the trainers, was an old champion. His arena name was Petraites and his many dreadful scars displayed Asklepiodes' expert stitching. He belonged to what we still called the Samnite school in those days. That meant he fought with the large, legionary-style shield and the short sword, usually with a helmet and at least one leg guard, and always wearing the wide, bronze belt of our old Samnite enemies. The biggest and strongest men fought in this category. Since the Samnites have been citizens for the last generation, the First Citizen has renamed this style of fighter the Murmillo. He has a passion for putting everything into strict categories.

"No, Petraites, I've come for a workout. I'm getting soft."

"Always a good idea to keep up your sword work. Some of your fellow senators are here today. With a big war coming up, a lot of them want to sweat a little lard off before they have to go off to Parthia."

It was not at all unusual for highborn men to train with the funeral fighters back then. That is another thing the First Citizen has cracked down on. He doesn't like aristocrats to mix with the scum. In those days the fighters were mostly volunteers and even condemned criminals and prisoners of war often re-enlisted after they'd survived their sentences, because it was a good life for a poor man with no marketable skills. You could get killed, but then senators got killed, too. Everybody else, for that matter.

For a while I watched the men train. Slave and free, volunteer fighters and condemned men, *equites* and senators, they were slashing and sweating with a will. Some of the highborn men were surprisingly expert. I saw the great senator Balbus practicing with a famous Thracian named Bato. That is to say, he belonged to the Thracian school and fought with the small shield and the short, curved sword, with both legs protected by armor. He was Illyrian by birth. Balbus of course used legionary weapons, similar to the Samnite.

"Senator Balbus could be a top professional," Petraites said admiringly. "I think he's the strongest man in Rome, and he fights like he was born with a sword in his hand. Maybe it's the Spaniard in him. They're great warriors." Balbus was a rare non-Roman in the Senate, a man who had gained his rank through his services to Rome and his personal friendship with Pompey and Caesar. "Your boy Hermes could make you a fortune in the arena, Senator, if you'd let him. He's an excellent light swordsman. Not enough bulk for a Samnite and he's not comfortable with Thracian armor, but as a Gaul, with the narrow, oval shield and light helmet and no armor, he'd be perfect."

"He'd like nothing better," I said, "but I've forbidden him to fight professionally. And he's not my 'boy' anymore. I freed him a while back. Luckily, I still have some control over his more foolish leanings." At that moment Hermes was sparring with a dreadfully earnest-looking youth whose tunic had the stripe of an *equites*, doubtless recently made a Tribune of the Soldiers and soon to join a legion. Hermes was a joy to watch. He fought with grace and style, but he lacked the true brutishness that a professional must have to survive for years in the arena. When they were done with their bout I joined them. Hermes looked only a little shamefaced.

"Senator, this is Publius Sulpicius Saxo, who will be serving with Voconius Naso next year." Naso was one of that year's praetors, and sure to be given a legion command if not a province. You could never tell, with a dictator in power.

"Family connection?" I asked.

"I'm his son-in law." He didn't look old enough to be married, much less hold a tribuneship. I wondered if I could ever have been that young. Then I recalled that I had been this boy's age when I was sent out to Spain as a military tribune to fight Sertorious. That was where I acquired the biggest of my facial scars.

"Hermes is a good instructor to teach you swordplay," I told him. "Have you considered the gear you're going to take with you?"

"Ah, I am not sure I understand," the boy said.

"Simple enough. If it's Spain or Gaul, you want the best sword you can buy. Get Gallic swords if you can, both a short sword for foot-fighting and a longsword for horseback. If it's Macedonia, you want the best horses you can get. If it's Parthia, don't stint on your armor, because those buggers love to shoot you full of arrows. Greek plate armor is the best over there, the arrows just glance off."

"Ah, thank you, Senator. I shall remember your advice."

"No you won't. You'll probably just get killed like all the other young fools who go out to join the eagles with their heads stuffed with Homer and stories about Horatius."

He wandered off, shaking his head. "A little rough on him, weren't you?" Hermes chided.

"I just gave him almost the same advice my father gave me when I went off to Spain. Only the probable theaters of operation are different. I didn't listen, why should he?"

I went to one of the equipment racks and tossed my toga atop it, then selected a wicker practice shield and a wooden sword. These were weighted to give them the feel and balance of real arms. Gladiators often trained with double-weight and even triple-weight arms, to build up strength and to make the real arms feel light when they went to fight seriously. I had always considered this a questionable practice and Asklepiodes concurred. He said that it caused more injuries in training than anything else.

"All right," I said to Hermes, "Let's fight."

"I'm tired!" he protested. "I've been here all day!"

"That's your fault," I told him. "Now suffer for it." I launched an attack at his face, forcing him to raise his shield, then I went low with a stab at his leading thigh. He evaded both easily. Tired or not, he was about fifteen years younger and trained daily with the sword. We contended for a long while, and I almost got the better of him a few times, but in the end he wore me down and I had to call a halt.

We got a polite round of applause from the spectators and Balbus relieved me of my shield and sword, which I could barely lift by that time.

"You're not too far off your best form, Decius Caecilius," he said.

"You are too kind. I'm getting old and slow."

"But you have a lot of sneaky and treacherous moves. That makes up for a bit of slowness brought on by age."

"I've always prided myself on my utter lack of honor on the battlefield." I saw Asklepiodes standing by in the crowd that had been watching. "Please excuse me, I need to speak to the physician."

"I need to confer with him myself," Balbus said. So we went over to him.

"Fine fighting on both your parts," the Greek commended.

"I'm not a patch on Senator Balbus," I said truthfully.

"Doctor," Balbus said, "I have some sort of strain in my right leg that needs attention. Come, I'll treat all of us to dinner."

"I've been out all day," Asklepiodes protested. "Let's go to my apartments and I'll have dinner brought in." Physicians are usually eager to sponge dinner off somebody else, but Asklepiodes had grown wealthy with his uncanny ability to cure wounds. Treating the gladiators of the school took up no more than half of his time. There was so much fighting among Romans of the ruling class in those days that he made a fortune sewing up the cuts and stabs that adorned aristocratic hides like military decorations. He once reduced a depressed skull fracture right in the Curia Hostilia when the clubbed senator was too severely injured to be moved.

In his spacious receiving room we sat and relaxed among his vast collection of weapons. He gave orders to his silent slaves in their incomprehensible Egyptian dialect and then he went to Balbus. "Let's have a look at that leg."

Obediently, Balbus put his foot on a sort of footstool that Asklepiodes had devised for displaying and immobilizing the leg. The Greek set about feeling that brawny limb and making wise noises.

"What will it be, Balbus?" I asked. "Parthia?"

"Almost certainly. Caesar is my patron, and just now he's on the outs with Antonius, so I'll probably go as his legate, if not Master of Horse. Antonius is to stay in Rome."

"So I've heard. My wife thinks he'll loot the whole city."

"Unlikely. He'll squeeze, but he's a better politician than that. Caesar will return someday, and Antonius will want to be in his good graces."

"I am not so sure. Antonius's propensity for extreme behavior has astonished men even more cynical than I."

"Then we shall see how much he fears Caesar."

Asklepiodes finished with his examination. "You will have to give this limb a rest for at least a month. You have strained the tendons of your knee and they need time to heal. I know it is difficult for a man as active as you to rest and relax, but I must insist upon it: no running, wrestling, or fighting for at least a month. You may ride, but be very careful in dismounting and remember to favor this leg."

"That sounds like a bore," Balbus said.

"Nonetheless, it is what you must do," Asklepiodes insisted. "If you injure it further it may give you trouble for the rest of your life."

Balbus eyed his thick knee dubiously. "It looks all right."

Asklepiodes sighed like any other expert having to put up with the objections of an ignoramus. "The damage is internal and therefore not visible, but you can feel it, can you not? It needs time to heal just like a cut or a broken bone. Therefore I adjure you to do as I say."

"I'll do it," he grumped.

"Some people must be convinced to stay alive and well," the physician observed.

"Any progress on the neck-breakings?" I asked.

"I've heard some talk about this," Balbus said. "What is the problem?"

So yet again we had to explain about the broken necks and the strange marks and the physician's puzzlement over the leverage applied. Like Brutus, Balbus pantomimed the act with his enormous hands, with which he could probably have twisted a man's head clean off had he so wished. "I see what you mean," he said. "I've never seen anything quite like it. Somehow you have to bring the two first knuckles of each hand to bear against the spine just below the skull, one hand to each side of the spinal column, and exert enough force to separate the vertebrae."

"You have a fine grasp of anatomy," Asklepiodes commended.

"My old wrestling instructor probably knew as much about the subject as you, doctor."

"A Greek, I presume?" Asklepiodes said.

"No, a Phoenician from Cartago Nova."

"I see. They are also quite expert in the anatomical arts, for barbarians."

"I can almost picture in my mind how it could be done," Balbus said, frowning, "but somehow it will not become clear. Tonight I'll sacrifice to my family gods and maybe they'll send me a dream that will reveal the technique to me."

"I hope your gods are more cooperative than mine," said Asklepiodes. "I've been sacrificing regularly with no results so far."

The slaves brought in our dinner and we applied ourselves to it, speaking of gossip and inconsequentialities for a while. My mind wandered to my recent conversation with Archelaus.

"What do you think of that extraordinary scene in the Senate, Balbus?"

He set his cup down. "You mean Caesar's dressing down of the Parthian ambassador? It was rough, but I've known Spanish kings to skin an offending ambassador alive and send his tanned hide to his sovereign as an answer."

"We are a bit more sophisticated here in Rome," I said, "and Caesar is sophisticated even for a Roman."

"Caesar isn't a young man anymore," Balbus observed. "Old men sometimes get cranky."

"That's just what Rome needs," I said. "A cranky dictator. Peevishness isn't something you want in a man who holds absolute power." It made me think of all those oriental tyrants to whom the anti-Caesarians were always comparing him.

"Do you think Caesar may be ill?" Asklepiodes said.

"Eh?" said Balbus.

"I have known him only slightly," said the Greek, "but he has always seemed the soul of congeniality, and of course he is famed the world over for his clemency. But any man's good nature can be warped by debilitating disease, especially so if it is one of the terribly painful ones."

"Now I think of it," Balbus said, "that day he came in by way of the door to the rear of the consular podium, and left the same way, instead of coming up the front steps."

"You're right," I said. "In all the excitement I forgot that. Maybe he didn't want to be seen looking infirm."

This gave me much to think about and that evening I spoke with Julia concerning this alarming possibility.

"Why would he conceal an illness?" she asked, frowning.

"Because a man who holds absolute power dares not show the slightest hint of weakness. It could be eating away at him, too. He still feels he has great things to accomplish, but the years and infirmity have crept up on him. It's the sort of thing that can make even Caesar ill-tempered. He hasn't yet outshone Alexander so he has to win this Parthian war and after that, I suspect, India."

"Nonsense! He only wishes to set the republic back in order. Then he will retire."

"Retire? Caius Julius Caesar? He'll retire when Jupiter retires from Olympus. I want to know about this. Pay a call upon your uncle. Pump Servilia for information. She's been with him more than anyone else lately."

"I'll do it, but I think you are wrong. This Archelaus must have done something to provoke him. You've said yourself that my uncle was rather sharp with Gallic and German envoys when their rulers had behaved haughtily."

"So Archelaus did, but a Roman citizen is not the same thing as a barbarian, and the king of Parthia is a monarch worthy of respect, even if he is an enemy. It is unlike Caesar to treat one he considers a peer disrespectfully."

"It does seem odd," she said, not protesting that Caesar would never consider a king his peer.

NOW I HAD ANOTHER COMPLICA-
tion in an investigation that was sufficiently complex as it was. Might
Caesar be seriously ill, and, if so, what might this portend? I mulled
this over as I crossed the Forum, closely attended by Hermes.

"I don't see how Caesar's being sick—" Hermes began.

"*if* he's sick," I said.

"—*If* he's sick—should have anything to do with some murdered astronomers."

"It shouldn't. But that doesn't mean there isn't a connection."

"That sounds very profound. What do you mean?" We found a
vacant bench just outside the enclosure of the Lacus Curtius and
sat. Since I wasn't very popular lately we weren't disturbed by too
many well-wishers.

"I've been concentrating on this almost to the exclusion of all
else since my conversation with Asklepiodes and Balbus yesterday.
Certain facts seem to come together and are probably related. Caesar
is determined to outshine Alexander the Great, but Caesar is getting
old. He may well be sick, perhaps deathly sick. He has always been

the soul of rationality, so much so that even his seeming follies always prove to be shrewdly calculated. Yet now he has begun to behave irrationally. His brutal treatment of Archelaus in the Senate was perhaps the most public example."

"Clear so far," Hermes said, "though I fail to see where this is going."

"Be patient. Asklepiodes noted that severe illness affects a man's nature. A great and thwarted ambition can do the same. Suppose both factors were present here."

"All right, I'm supposing it. I'm still not coming up with anything."

"You aren't thinking very clearly today. I think you need something to eat, maybe some wine to go with it."

"It would be ill-mannered to indulge myself alone, in front of my patron. You must join me."

"I accept your invitation." So we went to a nearby tavern and loaded up on sausages and onions grilled over charcoal and chunks of ripe cheese, along with plenty of rough, peasant wine. This is the sort of fare that promotes clarity of thought. At length Hermes sat back and belched with satisfaction.

"Has anything come to you?" I asked, downing the last sausage.

"I think so. I'm not well read, but I've heard a bit about great and ambitious men, and we've encountered a few of them. Most are very concerned with their greatness and reputation and how they will be remembered."

"I knew some food and wine would do you good," I commented. "Continue."

"Some of them, especially as they grow older, turn to oracles and fortune-tellers to reassure themselves that their fame will live forever. Marius and Sertorius were famous for it. Pompey, too."

"Excellent. Now connect that to our current investigation."

"Caesar may be consulting astrologers."

"On the day Polasser was killed, Cassius hinted that he was seeking a horoscope for Caesar. He didn't speak the name, but he could hardly have meant anyone else, and it was Polasser he wanted to consult with."

"Caesar also showed up with Servilia at the house of Callista," Hermes pointed out. "Do you think Callista may be involved somehow?"

"I would hate to think that, but it has crossed my mind, I confess. She knows all the Greek astronomers, all sorts of people attend her salons, not just intellectuals but politicians and wealthy parvenus and foreigners of all sorts. It's an excellent venue for carrying out a conspiracy."

"But a conspiracy to do what?" Hermes asked.

"That I haven't figured out yet."

Then he surprised me. "So where does all of this come together?"

"Eh?"

"Where do all the paths cross? Where is—what is the word?—where is the nexus?"

"That is an excellent question. There may be more than one. There is the Tiber Island, for instance. Both murders occurred there. And there is the house of that odd foreign woman. A lot of the women involved went there."

"Maybe we should talk to her."

I didn't know why I hadn't thought of it first. "Splendid idea. Let's go call on her."

From where we were, the shortest way across the river was to take the Aemilian Bridge, which leads to the via Aurelia, the highway that goes north along the coast of Latium and Etruria. Once over the bridge we turned left, away from the via Aurelia and into the sprawl of the Trans-Tiber district, and thence up the slope of the Janiculum.

The crest of this "Eighth Hill of Rome" was the site of a fort erected in the old days to guard against attack by our old enemies, the Etruscans. The fort had long since fallen into ruin but its great flagpole still stood, flying its long, red banner. By ancient tradition, the banner was to be lowered at the approach of an enemy. More than one politician had forestalled a vote or closed a court by having a confederate go up the Janiculum and lower the flag. At an opportune moment, the politician would point to the hill and proclaim that the flag was not flying. By ancient custom all official business had to halt while the citizens assembled in arms, even though they knew that there could not be a hostile army within a thousand miles.

Slowly, new houses were encroaching upon the slopes of the hill. It had been so long since a foreign army had attacked Rome that people had little fear of building outside the walls, and land here was much cheaper than within the City. Some imposing homes now stood on the Janiculum, mostly those of wealthy *equites* and foreigners, as an address outside the *pomerium* was considered unfitting for patricians and consulars.

We climbed until the buildings thinned out and found a fine, new house that looked as if it had to be the one Julia had described. It was surrounded by new and very expensive plantings. The formal garden was as impressive as Julia had intimated, with numerous fruit trees planted in huge tufa pots. I wondered how the inhabitants got water so high up, as the Trans-Tiber was not served by a great aqueduct in those days.

"I know land is cheap here, compared to the City proper," Hermes noted, "but somebody has spent substantially on this place."

"My own thought," I concurred. "This woman is not the sort who tells fortunes in the Forum for a few copper *asses*."

We went to the door and Hermes knocked. To my surprise, Ashthuva herself opened it. I knew it had to be Ashthuva, as Julia's description had been so thorough. Briefly, I wondered why someone so obviously prosperous had no doorkeeper for this task, but the woman herself had a way of driving all lesser thoughts from a man's mind.

In my life I had encountered many beautiful women, some of them exotic in the extreme, but I had never beheld one quite like this. Her regularity of feature and glowing, tawny skin were astonishingly set off by the dots and lines of color painted on her forehead, cheeks and chin. The gown, or rather wrapping, as Julia had described it, was gold this day, covering her as securely as an Egyptian mummy, but with tantalizing glimpses of flesh here and there. The huge red navel jewel was in place. But most enticing of all was her perfume, which Julia for some reason had not mentioned. It was an amalgam of flowers and spices and something indescribable, just below the level of consciousness, but not above the level of the testes, which this fragrance sent into an uproar.

"Yes, Senator?" the woman said in a voice so furry that it constituted a full-body caress. She placed her hands together, scarlet nails pointed upward just below her chin, and performed that serpentine bow Julia had described as wonderfully graceful, and that I perceived as unutterably lascivious. I had never seen every part of a woman's body in such enticing motion except among certain supremely accomplished Spanish dancers of the sort that were frequently forbidden by the censors to enter Rome lest they endanger public morals.

"Ah, well, I am Senator Metellus and I—ah, that is to say—" I had been more articulate in the presence of German chieftains bent upon my torture and slow death.

"Good lady," Hermes said, no less stimulated than I, but in

better control of himself, "the senator is engaged in an investigation on behalf of the dictator. We must ask you a few questions, if we may."

"Of course. Please come in." We passed within and like Julia I smelled fresh paint and new plaster. The decorations were astrological and clearly had been done by artists trained in the Greek tradition; I saw no Chaldean or Egyptian influence.

We followed her and the rear view was as maddening as the front. Hermes' eyes popped and his breathing became labored. I nudged him in the ribs, but I had no cause to pride myself upon my self-control. I found that I had to adjust the front of my toga for the sake of decency.

She led us to a room Julia apparently had not seen. It was illuminated, amazingly, by a skylight composed of a framework of lead strips in which were secured hundreds of small panes of colored glass. They formed no recognizable picture, but they seemed to be arranged in some subtle pattern I could not quite make out. It shed an unsettling light.

"Please be seated, gentlemen," she said in a way that turned that commonplace phrase into something sublimely seductive. There was no proper furniture, but the floor was nearly covered by heavily stuffed cushions, colorfully dyed. We collapsed with unseemly haste. Fragrant herbs were included in the stuffing of the cushions. It seemed that no sensual refinement went overlooked in this household.

"Please excuse me while I go see to your refreshment." When she was gone Hermes turned to me.

"Did Julia mention that this woman is like some sort of Syrian fertility goddess?"

"No, but that was an all-female group that night. Maybe her magic only works on men." But I remembered that Callista had said Ashthuva had exercised seductive tactics upon her.

Moments later the woman was back with a tray of delicacies

and a pitcher. We had just eaten, but the formalities had to be observed. The snacks seemed to be an amalgam of meats, fruit, vegetables, and eggs, chopped and mixed so that nothing was recognizable, fried and served on tiny squares of crisp, unleavened bread. It was highly seasoned and I found it delicious. The wine was excessively sweet and I judged it to be Syrian. Might that be where this woman was from?

"What interest might so exalted a person as the dictator Caesar have in me?" she asked when we had downed a few bites.

"The dictator has assigned me to investigate the murders of two astronomers on the Tiber Island."

"Oh, yes, I had heard about that. How terrible." She made a strange gesture of head and one shoulder that is difficult to describe. I remembered my conversation with Callista about how each culture has its own vocabulary of gestures and I wondered what this one might signify. Horror, perhaps.

"One of the victims was a notable astrologer, the one who called himself Polasser of Kish. Did you know him?"

She made another gesture, this one a flick of her right hand, which I guessed to denote denial. "No, Senator. There is no guild of astrologers. We tend to be solitary, not gregarious. An astrologer may have apprentices, but rarely colleagues."

"That seems odd," I said. "Astronomers are always flocking together to talk and argue."

"That is because, like philosophers, they are always coming up with something new and want to discuss it with their peers. Astrology is a very ancient art, and it never changes. All was discovered before human memory, and there are no new findings."

"I never thought of it that way," I admitted. "That is an observation worthy of Callista herself."

She inhaled sharply. "Ah! I met that learned lady just a few nights ago. She is the most remarkable woman I have ever encountered."

"She was quite impressed by you, as well," I said. I could have bitten my tongue. It was stupid of me to let her know that I had been discussing her with Callista. This woman's awesome sexuality drove my cautious instincts clear out of my head. "But I fear she has little regard for your art," I went on.

She smiled unsettlingly. "But, Senator, I have many arts."

I'll just bet you do, I thought. "She has a philosophical aversion to astrology, I fear."

"And I have little use for Greek philosophy. People need not agree on everything to find one another appealing."

"Just so," I said, wondering how our conversation had taken this odd turn. Then I remembered that I had started it by mentioning Callista. "So, you never met Demades?"

"Demades?" she said.

"The senator meant Polasser," Hermes said, coming to my rescue. "Demades was the other murdered astronomer, the one who did not practice astrology."

"I knew neither of them," she said. "In fact, I know none of the men who have been working on Caesar's new calendar."

"Is this because most of your clients are women?" I hazarded.

"No, because they are Greek philosophers and would seek out an astrologer of their own nationality, should they have need of one. But it is true that most of my clients are women."

"Rich and well-born ones at that," I said.

She surprised me by not denying it. "Such women have the greatest concerns, especially for their husbands and sons. Not all are well-born, though. Some of my clients are freedwomen, especially those whose men are risk-taking merchants and travelers. The well-being of such people is always precarious."

"Servilia is one of your clients," I said. "I assume she is concerned for the future of her son, Brutus. Does she want to know if he is to be Caesar's heir?"

"Senator, you must understand that I cannot discuss the affairs of my clients. It would be unethical."

I wondered of what the ethics of an astrologer might consist. "Ashthuva, I am here at the behest of the dictator. I am empowered to demand the cooperation of anyone I feel it necessary to question." As long as they are not too powerful and influential, I failed to add.

"I assure you, Senator, that the dictator Caesar would not wish me to answer that question, nor any other about either himself or the Lady Servilia." This was accompanied by a gesture of her whole body that put me in mind of several venomous serpents I had encountered in Egypt. This was one gesture, however unfamiliar, the meaning of which was unmistakable: It was pure threat.

I knew when to back off. "I'll discuss it with him, then."

"I regret that I can be of so little help to you."

"Your presence alone is gratifying," I assured her.

She beamed, all menace gone and the seductiveness back in full force. "And it is a great pleasure to me to meet one of the most interesting men in Rome. I have been hearing about you for some time, and meeting your wife made me even more intrigued with you."

"The horoscope you cast for Julia predicts a rather dreary future for me," I said.

"Only at the end. And, Senator, I have foreseen far worse futures than yours."

Something occurred to me. "Is Queen Cleopatra among your clients?"

"I have met her," she said, "but not in a professional capacity. I was invited to one of her parties shortly after her arrival in Rome."

"Invited personally by the queen herself?"

She put her palms together and bowed over them. "I am far too lowly a person to merit the personal attention of a great queen. I attended as the guest of one of my clients, a lady of high position. It seems that, at Queen Cleopatra's parties, it is customary for invited guests to bring along as many friends as they please. It is expected that such persons should be interesting and amusing."

"This lady could hardly have chosen a more interesting person," I assured her.

"You are too kind, Senator."

"Not at all," I said, rising, "and now I fear I must tear myself away from you. I have other calls to make."

She rose, but far more sinuously than I. "Please call again. If you like, I can cast a far more detailed horoscope for you."

"Please do not," I urged. "The last thing I want is to know what is going to happen to me. Some forms of ignorance are a blessing, and that is one of them."

She smiled again. Even her teeth were dazzling, the whitest I had ever seen, beautifully set off by her dark complexion and red-stained lips. "More people should possess your wisdom, though it would ruin my profession."

Once outside, we walked a few paces from the house, then I stopped. "Wait a bit," I told Hermes. "I have to get my breathing back to normal."

"Maybe a plunge in the *frigidarium* would help," he said.

"That woman could turn an Egyptian eunuch into a stallion."

"She could inspire an erection from an Egyptian *mummy*," Hermes said. "She may be wealthy from her fortune-telling, but if she ever turns professional whore she'll be as rich as Cleopatra."

We started down the hill. "Hermes, I would rather hold a bridge single-handed against an invading army than meddle in an affair as full of dangerous women as this one."

166

"It doesn't help that Caesar is withholding information from you."

"That is the truth," I said bitterly, "but then, just about everybody I've questioned so far is lying and holding back. Nothing new about that. Cleopatra has me shot in the nose when Servilia's name comes up; Servilia gives me the viper treatment when I dare to question her about anything. Cassius drops dark hints about obtaining a horoscope for Caesar—" I threw up my hands in disgust. "So far, it seems only Brutus has been straight with me, not that he knows much. Even Callista—" Some fragments of memory clicked together.

"Callista?" Hermes said.

"Callista said that Brutus had been at one of Cleopatra's parties and he talked for a long time with that Indian astronomer, not about astronomy but about some Indian belief in the transmigration of souls."

"What of it?"

"She said that it was because Brutus was studying Pythagoreanism. The Pythagoreans also believe in transmigration of souls. Yet when I spoke with Brutus he spoke disparagingly of them. He said they were to true mathematicians what the astrologers are to true astronomers."

"Maybe it was a temporary interest and he grew disillusioned with them," Hermes said.

"That could be it, I suppose. One more anomaly to cloud the waters."

"So what next?"

"Something I've been trying to avoid. Now I have to talk to Fulvia." Hermes began to grin broadly. "It won't be much fun this time," I told him. "She lives in the house of Antonius now."

"Oh, yes," he said, his face falling. "I'd forgotten that." In previous years, when we had called on Fulvia she had lived in a house

167

famous for the beauty of its female and male slaves. The house of Antonius would undoubtedly be different.

We made our way to the Palatine where that domicile lay. The doorkeeper looked like a professional wrestler and the major domo who received us was clearly one of Antonius's soldiers. The atrium was full of war trophies, weapons, and other masculine accoutrements. On the other hand, the courtyard to which he led us was full of beautiful sculpture, some of which I remembered from Fulvia's other houses. Clearly, interior decoration was a matter of some contention in this household.

The lady herself came out to greet us and we went through the usual formalities. Fulvia was tiny, voluptuously formed, and had a husky voice. I had thought she was the most alluring woman in Rome, but having just come from the presence of Ashthuva, she seemed no more seductive than a rather pretty statue.

"Polasser of Kish?" she said, eyebrows going up. "Wasn't he murdered recently?"

"Exactly," I told her, "and Caesar has commissioned me to discover who killed him and another stargazer named Demades. How well did you know Polasser?"

"Scarcely at all. I met him at one of Cleopatra's gatherings, but I'd heard of him before then."

"Heard of him? How?"

She frowned with thought. "Let me see, somebody mentioned him . . . you realize that astrologers are all the rage in my social circle, don't you?"

"I've heard of little else since this business began."

"So the ladies I know are always babbling about this one or that one. Anyway, I heard about him, and when I met him at Cleopatra's, he seemed so fascinating and knowledgeable that I decided to consult with him about my dear Antonius's future."

"Weren't you put off by the fact that he was a Greek dressed as a Babylonian?"

She shrugged, making her abundant breasts quiver. "I've never seen a Babylonian. For all I know, that's what they look like."

"So you got Antonius's horoscope. I take it that Polasser predicted a glorious future for your husband?"

She beamed. "He said that Antonius would become the greatest man in Rome."

"Did he say for how long?"

"No."

"A grain merchant named Balesus has told me that you recommended Polasser to him."

"Did I? I suppose I might have. That would have been when I sold off the last harvest I had from poor Curio's estate. It's the only time I ever went to the grain market."

"It surprises me that a patrician lady would stoop to such a transaction. Why didn't you send a steward?"

"The only steward I had at the time was Curio's, and he was sure to be on the side of Curio's family. Selling grain is far from the most scandalous thing I've done." Fulvia was totally indifferent to her bad reputation.

"In any case Balesus didn't do as well as you. Polasser told him to buy when it was time to sell. He lost a fortune."

"Did he? Serves him right. Why should an astrologer be expected to give accurate advice to a petty businessman? The stars proclaim the fortunes of great men, not little money grubbers like Balesus."

"Spoken like a true patrician," I said.

"And why not? It's what I am."

"Now that Polasser is no longer among us," I said, "whom do you consult upon celestial matters?"

"Recently I've been seeing Ashthuva. I think her knowledge of the art is even more comprehensive than Polasser's and she is the most delightful company."

"I daresay," I said, remembering.

"Do we have visitors?" said Antonius, entering the courtyard from the direction of the street. He was dressed in his usual brief tunic, sweating abundantly, and covered with sand, straw, and grime.

"Marcus, have you been fighting again?" Fulvia said.

"Just wrestling. Hello Decius, Hermes." With this perfunctory greeting he stepped into the pool, sat, and began washing himself down. The word informal does not begin to describe Marcus Antonius.

"Marcus, dear, Senator Metellus has been asking me about that murdered astrologer."

"He's been pestering everyone in Rome about the matter," Antonius said. He ducked his head beneath the water and came up blowing like a porpoise. "But Caesar ordered him to do it so there's no help for it. Are you any closer to finding the guilty party, Decius?"

"I hope so. I've learned a great deal, it's just a matter of putting it all together coherently."

"Well, that's your specialty." He stood up, dripping. "I just went three falls with Balbus."

"Who won?" I asked. So much for Asklepiodes' advice, I thought.

"He did. He's the only man in Rome who can beat me consistently."

"From the look of you, you weren't wrestling at the baths or the gymnasium," Fulvia noted.

"No, I encountered him at the cattle market and proposed a match right there."

"How entertaining it must have been for the market idlers," Fulvia said.

"I suppose it was. You don't get to see two real experts contending every day. I don't suppose there's any wine in the house?"

"I will take my leave of you, then," I said. "I must be about Caesar's business."

"Oh," Fulvia said. "I just remembered."

"Yes?"

"I remember now who told me about Polasser. It was Servilia."

We left the house and I stood in the street a moment, pinching the bridge of my long, Metellan nose. "My head hurts."

"This business is fit to give Hercules a headache," Hermes said.

"Everywhere I turn I encounter Servilia, the one woman in Rome I don't want to face without a legion at my back."

"Not to mention she's the woman Caesar doesn't want you to suspect of complicity in the murders. If she doesn't have you killed, he *will*."

"You do know how to brighten my day. What are we to do now?"

"It's as if we've walked down a blind alley with enemies chasing us," Hermes said, "and there we are staring at a blank wall and no place to go."

"A simile worthy of Homer," I commended. "So, what do we do when we're stuck in a blind alley?"

He grinned. "We duck into the nearest doorway."

"Right. Let's stop attacking this problem head-on and approach it obliquely."

"Whatever that means, I'm all for it. What now?"

"I've set a number of things in motion. Let's check on one of them. Let's go down to the docks and visit Ariston."

The big seaman looked surprised when we walked through his doorway. "Senator! This is convenient. I was just about to send a boy to track you down."

"You've found something?" I said eagerly.

"I may have. Take a seat." We sat and he bawled to a servant to bring wine for his distinguished guests. Moments later we were sipping a fine rose-colored Judean. These wines lack the body for drinking with meals, but they are an excellent light, refreshing afternoon pick-me-up.

"I put out the word as you asked," he began, "and pretty soon a sailor named Glaucus came to me with an odd story. A year ago he was on a ship called the *Ibis*, that sails a regular route between Alexandria and Rome, going up the eastern seaboard to Greece, then across to Italy. Seems that in Tyre they picked up a pair of passengers, easterners of some sort, a man and a woman. The woman was so swaddled in veils that they couldn't get a real idea of what she looked like. The man was tall and sort of willowy, in robes and a headcloth. The two of them spent a good part of each day sitting crosslegged on the deck, chanting long, monotonous prayers that got to setting the sailors' nerves on edge." He took a drink of his wine.

"Anyway, some of the men got to thinking it'd been a long time since they'd had a chance to visit the whores ashore, and here was this woman who wasn't a citizen protected by any laws that applied at sea. They had no idea what she looked like under all those veils but . . ." he spread his hands eloquently.

"Sailors are famously undiscriminating in such matters," I said. "So, these sea-lawyers decided that rape was a good idea?"

"Right. But it turned out it wasn't such a good idea after all. Somebody must've tipped the man what was afoot, because one morning they found three men dead on the deck, all with their necks broken. They were the ones who'd been doing the plotting."

"Didn't the surviving crew take any revenge?" I asked.

"I suspect the dead men weren't the most popular aboard, and who wants to face up to a man like that? They were sure that he was in league with some god or demon. What kind of man can break the necks of three strong men without alerting the men on watch? Would you want to deal with such a man?"

"It looks like I may have to," I said.

"Ah, Senator," Ariston said, "would you like for me to accompany you for a while? I can leave my business to my freedmen for a few days."

His offer was tempting. Ariston was a fighter of stupendous ferocity. I had once seen him kill a man in a manner I would have thought to be physically impossible. In sheer deadliness he was very close to my old friend Titus Milo. Hermes bristled a little at the suggestion that I might need a more accomplished bodyguard, but only a little. He had been present when Ariston had performed that feat with his broad, curved knife.

"I thank you, my friend," I said, "but I think that this matter will take more cunning than muscle power."

"Whatever you say, Senator, but don't hesitate to call on me if you should feel the need of backup."

"I won't hesitate a moment," I assured him.

Back outside Hermes and I conferred. "Sounds like we have our man," Hermes noted. "If, that is, we had any idea who he might be."

"We still have to determine his identity," I concurred, "but this bit of information allows us to eliminate a few suspects. He boarded in Tyre and was traveling with only a single companion. That pretty well clears Archelaus of suspicion. Not entirely, of course. He could have hired the man here in Rome, but I no longer suspect that the assassin was a part of his retinue. He's been here almost a year and Archelaus has been in Rome no more than a month or two."

"Something doesn't add up."

"A great many things don't add up. What particular anomaly strikes you?"

173

He frowned. "This man is a professional assassin, yet he only struck a few days ago. Why did he wait so long to exercise his skill?"

"A good point. I can think of a number of possibilities." I loved this sort of thing. "One, he may use other methods of elimination, perhaps reserving the neck-breaking for special occasions. Two, he may have used it, but we never heard about it. Such a death can easily be made to look accidental, and not every killing in Rome comes to my attention. There may have been a number of such that we never heard of. I was only engaged to investigate these deaths because the murdered men were Caesar's astronomers. And three, there are other places in Italy besides Rome. He may have been working elsewhere for a while."

"I suppose we can cross Cleopatra off the suspect list, too," Hermes said.

"Why?"

"Because Servilia is still alive."

"You're getting good at this. You've been paying attention. Of course, the two of them might be up to something together."

"There is that possibility," he agreed. "Is there some way we can find out if he has been active elsewhere in Italy?"

"None that I know of," I admitted. "We hear of exceptional murders from time to time, but ordinarily they are none of Rome's business and are handled by local authorities. Plus, remember this man can make his killings appear to be accidents. It's a good thing he's been in Rome such a short time."

"Why is that?"

"A man so talented would never go long without employment in Rome. There would be entirely too much demand for his services."

10

Julia displayed little sympathy for my plight.

"I think your hostility to Servilia is foolish. She isn't a scandalous woman like Fulvia. She's just ambitious for her son. She doesn't frequent low haunts or have numerous love affairs."

"Why is it," I asked her, "that people pretend to be shocked by comparatively harmless transgressions like adultery and extravagance? I've seen far more people killed because of ambition and greed than for such trifles."

"Far more husbands have died because of adultery than you would guess," she said darkly. Meaning it as a warning, no doubt.

"Yes, well, matrimony is never without hazard."

"Remember that. Servilia keeps popping up in this because she is now close to Caesar, and somehow this business is all about Caesar. It's his astronomers being murdered. This is aimed at him."

"I agree. It's an uncommonly oblique way of attacking him, though."

"Easterners are involved and that is how they work," she asserted.

It was after dinner, our guests had gone home and we were enjoying a rather crisp evening by the pool, sitting with a brazier of glowing coals between us. The year had been uncommonly mild but a chill was creeping into the air. Julia was wrapped in a heavy woolen cloak, but I preferred to exhibit manly hardihood by wearing nothing over my tunic.

"This is complicated even for our usual eastern enemies," I said. "Maybe these people come from even farther east. What's that place where silk comes from? I think it's about as far east as you can go."

"Keep your thoughts closer to home," she advised.

"I know, the king of Parthia is the most likely contender for foreign action, but somehow I don't think so. I think we have an oriental assassin working for somebody right here in Rome."

"There is still Sextus Pompey," she reminded me.

"Last I heard he was in Spain and our suspects came from the opposite direction. Admittedly, he could have agents working here in Rome who might have hired the killer, but young Pompey has no more imagination than his father. This is beyond him. If we can't figure it out, how could he have dreamed it up?"

"We're missing something," she said.

"Of course we are. That's always how it is when people behave in such a deceitful manner. Later on, when you have all the pieces in your grasp, you wonder why you never noticed those obvious factors that were staring you in the face all along."

"Callista says you should write all this down. Perhaps you could give a course of lectures on your methods."

"I ought to. Future generations will thank me."

"What if the grain swindle was just practice?" Julia said.

"Eh? Where did that come from?"

"It just seems to me that they may have had something bigger in mind. Polasser and Postumius discovered their mutual criminal inclinations. Polasser was intrigued by the chariot race swindle Postumius boasted about, and perhaps wanted to give it a try himself."

I saw what she was getting at. "But Postumius cautioned him against it. Felix the Wise might find out and punish them. Polasser was undoubtedly the more intelligent and imaginative man. He saw that the same swindle could be used in other venues. He had traveled widely, lived some time in Alexandria where the world grain trade is centered. He knew that trading in grain futures can be as much of a gamble as betting on the races. But you think it might have been just practice?"

"I believe so. Polasser needed some experience in this sort of criminality. He was already a fraudulent astrologer and needed to build up his confidence in the wider world of business."

"What was he practicing for?" I asked, already thinking I knew the answer.

"What is the biggest, most profitable activity in Rome?" she asked.

"Politics," I answered. "Politics as it is practiced at the highest levels, among the great families. How did he expect to—" Then it struck me. "Fulvia."

"He already knew her as her astrologer. He asked her to pick out some likely grain merchants and recommend him to them, tell them that his predictions were infallible. It's a sordid business for a patrician, but I wouldn't put anything past Fulvia."

I thought about it. "The temptation must have been strong. That was last year. Her husband, Curio, was dead and there was no love lost between her and the rest of his family. She hadn't landed Antonius yet, and she's a woman with expensive tastes. She had to sell off his last harvest before his male heirs could get their hands on it. Polasser held out the prospect of a huge profit from very little effort, and I've found patricians to be no less larcenous than the rest of us. They're just more snobbish about it."

She let that pass. "The question is, what sort of fraud was he perpetrating?"

I pondered it. "As a foreigner Polasser couldn't hope to take an active part in Roman politics, but politicians can be manipulated. He couldn't manipulate them directly, but he could do so through their wives. He had the tools he needed already at hand since most of his clients were highborn ladies."

"That chariot race elimination scheme wouldn't work, though," Julia said. "He wouldn't have a large enough pool of victims to begin with. Plus, these are people who talk with each other constantly. The ones he'd given bad advice would complain about him to the others."

"Right. It was something else. There are a lot of profitable activities at the top levels of government, but we can eliminate most of them. There are the propraetorian and proconsular commands, but the loot doesn't come pouring in until the promagistrate returns more than a year after being given the office. There is huge money in the censors' apportioning of the public contracts, but it's five years between censorships and with a dictator in power, who knows when we'll have censors again?"

"There is one issue of enormous importance yet to be decided," Julia said after a long pause.

"I know. Caesar's heir. It is the one problem I would give anything not to get involved with. I'd rather try to conquer Germania with a half century of rebellious Greek auxilia."

"TIME TO WAKE UP." IT WAS Hermes' voice. I opened my eyes. It was black as the bottom of Pluto's privy.

"Are the Gauls attacking?" I asked, trying to get oriented.

"No, we're back in Rome. We have another body to look at."

"What's going on?" Julia said next to me. It was her half-asleep voice.

"Just another murder, my dear," I assured her.

"Did you have to wake me? Go about your business, but do it quietly."

I got up quietly, dressed, and armed myself without making a sound. The unquiet times in Rome and the years with the legions had taught me the useful art of keeping my clothes and weapons where I could lay hands on them quickly in the dark. I waited until we were outside on the street before speaking again.

"Who is it this time?" I yawned mightily. There was just a trace of gray in the sky to the east, barely visible between the towering tenements that lined the street.

"Felix the Wise sent a messenger. Felix says he's found Postumius."

"Postumius," I said, scratching absently. I still wasn't quite awake. "The missing figure in all this. I take it Postumius is the corpse we're going to see?"

"Apparently so. The messenger will guide us there."

I realized with a start that there was a man standing next to us. I am never at my best early in the morning. "How did you find your way here through these black streets?" I asked him. Few people ventured into the nighttime streets of Rome without a torch-bearing escort.

"I am Pelotas, Senator," the man said.

"Pelotas? The famous burglar?"

"I was, Senator, before I reformed and became an honest man."

"Right. That's why Felix the Wise keeps you around. Well,

lead on." We followed him. He was quiet as a cat and walked through the gloom as if it were noon.

"I've known guides in Gaul who could work in the dark like you. They ate owls to improve their night vision. Do you eat owls?"

"That's for barbarians, Senator. I have good eyes. My father and grandfather were famous burglars, too, but what gives you the edge at night is a drop of belladonna juice in each eye just before you go out. It brightens things right up."

"It's good to work with a professional who knows his trade," I said. "Is Felix at the Labyrinth?"

"Not far from there. It's a house by the river."

We went through the shadowed streets and crossed the Forum and the cattle market. The gray light increased and I could almost discern my hand at arm's length by the time we crossed the Sublician Bridge. On the other side we went down a narrow street and were immediately plunged into blackness again. Pelotas stopped at a door I couldn't even see and knocked with a strange rhythm, some bit of underworld craft obscure to me and my sort. The door opened and light spilled out. The doorman was an ugly thug with a bare sword in his fist. When he saw who was outside he stepped back and gestured us in with his sword. Inside, I found Felix sitting at a table and five other men standing around, all well-armed. There were several clear violations of the law in that room and I wasn't going to do a single thing about it. Nighttime in the Trans-Tiber was no place for a mere senator to be throwing his weight around.

"Welcome, Senator," Felix said. "Have a seat. Got some nice warmed wine here, just the thing for a morning like this."

I saw no problem with this and sat. Fragrant steam rose from the wine pitcher as he poured. The wine had herbs steeped in it and made me more ready to face what I knew was going to be an unpleasant duty.

"I have a feeling," I said, "that Postumius is not going to be able to talk to me."

"I'm afraid not," Felix said, "but I'm pretty sure he talked to somebody."

"Before I view the body, tell me how you found him."

"It was Pelotas that found him. He was paying a visit here when he saw the corpse."

"I smelled it first," Pelotas said.

"I don't want to ask why you were here," I said.

"Just as well. Anyway, when I came in—"

"I don't suppose you just knocked and come through the front door," I said.

"Well, no. I came in through the roof."

"All right, I'll assume you were doing some repair work up there, had to remove a few tiles, that sort of thing?"

"Exactly, Senator. Anyway, I dropped in and the first thing hits me is the smell. I looked around until I found the room with the body. As you know, I see good at night, and that hour there was moonlight coming in through the window. I saw right away it was Postumius. I knew him from the races. He knew his horses better than most, and he knew all the drivers, so he was always good for a tip. Felix had put the word out a few days back that anyone who saw Postumius should come tell him right away, day or night, so I ran right over to the Labyrinth."

"Why did you pick this house to visit tonight? Other than the necessary roof repair, I mean."

"Well, I'd heard it was a rich man's place. I'd looked it over the last few nights and never saw anyone here, nor any lights."

"Always good to do repair work when the owner is away," Hermes commented. "That way he's not disturbed by all the noise."

"That's how it is," Pelotas agreed.

"Does anyone know which rich man owns this house?" I asked. All I got were some shrugs. "Where did you hear that a rich man owned the place?"

"From the neighbors. I never asked his name."

"Er, Senator," Felix said, "what's all this about?"

"It's how he works," Hermes assured him. "He collects all the available facts before he makes any assumptions."

"Philosopher, eh?" Felix said. "I never would've expected."

I looked around. The house was of modest size, but even the houses of the rich were relatively small in those days. The wealthy spent money on lavish country houses, maintaining a pose of antique virtue in Rome. There was more room for sprawl in the Trans-Tiber, but this house was on one of the smaller streets near the river and was typical of the district.

Not that it was all that modest inside. The walls in the room where we sat were adorned with frescoes of the highest quality and the floor was tiled in intricate geometrical patterns. There was a statue of Apollo just outside the door that opened onto the *impluvium*. It looked like a very superior copy of the original by Praxiteles, probably a product of Aphrodisias, and I knew from experience how expensive Aphrodisian sculptures could be.

No sense putting it off any longer. "Well, let's have a look at him," I said.

We got up and passed through the colonnade surrounding the *impluvium*. In the rear of the house we took a stair to the second floor and walked a few paces along the balcony to where another armed man stood guard at a door. We went inside.

As Pelotas had hinted, the smell was awful. It usually is when someone has been tortured to death. The late Postumius had been bound naked to a chair and worked over by an expert, or more likely by a team of them. He had been burned, beaten, partially flayed, and bits of him hung loose, apparently torn by pincers.

"As a soldier and magistrate," I said, "I've witnessed a good many military and judicial tortures. I've never seen anything this comprehensive."

"Somebody wanted some answers from him," Felix said. "From the look of it, he didn't know what they wanted him to tell them."

"Why do you say that?" I asked.

"I knew the man. He didn't have the backbone to hold his tongue under a working over like this."

"Very likely. Hermes—"

"I know. Go get Asklepiodes." He turned and left the room, for once all too eager to run off on an errand.

There was a single window at the rear of the room. I went to it and opened the shutters and leaned out to breathe some clean air. Below was a short embankment, and beyond it the river. It was a good place to torture someone. It was upstairs in the center of the house, with a number of walls between this room and the neighboring houses. It was as far as you could get from the street and nothing was to the rear but the river. A man could scream as loud as he liked and not be heard.

"Any idea who owns this house?" I asked.

"None," Felix said. "I could find out."

"Don't bother. I'll just ask the neighbors as soon as the neighborhood is awake. Well, there's nothing to be gained standing around here."

We went back downstairs and I took another cup of the hot, spiced wine. I needed it. "It's dawn," I said. "You and your men can go now. I won't forget this favor, Felix."

"Always happy to be of service to the Senate and People,"

183

Felix said. He knew that I might again be a sitting magistrate and in a position to spare him serious punishment. His class and mine had an understanding in these matters. They left me alone with my thoughts and the remaining wine. It was almost gone when Asklepiodes arrived.

He was as cheerful as usual, despite the hour. "Murder never waits upon our convenience, does it, Decius?"

"I fear not. Hermes will show you where he is. Have a look and tell me what you think." They disappeared upstairs. From outside, I heard morning sounds as the neighborhood embarked upon the coming day. Birds sang and I heard distant hammering. They were not upstairs for long.

"That's enough to put a man off his breakfast," he said.

"Have some wine," I advised. "There's a bit left."

He held up a hand. "I don't drink wine before noon."

"That's an odd habit," I commented. I peered into the bottom of the pitcher. "Just as well. There really isn't all that much left. Were you able to learn anything?"

"Only that the torture was carried on far too long. Painful though they were, his injuries were not sufficient to kill him by themselves. Signs of suffocation are absent. He died from the pain or terror or a combination of the two."

"From the look of him they would have been sufficient for the task," I observed. "It seems Felix the Wise was right. He didn't have whatever information they wanted from him."

"You assume that this was a torture for information?"

"Naturally. That's the most common reason to give a man a working over like that."

"Might it not have been revenge?"

I thought about it. "He seems hardly the sort to have earned such enmity, but then, how much do we know about him? I suppose someone truly vindictive might have wanted him to expire with embellishments. Rome abounds in men qualified to deliver the treatment."

"I will take my leave then. I am still working on the neck-breaking puzzle. It seems to me that I must be overlooking something abundantly obvious."

"I've had that feeling for this whole weary business," I told him. He left with my thanks.

Hermes and I went outside to the now-awake neighborhood. A barber had set up his stool, his basin of warm water, and his vials of oil. A shopkeeper opened his shutters and dragged out his display cabinets of copper pans and platters. I walked over to this man.

"Good morning, Senator," he said. He didn't seem to recognize me as the infamous calendar tamperer.

"Good morning. Would you happen to know who owns that house?" I pointed to the one from which I had just emerged.

"It's been standing empty for quite a while," he said. "Last I remember, it belonged to that tribune of the people, the one who died in Africa a while back, fighting for Caesar's cause."

"Curio?" Hermes said.

"That's the one."

"Did he actually live there?" I asked him.

"I don't recall ever seeing him there."

"Has anybody lived there recently?" I asked.

He shook his head. "Not in months. There were some funny-looking people there a few months ago, foreigners of some sort, but they were only there for a little while, less than a month."

"What sort of foreigners?" Hermes asked.

"Couldn't say. Not Greeks, but that's as much as I can tell you.

They didn't show themselves much and never talked to anyone here that I heard of."

"Have you seen anyone go in or out the last few days?" I inquired.

"Not in the daytime," he said. "As for the nights, I couldn't say."

I thanked him and we walked away a few steps. "Curio again," I said.

"So this place belongs to Fulvia?" Hermes said.

"I hope not. Let's not assume so. It may have passed to someone else in his will. I hope that's the case. I don't want to have to haul Fulvia into court. She'd probably just have me killed, even if Antonius didn't."

We conferred for a while with the neighbors to either side and across the street. Nobody had seen or heard anything. All remembered some "foreigners" living there a few months previously, something that might or might not be significant. Much of the Trans-Tiber district catered to the river trade and there were many resident foreigners living there. It would not be at all unusual for such people to rent a house while its owner was away. On the other hand, we had the odd foreigners the sailor had told us of. Was there a connection between the two and this house?

The sun rose, the day grew warmer, and we headed back toward the City proper. Halfway across the bridge I sat on the coping and began to think. "What do we know about Curio?" I mused.

"He was a politician like a hundred others," Hermes said. "He was rowdier than most, good with crowds, and an extremely popular tribune of the plebs. For a little while he was more popular than Caesar or Pompey, but that's common with tribunes. While they're in office the people love them for their public works and the laws they whip up enthusiasm for. Usually their popularity fades as soon as they step down from office."

"That's how I remember him. His father was Caesar's deadly enemy, a strong supporter of Pompey and the aristocratic faction. For a while it looked like the younger Curio would follow the same path."

"But he ran up huge debts endearing himself to the voters," Hermes said. "Not unlike others." He grinned when he saw me wince. "But worse than most. Rumor had it that he was more than two and a half million denarii out of purse."

"So what made him come over to Caesar's side? I remember that Caesar covered his debts, which was no small thing, but he trumped up some sort of charge to desert the *optimates* and join the *populares.*"

"Maybe you should ask Sallustius."

I shook my head. "I don't want to be any more obligated to him than I am already. Besides, it may be nothing. The man's been dead for a couple of years now, fighting King Juba in Africa."

"Old Juba," Hermes mused. "There was bad blood between him and Caesar, so I guess it was his way of getting revenge. What was his grudge? Didn't Caesar insult him publicly?"

I chuckled at the memory. "He certainly did. It was just before Caesar left for Spain. He was representing a client of his, a Numidian nobleman, in a case before the *praetor peregrinus.* The old king, Heimpsal, claimed this noble as a tributary, and the man disputed it and went to Caesar for aid. Heimpsal sent young Prince Juba to represent his side of the case. Caesar got a bit carried away in his defense and he grabbed Juba by the beard and dragged him all over the court." I couldn't help but laugh. "Of course the court found in favor of the king after such a display, but Caesar smuggled his client out to Spain with him."

"We're used to rough-and-tumble in our courts," Hermes noted, "but that sort of thing is a mortal insult to royalty."

"Well, Caesar was young then, but it's no wonder Juba was just waiting to do him a bad turn. He went over to the aristocrats as soon as they set up shop in Africa."

"So a few days ago wasn't the first time Caesar roughed up a foreign representative publicly."

I thought about that. "It was different. Caesar was a young politician on the make, not dictator of Rome. Juba was just another prince. We've never made much over foreign princes, since their fathers breed so many of them and nobody gets royal honors in Rome. Archelaus is an ambassador, and we always observe the diplomatic niceties. Usually, anyway." I thought about it for a moment. "At any rate, Juba is dead."

"How did that happen?" Hermes wanted to know.

I had to think about it. Those were eventful years, packed with incident. There were powerful personalities and men had died in peculiar ways.

"Curio was victorious at first. He was a brilliant man, and he had a flair for military affairs as well as for politics, but he and his army were ambushed by one of Juba's generals. Curio decided to die fighting rather than surrender. When Caesar showed up in Africa, Juba went to join Publius Scipio, but Scipio was defeated and Juba fled with Petreius. When their defeat was inevitable, they decided to fight in single combat. That way the loser would have an honorable death and the winner could commit suicide to avoid capture by Caesar. Petreius won and promptly killed himself."

Hermes shook his head. "I'll never understand nobles and royalty."

"Personally, I'd have surrendered as soon as I knew Caesar was anywhere near. That's probably why I'll never be entrusted with command of an army."

"Well, the day is young. What next?"

"I hate this," I said.

"Hate what?"

"All this scurrying about, cornering people and asking questions, while all the time the killer or killers go calmly about their business, killing and torturing people as if I didn't worry them at all. As if I didn't even exist."

"It's probably just as well," he said. "If they were worried about you they'd probably kill you, too."

"They might yet. I would love to take some sort of direct action instead of merely reacting to what's already been done."

"We can't do a thing until we have a firm suspect," Hermes pointed out.

"I still haven't looked over Archelaus's staff on the via Aurelia," I said. "It's not far away and I want to arrive unannounced."

We walked along one of the roads that go northeast through the Trans-Tiber. It ended at the western end of the Cestian Bridge, which connects the Tiber Island to the west bank. This area housed a great many river bargemen, and we heard every accent and dialect to be found along the navigable length of the Tiber from Ostia almost to the Appenines.

The via Aurelia begins at the Cestian Bridge. Like all our highways it was lined with tombs, though it wasn't nearly as crowded with them as the far older via Appia. There were also some stately villas, most of them owned by *equites* who wanted to avoid the crowding of the City proper, especially in summer, while staying close to Rome and the exhilarating activity described by Callista. Aristocrats generally had their estates much farther from the walls.

We paused and took a breather at a small but exquisite temple dedicated to Diana and a priest there told us that the embassy from Parthia resided at a villa no great distance away, and that we should take a small side-road flanked by two herms. The villa was at the end of the road.

We found the road a short time later. The herms were draped with garlands of holly leaves, the greenest foliage to be found at that time of year. It pleased me to see these rustic devotions kept up. City people were getting more and more out of touch with their rural roots. We passed between them with a nod of acknowledgement.

The villa was old-fashioned, a rather modest house surrounded by a number of outbuildings, most of them converted into residences. There was some small commotion in the house as we approached and a well-dressed man emerged, holding a small, silver-topped staff. He looked Greek but dressed Roman. Another Bithynian, no doubt.

"Ah, Senator, welcome," he stammered. "We were not expecting so distinguished a visitor."

"You weren't? Didn't Archelaus send word to expect me?"

"I've had no communication from across the river in a few days. I am Themistocles, steward to Archelaus. How may I be of service?"

"I am on an investigation for the dictator," I told him. "I need to inspect the personnel of your mission. Please be so good as to summon them."

Now he looked alarmed. "I had heard that my master's interview with Caesar did not go well. Surely he will not take action against us?"

"Nothing of the sort," I assured him. "We are not barbarians. We respect embassies. Now, will you summon your people?"

Relieved but mystified, he went to do my bidding. A short time later we had almost a hundred people lined up before the house. I immediately dismissed the women, the young boys and the older men to go about their duties. This left about fifty men of an age to be dangerous. Hermes and I began looking them over, paying special attention to their hands. As at the town residence, there were some tough-looking specimens, all of the same tribe as the guard I had questioned there.

Toward the end of the line was a smaller man, dressed in a rough, dark-colored tunic. As we neared him, he looked about, his face whitening.

"There's a shifty one," Hermes said. He left the man he had been questioning and made for the suspicious one. The servant whirled and dashed off with surprising alacrity.

"Action at last!" Hermes said, grinning. He took off in pursuit, and I found myself wishing that I had someone to place a wager with. Hermes was an excellent runner and in top condition, but fear had lent the fleeing man the winged feet of Mercury. It would be a close thing.

"Are you a betting man, Themistocles?"

"Eh? I am sorry, Senator, what did you say?"

"Never mind. Who is that man?"

"Just one of the locals I hired to help in the stables. When we arrived here we required a few servants who knew both the area and the language. It was easier than buying slaves that we would have to sell when we leave. May I know what this is about?"

"All in good time. How long has he been here?"

"Not long, perhaps ten days. Is he wanted for some crime in Rome?"

"If he wasn't before, he is now," I said. "If he'd just brazened it out I probably wouldn't have suspected him. That's what a guilty conscience will do to a man. He condemned himself without a word."

"I daresay," Themistocles said, swallowing. "Will there be trouble over this?"

"That remains to be seen. I believe I'll go find my assistant. Maybe by now he's run the rogue to ground. Don't go anywhere."

I went off in the direction the two had gone. In moments I saw pursuer and pursued, made tiny by distance. The fleeing man leapt a low stone wall with great agility and Hermes cleared it moments later. All that money I spent sending him to the *ludus* was proving to be a sound investment. I didn't hurry. In this sort of tortoise-and-hare situation, I preferred to play the tortoise.

The hours are short in winter, and I spent the better part of one catching up with Hermes. He lay upon the ground, sweating abundantly and breathing heavily. I saw no wounds on him.

"Shame on you, Hermes," I said. "Letting an amateur like that get away from you."

"Amateur?" he gasped. "That man is a trained runner. I'm a trained fighter. There's a difference."

I sat down beside him. "I don't think that was our killer."

"I don't think so either," Hermes wheezed. "The killer would have made a fight of it."

"You're right. Pride would have demanded it. Our murderer is a superlative craftsman in the art of homicide. This one is just a flunky."

"One of the torturers?" he hazarded.

"He didn't look that brutish to me. Who is another missing man in this business?"

He thought about that for a while as he got his breathing under control. "The servant on the Tiber Island, the one who summoned all the astronomers to meet with Polasser, and then couldn't be found."

"That may be it. He was already established here. As a free laborer, he wouldn't need a pass to leave the estate. He just went down the via Aurelia to the Cestian Bridge, across to the island, did his job, then hurried back here while we were all gaping at Polasser's body."

"Was the killer with him, do you think?" He tried to sit up, then fell back, groaning.

"Unlikely. I suspect that his task was arranged by a go-between. If he could identify the assassin by sight, he would have been killed as soon as he was no longer useful."

This time he managed to sit. "He looked local."

"That's what the steward said he was."

"So he's not one of Cleopatra's people." He felt his abdomen gingerly.

"Can you get up?" I said, rising myself.

With my help, he managed to struggle to his feet and stay upright. He retched a bit, then steadied. "Let's take it easy going back, all right?"

So we ambled back to the villa, admiring the pleasant countryside.

"So is Archelaus our main suspect now?" Hermes asked.

"I don't think so. Archelaus knew I was coming out here to inspect his staff, yet he didn't warn the man to get out quickly. Apparently he had no idea he was harboring someone involved with the murders."

"But there has to be some connection," Hermes protested. "Out of ten thousand hiding places near Rome, he picked the Parthian embassy."

"It bears thinking about," I agreed.

When we arrived at the villa, Themistocles had assembled the servants who had worked with the fugitive.

"His name is Caius," the steward said.

"That's not very imaginative," I said. "It's the most common of Roman names."

We questioned the servants but they all said the same thing, exactly what I suspected: They barely knew him. He did his work and kept to himself.

Just like all the thousands of humble, near-invisible people all around us.

11

"YOU LET HIM GET AWAY?" JULIA said witheringly.

"I didn't let him get away," I protested. "Hermes did."

"The man ran like a gazelle," Hermes said defensively. "I was catching up to him at first, but he vaulted the field walls without slowing down a bit. I had to take them slower. In the end I ran out of wind, and he didn't." We were back at the house. It was late afternoon.

Julia looked from one to the other of us as if at a pair of not-too-bright children. "And that doesn't tell you something?"

"Enlighten us," I said, nettled.

"It means he's probably a highly trained athlete. Maybe even a professional. If so, he probably trains at a gymnasium. There are only a few in Rome. Check them all. Someone may know him."

"I was about to suggest the same thing," I said. She just snorted disgustedly. "All right, what else are we missing? Does the torture and death of Postumius suggest anything to you?"

She thought about that for a while. "Your friend Felix was right.

It went on far too long just for information extraction. Whatever he knew, he must have spilled at the first threat. He had no sense of honor or loyalty, and what was anyone going to do to him that could be worse than what was coming? Someone was very, very displeased with Postumius."

"You have a gift for understatement," I commended, "but where does that leave us? Men like Postumius always have enemies. People resent being cheated, and sometimes they get carried away in their eagerness for revenge. It went far beyond mere punishment, but a touchy sense of honor causes some people to lose their sense of proportion."

"That suggests patrician involvement," Julia said. "Plebeians rarely have so extreme a sense of honor."

"Back to Fulvia again," Hermes said. "She may be shameless and scandalous, but you just can't get more patrician."

"That is true," Julia concurred, "and she is just the sort to enjoy such a thing. She probably made use of a pair of hot pliers herself."

"Let's not make unwarranted assumptions," I cautioned. "Just because you dislike Fulvia is no reason to place her in that room, wielding torture instruments with style and panache."

"You are hopelessly naïve. The woman is evil."

"What of that? I've known a great many evil women in this city."

"So you have," she said ominously. It had been the wrong thing to say. She rose. "I am going to the evening ceremony at the Temple of Vesta. After that, I am joining Servilia and some other ladies for dinner and gossip. I'll see if I can get anything useful from Servilia."

"Excellent," I said, happy for the change of subject. "If you see Brutus while you're there, see if you can pump him about this transmigration of souls stuff. Something about what he's been saying doesn't add up."

"I'll do that. This has been a long day for you two. Don't go out carousing. Get to bed early and look into the gymnasiums first thing in the morning." She went out, followed by two of her serving girls.

"Between Julia and her uncle," I said, "throwing in this mysterious assassin and the conspiracy that seems to surround him, I'm at a loss to know who terrifies me more."

The next morning we set out to make the rounds of the gymnasiums. As Julia had said, Rome had only a few at the time. Recently the First Citizen has tried to revive interest in Greek-style athletics, but back then Roman men usually exercised at the baths, or went to the Field of Mars for military exercises like drilling and javelin-throwing or to the *ludus* for sword practice. The gymnasiums were patronized mainly by Greeks or people from Greek-influenced parts of the world.

The first we tried was located just outside the Lavernalis Gate, at the southwestern extremity of the city. It was always easier to find spacious, inexpensive land outside the walls than within, so if you needed generous grounds, that was where you went. Your place was likely to be destroyed if an enemy invaded, but that hadn't happened for a generation, not since the Social War in Sulla's day.

This one was located in a pleasant grove of plane trees and tall pines. In its forecourt was a fine statue of Hercules, the patron of athletes. A large field to one side offered facilities for those sports requiring space: running, the discus, and the javelin. Inside, it consisted simply of a long exercise yard floored with sand, where men and boys went through a number of exercises under the supervision of instructors. Here they vaulted, wrestled, and tossed the heavy ball.

In one corner a pair of burly men practiced pugilism. For sparring they wore leather helmets and their forearms were thickly wrapped with leather. Their hands were wrapped in padding as well. In a real bout their hands would be wrapped in hard leather straps, perhaps featuring the bronze *caestus*. They were finishing their bout as we came in, the trainer separating them with his staff. They removed their helmets and one of them wore the small top-knot that identified a professional boxer.

It was easy enough to separate the Romans from the Greeks and would-be Greeks. The former wore loincloths and sometimes tunics while exercising. The latter worked out naked. The head trainer, carrying a silver-topped wand, saw us and approached.

"How may I help you, Senator?" He was sixty if he was a day, but as lean and hard as a legionary recruit after his first six months in the training camp, and he moved with an athlete's springy grace. He made me ashamed of myself. I made a mental note to go to the *ludus* or the Field of Mars every day from now on until I was in good shape and the flab was gone from my waist. Julia was right.

"We are looking for an outstanding runner, a man about twenty-five to thirty years of age, medium height, dark hair, spare build. He is probably a native Roman."

"Except for the Roman part you've described most of the best runners I know. Some are younger, of course."

"This one is exceptionally good at vaulting while running full speed," Hermes put in.

"That narrows it." He scratched in his grizzled beard. "A couple of years back a man trained here for a while. Ran like the wind and loved cross-country racing. That calls for lots of vaulting, of course. He answered your description, too. A Roman. What was his name, now? Domitius, that was it, Caius Domitius."

The man had been using the praenomen Caius, not that it meant much, but it was a possibility. "Do you have any information on him?" I asked. "Any records?"

He shook his head. "If he'd been a member who paid by the year or the month we'd have some record of him, but he just came in and paid by the day for use of the facility. Half the men who come through here are day users."

Hermes had been scanning the athletes in the yard. "Did he work with a particular trainer?"

"He mostly worked out alone, like most cross-country runners, but I know he worked with at least one for technique drill. Let me see." He whistled loudly and all activity stopped. Everyone looked puzzled as he crossed the yard, calling the trainers to him. When they were gathered he talked to them in a low voice.

"He doesn't seem very curious about these questions," Hermes noted.

"He's a foreigner," I said. "Ionic Greek, by his accent. Aliens are usually reluctant to delve too deeply into what looks like Roman trouble."

The head trainer returned with another man, this one small and thin, the classic build of the long-distance runner. He was sandy-haired and had blue eyes, his skin deeply tanned.

"This is Aulus Paullus. He worked with the man you are asking after."

The euphoniously named man nodded. "What do you need to know, Senator? I'm afraid I can't tell you a lot. He wasn't here long." His accent was pure Latium: from the district around Rome. I took this as a good sign.

"First off, was the man a real Roman?"

"Talked like he was born within the *pomerium*, which is unusual for a long-distance runner. They're usually from the rural areas or work as messengers for the big estates. City boys more often train for the dashes. You have to be able to endure a lot of pain to be a distance runner."

"Yes, we urban people are soft and degenerate," I agreed. "Do you have any idea of his status? Was he born free or a freedman?"

He thought about that for a while. "He spoke well, when he spoke at all. I think if he was born a slave, he must've been schooled with the master's children."

"But he didn't speak much?" I asked.

"Mostly he was saving his wind for running."

"Do you know if he competed in any of the major games?" Hermes asked. I should have thought of that.

"If you mean the Olympics or the Isthmian or any of the great ones in Greece, I don't think so. Everyone who competes in those brags about it for the rest of his life, and Domitius never mentioned it."

"There was a time," the head trainer said sourly, "when only full-blooded Hellenes could compete in the great games. Now Romans can compete."

"There was a time," Hermes said, "when foreigners couldn't be Roman citizens, too. Times change."

"Let's stick to the subject at hand," I admonished.

"Sorry, Senator," the head trainer said.

"Did he mention competing in games around here?" I pressed on.

"He said a couple of times a year he went south to run in the Greek games at Cumae. Most of the Greeks in Italy live down south. Didn't mention taking home any prizes, though."

"Are there any such games held at or near Rome?" I asked.

"None that feature cross-country running," the head trainer said. "There's an informal meet held at the Circus Flaminius on the calends of every month. Nothing official, no prizes or palms or wreaths awarded, but most of the serious athletes attend, to keep in practice for the major games. But the running events are all of the stadium sort. No long-distance races."

They had no more to offer, and I thanked them. Hermes and I made our way to three other gymnasiums but none had any better prospects.

"So you think this Domitius is our man?" Hermes said as we lounged in the baths just off the Forum.

"It isn't much," I said, "but it's the best lead we've got."

"Domitius is a patrician name, isn't it?"

"Only the ones surnamed Albinus, and that family is almost extinct, though their plebeian branch is still prominent. The rest are all plebeian. The Domitius Ahenobarbus and the Domitius Calvus families are plebeian. And there are plenty of plebeians named just plain Domitius."

"Good. We don't need more patrician involvement in this. It's too bad there's no long-distance running at the Flaminius on the calends. We might have caught him there."

"I've been thinking about that," I told him. "If he's an enthusiast about Greek athletics, he might show up anyway, to watch the others compete. When is the calends?"

He shrugged. "Is this one of the thirty-one day months?"

"I've forgotten. It's not that far off, but I hope we get this cleared up before then. Caesar was never a patient man and lately he's become even less so."

"Do you think Asklepiodes is right and Caesar is ill? What's going to happen if he just drops dead?"

"I don't like the prospect," I admitted. "Everybody dies and Caesar is no exception, but if he dies now, the sort of men who will contend over the government fill me with dismay. Cicero is the best of them, but he has no real influence anymore, he's just a senior voice in the Senate. It will be the likes of Antonius and Lepidus,

201

maybe Cassius, and he's not a bad man, just too reactionary. Sextus Pompey could return to Rome and have a try. With Caesar dead nobody would stop him and it would be civil war between him and Antonius inside a year." I shook my head. "It's a bad prospect."

"So what happens if Caesar lives?" Hermes asked.

"Not good, but better. I don't care about his building and engineering projects, but I'd like to see him finish his government reforms and his reordering of the constitution. Sulla did that and it's served us well for a long time. If Caesar would do that and back down from office, handing off his powers as he retires, we just might make it through the next few years without a war of Roman against Roman and emerge with a stable political order. If he accomplishes that, Caesar's name will live forever."

"And if he dies soon?"

"He'll be forgotten in a few years," I pronounced, "just another failed political adventurer." A fat lot I knew.

THE MAN IN QUESTION WAS RE-cruiting manpower for his upcoming war. Most of the veterans of the long wars in Gaul had been given their discharges, though many were eager to rejoin the standards. Caesar had proven that he brought victory and loot, the two most important things to a Roman soldier. He was brilliant and he was lucky, and the latter was the most important qualification a general could have. Give a legionary a choice between a strong disciplinarian who is also a skilled tactician and a commander who is lucky, and he will pick the lucky one every time. To his soldiers, consistent good luck such as Caesar displayed was a sure sign that the gods loved him, and what more than that could one ask?

The legions numbered First, Second, Third, and Fourth since

ancient times had been under the personal command of the consuls, and all four fell to Caesar's command as dictator. It was these legions he was bringing up to full strength. The time was long past when a large army could be raised from the district around Rome, so Caesar was combing all of Italy and Cisalpine Gaul for recruits and sending them to his training camps. Most of these were located in Campania, since that district was extremely fertile and could support the troops, and because there were still wide public lands there, unclaimed by our greedier senators and *equites*, though they were hard at work on that problem. Good land never stayed out of aristocratic hands for long.

I, personally, thought that Caesar had finally taken on too great a task. Fighting brave but ill-organized Gauls was one thing; Parthia was quite another. Parthia was a vast, sprawling empire, and heir to the Persian Empire of the Great Kings. Of course, that was part of Parthia's charm, as far as Caesar was concerned. Only Alexander had ever conquered Persia, and Caesar would inevitably be dubbed the new Alexander, should he succeed in doing the same.

Unfortunately, King Phraates was no Darius. Darius had been a palace-bred monarch who brought his harem with him on campaign and ran at the first reverse in battle. Phraates was a hard-living soldier-king. His Parthians were tough horse-archers recently off the eastern steppes who had invaded the empire and reinvigorated the tired old Persian blood.

Romans have always excelled in open battle, where we can close with the enemy and defeat him hand-to-hand. The Roman soldier with pilum and short sword is unmatched at this sort of combat. We are also preeminent at engineering and siege warfare. Unfortunately, the Parthians refused to oblige us by fighting our way. They are nomadic bowmen and think hand-to-hand combat undignified.

At Carrhae they rode around the legions of Crassus in circles, pouring in volley after volley of arrows. The Romans crouched under their shields and waited for them to run out of arrows. Thus it had always happened before, but not this time. The Parthians brought up camels loaded with arrows and the storm never stopped. The Roman army couldn't fight and it couldn't run, so it died. A small band under Cassius managed to cut their way free and escaped. A pitiful remnant surrendered and was marched off into slavery.

If Caesar had some plan to negate this little advantage he wasn't telling me about it, nor anyone else. He seemed to assume that his legendary luck would overcome anything. This was another reason I was determined not to follow him into any more of his military adventures. I had rolled the dice too many times to believe that good luck lasts forever.

That day he was on the field of Mars reviewing a cohort of his new troops that had marched in from Capua the evening before. They were bright in new equipment and their shields shone with fresh paint. Something looked odd about them and it took me a moment to realize that their helmets were made of iron instead of the traditional bronze. They had been made in the Gallic armories Caesar had captured in the war. The Gauls are the best ironworkers in the world.

I was not surprised to see a large number of senators standing about, observing. Besides the general Roman fascination with all things military, they were all curious about the latest manifestation of Caesar's ambitions. They commented on equipment, on drill and discipline, on the alacrity with which the men obeyed orders conveyed by voice and trumpet. On command the soldiers advanced and hurled their *pila*, then drew their swords and charged upon their invisible enemy. Senators and other veterans in the crowd tut-tutted and lamented the decline in strength and fortitude since the days when they were legionaries in service against Jugurtha or Sertorius or Mithridates.

Some commented that the shorter, wider sword carried these days was not as effective as the old one, while others said that it encouraged aggressiveness, since a man had to get closer to use it. Someone thought it odd that men so young had weapons adorned with silver. Someone else said that Caesar issued them expensive weapons so they'd be less likely to drop them and run, raising a general laugh.

I had been hearing talk of this sort all my life, the old-timers forever denigrating the new recruits. In truth, they looked like excellent material to me, and sore experience had given me a good eye for soldiers. Most were just young and inexperienced, but there was a good salting of grizzled veterans among them. These would provide a steadying influence when the arrows started to fly and slingstones rang from the fine iron helmets. They would probably prove to be as good as any other soldiers Rome had fielded.

Caesar was resplendent as usual, sitting in a leopardskin-draped curule chair upon the big, marble reviewing stand dressed in his triumphal regalia complete with golden wreath. This time I saw a new touch to his turnout, and I was not alone.

"He's wearing red boots!" said a scandalized old senator.

"What's wrong with that?" demanded an idler. "Caesar can wear anything he wants!"

"Not red boots," the old man insisted. "There was a time when only kings of Rome were allowed to wear them."

Caesar's impressive footwear resembled the thick-soled buskins worn by actors on the stage, elaborately strapped and pierced, and topped with spotted lynx skin. They would have been merely a showy affectation had not the color been an affront to the Senate, as I had no doubt was Caesar's intention.

"He's asking for trouble, isn't he?" Hermes said in a low voice.

"He's done little else for the last ten years," I affirmed. "He adds a bit more royal glitter to his appearance from time to time, testing the waters. If the Senate is outraged, so what? Just so the people stay behind him. That's where his power lies."

"You think he really intends to be king?"

"I've tried to deny it for a long time," I said, "but those boots may be a bit too much. He's outdone the consuls of the past. Now he wants to outdo Alexander. What's the one thing left that will place him unassailably ahead of every Roman who has ever lived?"

"King of Rome. But there have been kings before."

I shook my head. "They were petty kings, lording it over an Italian city-state still being regularly whipped by the Etruscans. With Parthia added to his conquests and Cleopatra making him Pharaoh, he'll effectively be emperor of the world." I shrugged. "Well, never let it be said that Caesar lacks ambition." I shut up when I saw a little band of senators heading my way. I plastered a silly smile on my face but I was too late. Cicero was among them, and he was steeped so deeply in the rhetorical arts that no nuance of facial expression escaped him.

"So, do you believe now, Decius?" Cicero said, gesturing toward the podium. Brutus and Cassius were with him, as on the day when Caesar had rebuked Archelaus. Lucius Cinna, Caesar's former brother-in-law, was with them, and some others I did not know as well.

"What Caesar wants and what he can accomplish are not the same thing," I said.

"Then it behooves us all," Cassius said, "to assure that he does not accomplish his ambitions."

"And how do you propose to do that?" I asked him.

He glanced at Cicero, but Cicero didn't catch it. "Roman patriots have always found ways to frustrate the designs of tyrants."

"Let me know as soon as you've found a way," I told him.

"At least his soldiers look fit for battle," Brutus said, changing the subject clumsily.

"So they do," Cicero agreed, "and perhaps this war of his will be the best thing for all of us. It will keep him out of Italy for some time, perhaps a few years. Much can happen in that time."

"And much will, I've no doubt," said Cinna, "but not an election. Not as long as Caesar is dictator in perpetuity. All offices with *imperium* will go to men nominated by Caesar and confirmed by his tame assemblies. We'll have tribunes of the plebs, but their power of veto is suspended while he is dictator, and what is a tribuneship without the veto? All they can do is propose the legislation he has already laid out for them."

That was the real reason for the resentment of these men. Caesar was frustrating their own ambitions and humbling their pride. Except for Cicero, they were all men from the great families, men who thought high office to be their natural right, inherited from their ancestors. I had been such a man myself, once. When men prate of things like patriotism, you can be sure that self-interest is at the root of it.

"Caesar is not immortal," Brutus said, a pronouncement that could be banal or fraught with meaning, depending on how you looked at it.

"He thinks himself godlike," Cicero said lightly. "Let us hope that his fellow deities see fit to call him to join them soon." The rest laughed, but without much humor.

They turned back toward the City gate and left me pondering. "Cassius is plotting something," I said to Hermes, "but he doesn't want to talk about it in front of Cicero."

"I caught that," he said. "But why, do you think? They all seem to be of a mind on the subject of Caesar and his power and ambition."

"He could be planning something desperate, and Cicero is not a man you want to involve in desperate action. He'd lose his nerve at the last minute. He acted decisively and against popular opinion once in his career, when he put down the Catilinarian revolt. He's been conservative and vacillating ever since. He'd be the weak reed in any conspiracy."

"What is Cassius up to?"

"I don't want to know." It was all a great distraction. I had other things on my mind.

That evening Julia filled me in on what she had learned the previous night.

"Servilia is definitely on the outs with her dear little Brutus, and she doesn't really approve of his friends lately, Cassius and Cinna and that lot."

"Why not? They positively reek of nobility and old-fashioned Roman virtue."

"I think it's because they're so vehemently anti-Caesarian. I, on the other hand, am most definitely in the Caesarian camp so she feels she can confide in me. She wants Brutus close to Caesar and wishes he'd go back to his old moneylending habits. She loathes the business as ill-bred, but at least it's politically neutral."

"Anything about the astrologers? The exotic woman in particular?"

"No, and every time I tried to bring the subject up—discreetly, of course—nobody seemed much interested. Atia was there and she had a whole collection of omens from all over Italy. She must employ people just to collect them. So everybody was talking about a two-headed goat born in Bruttium and an eagle that snatched a child in Cumae and a statue of Scipio Africanus in Nola that wept blood."

"And what did these ladies discern from such prodigies?"

"That something dreadfully important is going to happen."

"Something dreadfully important is always going to happen. What of that?"

"They all believe that it will concern them personally."

"Did they say why, other than that this lot never needs much excuse to see the will of the gods at work in all their doings?"

"They were noticeably reticent on that point."

"Because they fear what they say to you will get back to Caesar?"

"Most likely."

"At least Atia should be in your camp, since she wants her vaguely Caesarian brat to inherit. She may want to call upon you privately soon."

"In fact, as we were leaving she asked if she might do exactly that tomorrow after the morning ceremony at Vesta's."

"Do you patrician women do anything that doesn't revolve around that temple?"

"It's convenient. Common women get together at the corner fountain or the laundry to meet and gossip. The rich freedwomen and wives of the *equites* gather at the expensive shops on the north end of the Forum. We have the Temple of Vesta. To be terribly honest, very few even pay attention to the ceremonies except on special days."

"I always thought it must be something like that. Like senators at the baths in the afternoon."

I told her about our barely productive visit to the gymnasia, then about the military review on the Field of Mars. Her face fell when I told her about the boots.

"He's giving his enemies a sword to use against him, isn't he?" she said.

"I'm afraid so. Everything else they've been able to swallow, albeit with poor grace: the triumphal regalia, the ivory staff, the wreath—they're all the things we allow a triumphing general, although only for a day. But the trappings of royalty? That's different. The day he shows up in the Senate wearing a diadem there will be a revolt."

"Do you think he'll go that far?"

"I fear that the day isn't far off," I assured her.

One of Julia's slaves came in. "There is a messenger outside. He says he bears a missive for my mistress from Callista of Alexandria."

My eyebrows went up. "What might this portend?"

"I can think of a very easy way to find out," Julia said. "Send him in."

The messenger was dressed in the tradition of his guild in a white tunic that exposed one shoulder, brimmed red hat with the silver wings of Mercury attached, sandals with similar wings, and a wing-topped wand twined with serpents. He handed Julia a rolled and sealed letter. I tipped him and told him to wait in the atrium in case she should wish to return a reply. Julia unrolled the thing and read it for an unconscionably long time.

"Well," I fretted, my patience at an end, "what is it?"

"Don't rush me, dear, you know I don't like that."

So I snapped my fingers at a slave and the well-trained man instantly refilled my cup. It was, as I recall, an excellent Massic.

"It begins with the usual pleasantries. She calls me her sister and says that I have not called upon her in far too long, that she has missed my company dreadfully, yet she doesn't overdo these formalities the way so many women do. She is a woman of the most exquisite taste."

"I daresay," I muttered.

"She invites us to a salon to be held the evening after tomorrow and apologizes for the short notice."

"Aha!" I said, my ears pricking up finally.

"Aha what?"

"Just aha. Do go on."

"She says that some astronomers of her acquaintance will be attending."

"This sounds promising. Perhaps she's found out something for us."

"But here is the most interesting part. She says that at sundown, the whole group will go to a small banquet at Cleopatra's villa."

"Interesting, indeed. What is the woman up to?"

Julia smiled. "I just can't wait to find out."

12

THE NEXT MORNING I WOKE UP realizing what I had missed the previous evening. That messenger with his Mercury garb. I should have thought of it much sooner, but I was finding that, as I got older, some mental processes seemed to be slowing down. The baleful influence of a hostile god, no doubt.

I sent for Hermes, and he arrived while I was about my morning ablutions.

"Hermes, we're going to the headquarters of the messenger's guild this morning." I thrust my face into the bowl of cold water and blew like a beached whale for a while. I straightened and groped for a towel, which Hermes thrust into my hand. The cobwebs and smoke seemed to clear from my head as I dried my face.

"I should have thought of it myself," Hermes said.

"My thought exactly. What more logical than that our fleet-footed fugitive should work as a messenger? He can keep in training and get paid for it in the bargain."

"But the guild members are mostly slaves," he pointed out.

"He could be working as a messenger at one of the great houses instead of at the public service."

"That's likely," I said, knowing that men like Cicero carried on huge correspondence and employed full-time messengers. Businessmen sometimes had scores. "But it's a place to start and there has to be network of information among the community of messengers. It's not that large a group of men, even in Rome."

After a few bites of oil-dipped bread we were out the door just as the sun was clearing the roofs of the lowest buildings. Then we turned our steps, as on most mornings, toward the Forum. The headquarters of the messenger's guild was located near the Curia, since they got a great deal of business from the senators.

It was a modest building, the carving above its portal proclaiming it to be, logically enough, the Brotherhood of Mercury. There was a rather fine statue of that deity out front, and a number of members lounged about on the steps. Ordinarily, a great many more occupied the tavern just across the narrow street, but it was all but empty at this early hour. We climbed the short flight of steps and passed within.

As a guild whose only stock in trade was its membership, the place needed no elaborate facilities or warehousing space. There was a single, spacious room, its walls decorated with tasteful frescoes, a fine marble desk in its center. In the rear wall was a doorway leading to what appeared to be a smaller room lined with honeycomb shelves for record-keeping. That was all. A substantial man rose from behind the desk.

"Welcome, Senator Metellus!" he said. "How may I help you? I am Scintillius, *duumvir* of the Honorable Guild of Mercury at Rome." Actually, the word "substantial" is a weak one to describe the *duumvir* of the guild. He was grossly corpulent and wheezed as he rose. If he had ever been a messenger himself, those days were long behind him.

"Ah, my friend Scintillus!" I said as if I wanted his vote. "Well met! This morning I find myself in need of your services. That is to say, I am trying to locate a man who might be a member of your guild."

"Eh?" He looked a bit hesitant. "I mean, I shall be most happy to help you and the noble Senate any way I may." He sweated slightly but that might have just been all that fat. "I do hope there is no, ah, irregularity involved?"

"None at all, none at all!" I assured him heartily.

"The senator is looking for a man who may be going by the name of Caius Domitius," Hermes rapped out. "We think he works here." This was a routine we had worked out long before. I was all hearty geniality, and he came across as threatening. Sometimes if you keep people off-balance you learn things you might not otherwise.

"I see. Caius Domitius, you say? I can't say that I know all of the messengers by name, but with two names he must be a citizen so that narrows it, and we have records, of course. Why did you say you wanted him?"

"We didn't say," Hermes told him forcefully. "Records, you say?"

"Yes, yes," he gestured toward the door behind him. "Right back here. Records of our purchases and discharges, payrolls, important commissions and so forth."

"Show us!" Hermes barked.

The man whirled and now it was time to do my bit. I took him by the arm. "This fellow should be distinctive. He's a great cross-country runner, surely an asset to your magnificent, ancient, and very honorable establishment. Such a man as you might use to run messages to country estates, or even hire out to the legions for war-time service. Why, when I was in Gaul with Caesar a few years ago we had a company of men hired from this very guild for routine communications between far-spread cohorts, all those daily missives that don't call for a detached cavalryman, you know." While I babbled on thus we entered the smaller room which was jammed full of cabinets, the nests of cubbies stacked to the ceiling.

"As you see, Senator, we keep very careful records."

I could see nothing of the sort, but I hoped they were in better order than those at the public archive. "So I see. A splendid facility indeed. And among these heaps of scrolls do you have the employment record of our Caius Domitius?"

"I truly hope so, Senator. As you can see these records go back many, many years, but I presume that the man you seek will have been employed here, if indeed he was, in rather more recent times?"

"Certainly within the last few years."

"Then the payroll records are the place to look," he said, taking down a large scroll. "Since most of our staff are slaves, those receiving a free laborer's pay are a decided minority."

"Why do you employ free men at all?" Hermes demanded.

"It's a matter of law," he said, "laid down by the censors in the times of the wars with Carthage. In businesses that employ more than a hundred persons, no more than eighty percent may be slave. It is the same for the construction industry, the stevedores, brickmaking, and so forth. In fact, only agriculture is exempt, and certain occupations that free men won't do for any pay, like mining."

This was a law dating from the earliest days when cheap slaves began to pour into Italy. There was fear that free labor might be totally displaced and the censors acted to stem the tide. Their success has been partial, at best. Caesar had recently passed a law requiring those who grazed their herds in Italy to employ not less than one-third freemen as herders. It was the least he could do, considering how many Gallic slaves he had dumped on the market.

He went to a table beneath an east-facing window and began to unroll the big scroll. "The first part," he explained, "records the contributions we make to each man's *peculium*. These vary in size and frequency according to the man's length of service and diligence at his work. One who works hard and stays sober can expect to buy his own freedom from the savings in his *peculium* in five to seven years." This is the traditional means of assuring obedience and good work from a slave. "They can, of course, keep any tips they receive." He unrolled the scroll further, revealing figures in a different color of ink.

"Now here," he went on, "are the records of the free employees' pay. Men are paid on the day before the calends of each month. Of course," he grumbled in a lower voice, "with this new calendar, we must refigure everything."

"Just see if he's in there," Hermes growled. He was beginning to overdo it. The man was cooperating after all. I made a signal to back off and Hermes complied, reluctantly. This was one of his favorite games.

"Certainly, certainly. Ah, here he is!" He stabbed a pudgy, beringed finger at a line on which in large letters was written "C DOMIT CIT."

"You see? Caius Domitius, citizen. This accounts for his slightly higher grade of pay than that of a foreigner, of which we employ a number."

"Dates?" I asked.

"Last worked for us in Quinctilis of that year." For those too young to remember, that is the name of the month that Caesar had that very year obtained consent from the Senate to name after himself, July. The Senate would grant him almost anything in those days.

It was looking like another blind alley. "Did he quit or was he dismissed?" I asked him, all but discouraged.

"Hmm, let me see, there's a notation here. Ah, he went on detached service. That is something we do frequently. A great house or business will lease a man from us fulltime, sometimes a whole company of our messengers, as you mention your legion in Gaul did."

I felt a tingle. "Who hired him from you?"

"Let's see—ah, yes, now I remember it. A foreign steward hired him for the household of Queen Cleopatra for the duration of her stay in Rome."

I thanked him effusively and we went back outside. "I knew it!" I said.

"Knew what?" Hermes asked.

"I knew that scheming Egyptian was up to something." Have a pygmy shoot me in the nose, would she? We'd see about that.

"But what is she up to? Do you think she ordered the murders?"

"Well, we don't really know that, but she's involved somehow."

"We've suspected that for some time. In fact, we still really don't know much at all, do we?"

"We know that Cleopatra hired Domitius. What we need to find out now is how he got from her household to the stables of Archelaus, and why." I looked across the street to the tavern catering to the messengers. The painting to one side of the door featured, unsurprisingly, Mercury. On the other side was painted a gladiator. For reasons I have never been able to understand these luckless men have become a popular symbol of good luck and you see them painted everywhere, usually at entrances. "Hermes, I want you to come back here this afternoon when the tavern is crowded. Hang about and see if you can learn anything about our friend Domitius."

He beamed. "Certainly."

"You are to stay sober."

"How can I do that without losing all credibility?"

"You'll find a way. You are clever. That's one reason that I gave you your freedom."

"It wasn't because of affection? Because of my years of hard work and faithful service? Not to mention the numerous occasions upon which I've saved your life or the awful perils we've gone through together?"

"No."

"I didn't think so. What now?"

By this time we had turned a corner and entered the Forum. It was even more noisy and chaotic than usual due to Caesar's building projects. Great cartloads of marble rumbled along the pavement. Others carried wood or brick or the powdery cement which, mixed with gravel and water, made Rome's uniquely ugly, pinkish concrete. People crowded one another and loudmouths sounded off from the bases of monuments. Unsupervised children darted between the legs of adults, bound upon missions of mischief. Farmers led asses piled with produce toward the vegetable markets beyond, peddlers hawked their wares in blissful violation of the laws banning such activities in the Forum. Mountebanks performed with equal contempt for the law, and fortune-tellers had their booths set up along the porticoes, tempting the anxious with prophecies of good luck and the favor of the gods.

It was a familiar, comforting scene, one I had enjoyed most days of my life. Had the heat and smells of summer contributed to the ambience, it might not have been so pleasant but, just then, it was the Forum the way I liked to see it. However, somewhere out there, perhaps in the Forum, certainly within the city or its suburbs, an assassin moved freely, concealed as a shark is concealed beneath the surface of the sea.

"What next?" I echoed. Over the roof of the Temple of Saturn

I eyed the towering façade of the Archive, its rows of arches on three levels seeming from this angle to support the temples of Juno the Warner and of Jupiter Best and Greatest, which watched benignly over all. A pair of eagles circled high above the temple rooftops. Doubtless many idlers were reading an omen into the flight of these birds, despite the fact that eagles flew over the capitol all the time. "What, indeed?"

I had just espied a little knot of men gathered beneath a statue of Caesar and recognized them as some of the year's tribunes of the Plebs. They were arguing loudly and drawing a minor crowd of their own. These men were understandably peeved that year. Their office was one of the most powerful, with the authority to introduce legislation to the Plebeian Assembly and to veto acts of the Senate, but not with a dictator in power. Now if they wanted to introduce a law it hadn't a hope of passing unless it was proposed first by Caesar and their power of veto was suspended. They were barely even time servers.

"This looks like amusement in the making," I said. "Let's see." So we made our way toward the disputatious legislators. They were growing red-faced, and one of them, a beak-nosed individual who looked vaguely familiar, was waving a gilded object that appeared to be made from thin metal. I barged in as if I had some business there. "What's going on, gentlemen?" I asked jovially.

The beak-nosed one glared at me for a moment. "Oh, it's you. You're just another of Caesar's lackeys. Stay out of this."

I stuck my right hand into a fold of my tunic and slipped the bronze cestus over my knuckles, just in case. "No need to call names, ah, Flavus, is it?" At last I recognized him as Caius Caesetius Flavus, a tribune decidedly in the anti-Caesarian camp, meaning he was a man with few allies. One of these, another tribune named Marullus, now spoke up.

"You should have died with the rest of your family, Metellus. They were better men."

I decided the bridge of his nose would do nicely for a target. One smack for him, then a half-turn and lay another one on Flavus's jaw. I bet myself that I could put them both on the pavement in the same moment, but this time Hermes played peacekeeper.

"What's that thing you're waving around?" he asked.

Flavus held it up. "Last night someone put a crown on the head of Caesar's statue!"

"What of it?" I asked. "The Senate has granted Caesar the right to adorn his statues with the Civic Crown and the Siege Crown." I gestured around the Forum, where a minor crowd of Caesar's statues stood in prominent places. He really was overdoing it in those days.

"This is not one of the crowns of honor," Marullus hissed. "It is a diadem, a royal crown!"

"Put it back," yelled yet another tribune. I did not recognize this one. You hardly saw them in the Senate since they lost their veto.

"Shut your mouth, Cinna!" Flavus bellowed. Cinna charged and for a while a good-sized brawl erupted at the base of the statue, with numerous bystanders taking part. Hermes and I kept out of it. A tattered golden object came flying from the pile of struggling men and Hermes caught it adroitly. I examined it and found it to be made of gilded parchment, not metal.

Eventually the disputants were separated. Flavus and Marullus were taken off to their houses, much the worse for wear. Cinna sat on the steps blotting at the blood running freely from his nose. I handed him a kerchief and he pressed it to his nose, tilting his head back for a while. When the bleeding stopped he stood.

"Many thanks, Senator Metellus."

"Think nothing of it. You're not Cornelius Cinna, I know him. Are you Cinna the poet?"

"Helvius Cinna, and yes, I flatter myself that I write verses of some merit. Come, I need a drink, and I'll stand you to some wine as well."

"Bacchus lays his curse on a man who turns down a free drink," I said. "Lead on."

We went down an alleyway that led to a small square with a fountain in its center. The tavern had outdoor tables covered by arbors that provided shade in summer. Just then the sun overhead and the buildings on all four sides kept the temperature tolerable for dining or drinking in the open.

He ordered a pitcher with some snacks to go with it, and we filled our cups, poured a libation on the ground, and pledged one another's health. It was the raw red stuff of the country, a welcome change from the rather effete vintages I had been imbibing of late. At least so I told myself. The fact was, I would drink just about anything. Still do, for that matter. The girl came back with a large bowl of crisp-fried nuts and dried peas, liberally salted.

"I know you of course, Senator Metellus," Cinna said, his voice slightly distorted by his swollen nasal passages. His nose, doubtless handsome in its usual state, was rapidly assuming the shape and color of a ripe plum. "I know that you are married to Caesar's niece, and that you've been his friend since you were both boys."

I took a long drink, pondering how to play this. It was a distinct exaggeration to style us boyhood friends. I barely knew him until I was in my twenties. He was about ten years older. We had worked closely together many times in the years since, though. To a recently arrived man like this obscure Cinna, it might well seem that Caesar and I were old cronies.

"Caesar trusts no other man the way he trusts my patron,"

222

Hermes said with smarmy sincerity. He had already decided the best approach and I thought it best to play along.

"That's good to know," he said. "Caesar has a great many toadies, but only a few true supporters."

"Hence your lack of objection to the crown on the statue," I observed.

He chuckled. "I put it there."

This was interesting. "And you would have no objection to a real crown on the dictator's head?"

"Why not? The Republic of the old days is dead, anyone can see that. Since Marius it's been one strongman after another taking dictatorial power, whether or not he held the title. When there's none in power, the rest are all fighting to gain that power. It's messy and it's stupid and destructive. Caesar is the first man of true talent and genius to pick up the iron rod and wield it over lesser men. Why not let him have the throne and crown to go with it? We had kings in the past, and they were good ones. It wasn't until we had Etrus-cans for kings that we rejected monarchy."

"Feeling runs deep against unlimited one-man power, espe-cially if it can be inherited." I munched on some nuts.

"But that's foolish," he objected. "A republic worked well enough when Rome was a little city-state like dozens of others in Italy. A panel of wealthy farmers could rule well enough in those days, when all their retainers lived within a day's march of the City. But now Rome rules a world-spanning empire and our provinces are so far away that a man sent out to govern travels so long to get to his province he practically has to turn around on arrival to be back in Rome for election time. It's foolish!"

"Very true," Hermes said, nodding. "He should have all the trappings of a king, so he can deal with foreign kings on an equal footing."

"Right," Cinna said. He smiled slyly. "In fact, this is supposed to be secret, but the whole city will know about it soon enough. I have the bill all drawn up in legal fashion, I'm just waiting for Caesar to give me the word to introduce it—"

"Tell us!" I pleaded. He looked satisfied as only a man who holds a secret can. I slugged down some wine and tossed a handful of the snacks into my mouth.

"Well, this is for your ears only, right?" We nodded with wide eyes like a pair of idiots. "All right. This bill, which I will bring before the Plebeian Assembly, empowers Caesar to marry any woman he wishes, and as many of them as it pleases him to marry, simultaneously, not sequentially."

There is a great art to not choking on a mouthful of dried peas and nuts when news like this gets dropped on one. Fortunately, I am a master of this art. It has saved my dignity at many a political banquet. I continued chewing and turned that into a nod.

"Makes sense," Hermes said.

I swallowed. "Absolutely. Kings do that sort of thing all the time."

"It's traditional for sealing alliances in the east," Cinna pointed out, "and Caesar plans further conquests in that direction. Alexander had no problem with marrying some kinglet's daughter when he needed an alliance."

"And we all know Caesar has taken Alexander as his model," Hermes said with an air of great wisdom. He was laying it on a bit thick, but Helvius Cinna seemed like the sort of man who wouldn't notice such a thing. Typical poet.

"Has he given you any idea when he wants you to bring this before the *consilium*? I asked him.

"No, but I think it can't be much longer. He will be leaving for his Asian campaign soon."

We finished our wine and traded a few more pleasantries and parted with hearty handclasps and tokens of good friendship. Without exchanging a word Hermes and I walked down to the embankment by the side of the Tiber, a handsome park above the retaining wall that had been built by the aediles after the last big flood. There we found a fine marble bench between shade-trees and sat, watching the river flow by.

"All right," Hermes said at length, "what's this mean? I can guess part of it but there must be more."

"What have you guessed?" I asked him.

"That he's going to marry Cleopatra. She'll be a legal wife, not just a concubine. I don't know the Egyptian custom, but with the legions to back him, that will make him pharaoh as far as we're concerned."

"Yes, and how did the pharaohs keep it in the family, so to speak?"

"They married their sisters so as not to sully the royal bloodline, but Caesar has no living sisters and his only daughter is dead."

"So who does that leave?" I prodded.

He thought. "Atia?"

"Yes, his niece. Then her brat, Octavius, becomes young Caesar, heir not only to his fortune but to his power. He will have our empire in his hands on Caesar's death."

"Then Servilia and all the others are out."

"Under this law he can marry her if he feels like it, but Servilia will not be a cowife. Not to Cleopatra or anybody else."

"Will people put up with this?" Hermes wondered. "The purple robe, the red boots, even the crown are just baubles, but overturning the custom of centuries and the power structure founded by the first Brutus, that's different."

"I don't know," I admitted. "The commons love him, and part

of that is seeing how he's humbled the aristocracy. I'm not sure many of them see much difference between being ruled by a king and being ruled by a Senate composed of the likes of Lucius Cinna and Brutus and Cassius, aristocrats who have always treated them with contempt. It's not as if their votes really count for much. Caesar has given them splendor and foreign conquest and public banquets and the grain dole. They might just back him in this."

Hermes was quiet for a while. Then said, "Do you think Caesar has gone insane?"

"If so, he wouldn't be the first to rise to absolute power and lose his grip on reality as a result." I got up. "Then again maybe this Helvius Cinna, poet, is lying. We can always hope so."

I dismissed Hermes to go snoop in the messengers' tavern, little hoping that he would return sober. For a while I sat and watched the river. It was a familiar, soothing sight, as the Forum had been. Citizens crossed the busy bridges or leaned on their balustrades, brooding on the water just like me. Ducks paddled about while men with poles and lines fished for dinner. More serious fishermen were out in boats with nets and barges plied the water. Pleasure craft sailed about, carefully staying upstream of the sewer outlets.

While I watched the river I thought about Egypt. The land of the Nile, Cleopatra's kingdom, was incredibly rich yet the Ptolemies, the Macedonian usurpers to the ancient land, were often penniless. This was partly due to their own fecklessness but also because Egypt's vast wealth, product of its incredibly fertile land, went into the coffers of its priests and temples. Even the greatest pharaohs and their Macedonian successors had been unable to break the stranglehold of the priesthoods of the many beast-headed gods of that superstitious, benighted land. I have always been grateful that Romans would never submit to the rule of priests.

In truth, Cleopatra, last descendant of that degenerate line, was ruler only of Alexandria and much of the Delta. Those alone made her richer than all other monarchs save a Great King of Persia, but she would have been ten times richer had the produce of the interior been hers.

Did Caesar truly aspire to be the first pharaoh in more than five hundred years? If so, he would have all that wealth because unlike any Egyptian or Greek he would not hesitate to make those priests pay up. We Romans respect other peoples' gods, but that has never stopped us from looting their temples, even those of gods to whom we pay the highest honors. Sulla and Pompey had plundered temples all over Greece and the East, their excuse being that they were collecting from rebellious or resisting cities, not from the gods themselves. They left the images and insignia of the gods alone but took everything else of value. No Roman had even that much respect for the ridiculous deities of Egypt.

How much ambition was it possible for one man to have? To surpass Alexander in conquest, even to surpass Romulus in prestige and honor, these were ambitious enough. Romulus had been deified. Did Caesar aim that high? Did he think to place himself among the immortal gods? The thought sent a shudder through me. This is what the Greeks call "hubris" and its consequences are famously terrible, not just for the offender but for the whole community. This is why a triumphing general has a slave standing behind him in his chariot to whisper from time to time, "Remember that you are mortal." I am not superstitious, but there is such a thing as tempting the gods too far.

From the river I made my way back to the Forum. It was as good a place as any to be, since I had run out of leads to investigate. The political gossip being bandied about from end to end of the Forum was no less lively for the overbearing presence of a dictator. There were plenty of lesser offices that were still desirable because they were too small for such a man's attention, others that were coveted for their prestige.

Consul was one of these. Though the dictatorship usurped the consular powers, Caesar kept the office alive. Each year, he was always one of the consuls, with some chosen politician acting as his colleague. At that date his colleague as co-consul was Antonius. There was much talk of who would take Caesar's place as suffect consul when he left for Syria.

It seemed, if I was collecting the right gossip, that Caesar had chosen Publius Cornelius Dolabella, and according to report (unattributable, naturally) Antonius was furious about it. I remembered the man slightly. Three years previously he had been a tribune of the people and had proposed legislation canceling debts and remitting house rents, always a winner with the commons. His proposals had gone nowhere of course, but he had gained much popularity thereby.

It was entirely possible that his choice of causes was not lacking in self-interest. Dolabella was a notorious wastrel and many of the debts cancelled would be his own. Like many another such reprobate, Caesar, upon his return from Alexandria, had taken him under his wing, covered the worst of his debts, and hauled him off to Spain for some personal training and education. He was now firmly in the pro-Caesar camp. In just such a fashion had Caesar attached Scribonius Curio to his cause. Curio made him another useful tribune.

I couldn't see that the choice could make much difference. Antonius's prefecture of the City was where the real power lay and Caesar would undoubtedly leave Dolabella a minutely detailed list of every action he expected the second consul to take and a very long list of things he forbade him to do. Antonius would get his own list, which he would ignore, but Dolabella would never dare.

I crossed the broad pavement and pushed past some oxen

hauling a wagonload of marble to the new basilica. There was a great crowd of people standing about before the huge building, and many of them were foreigners. Some were truly exotic specimens and I knew these were not the usual travelers come to see the sights of the famous city. The lictors on guard pushed them back if they got too close. I walked up to one of the fasces-bearing men I recognized.

"Hello, Otacilius. I've come to see the dictator. I take it from your presence that he's here?"

"Certainly, Senator. Your name is on the list of those allowed in." He stepped aside for me.

I suppose I should have felt uniquely privileged to have my name on that list. Perhaps I should have preened. It was certain that many other senators preened to be thus singled out. At that time I could only reflect that there had been a time when any citizen could walk into a basilica any time it struck his fancy to, even if the thing was under construction.

I found Caesar inside, and Cleopatra was with him, which came as no surprise to me, having seen the crowd of exotics loitering about outside. Caesar, uncharacteristically, was seated and looked rather drawn.

"Well, Decius Caecilius," Caesar said when he saw me, "I hope you have brought me some good news. I could use some."

At that moment some things began to fit together in my mind. They did not give me anything complete, but it was as if some bricks had been added to what was still a very incomplete wall. I must have looked strange because Cleopatra said, "Well? Can you not speak?"

Caesar raised a hand. "Patience. The gods are speaking to him. It happens sometimes. I've seen this before."

"Caius Julius," I said at length, "I think that in, oh, two days, I shall have the answer to these murders."

"That is oddly imprecise, but if you have the killer for me, I shall be content."

Cleopatra looked at me sharply. "You are certain of this?"

"I am," I assured her. Actually, I had no such confidence, but I was not about to admit it in front of her. I smiled as if I knew something that she didn't. I always hate it when people do that to me and was gratified to see her look of discomfiture. It might mean something. Or perhaps not. Everyone has something to hide and a person like Cleopatra has more than most.

"I'm sending the astronomers back to Alexandria," Caesar said. "They've been here long enough."

"I rejoice to hear it," I assured him. "I'd hate to lose Sosigenes. The rest I don't care much about." As we spoke I noticed a man hovering in the background, beneath one of the interior arches. He was a tall, thin man, coiffed and bearded in Greek fashion. Beside him was a boy who carried a large, leather-covered chest slung from his shoulder. I knew the man well, as he had worked on me upon occasion in Gaul. He was Caesar's personal physician.

The two showed no further interest in me so I took my leave of them and walked back out to the Forum with much to ponder about. Having made my boast, I now had to deliver. Caesar would be very displeased should I fail to hand him the killer on the day following the next. Not only the killer, but some sort of comprehensible explanation for what had been going on.

Hermes found me in the tavern near the old Curia where we ate frequently. It enjoyed a fine view of the ancient building, the meeting-place of the Senate since the days of the kings. At that time it was still gutted, its upper façade black-smudged, the marks of the rioting that followed the funeral of Clodius.

How like Caesar, I thought, to erect his immense basilica to his own glory practically next door while the most sacred of our ancient assembly-places stood derelict for want of someone to pony up the cash for restorations, forcing the Senate to meet in the Theater of Pompey. Maybe it was another way for him to display his contempt for the Senate. Or maybe he planned some unthinkably vast and elaborate new Curia, one that would outshine anything built by Pompey.

Hermes plunked himself down and began helping himself to my lunch. "Domitius drops by the messengers' tavern from time to time."

"I thought so. Men who share a profession or specialized skill usually like to get together with their fellows to talk shop. What do the others know about him?"

"He regales them with stories of Cleopatra's house. They love to hear about the extravagances that go on in that place."

"Everybody does. Anything else?"

"Lately he's been working for someone else as well. Someone he calls 'the easterner' or 'the star man.'"

"Polasser!" I said, thumping the table with my fist. "Worked for him, all right, but he set him up to be murdered."

"Maybe he's the killer," Hermes suggested.

"I thought about that, but somehow I doubt it. I didn't get a good long look at him, but I don't think he had the hands and arms of a wrestler. Pure runner, that's all. Did you get anything else?"

"Just that he hasn't been by for more than ten days, which they think odd. I didn't press it. They already thought I was being suspiciously snoopy, even though I was buying the drinks."

"A conscientious lot," I said. "Most men will sell you their mothers as long as you keep the free wine flowing." I told him of my little meeting with Caesar and the queen of Egypt.

"So maybe he really is sick," Hermes mused.

"Or maybe Cleopatra is just being oversolicitous of his health and insists on having a physician present, and Caesar would trust nobody but that Greek. It's like her. Still, he didn't look all that well. Not really sick, but lacking in his usual vigor, like that day in the Senate when he was so undiplomatic with Archelaus."

"Do you think Caesar will live long enough to take his expedition to Syria?"

"If King Phraates has any brains at all," I said, "he's sacrificing to Ahura-Mazda right now that he will not."

13

IT WAS BARELY MIDAFTERNOON
when we set out for Callista's. Respectable gatherings always began early. Only disreputable ones went on after dark. Of course,
this party was going to move to one of the most dissolute households
in Rome. I mentioned this strange juxtaposition to Julia as we
were carried off.

It annoyed me that she insisted that I ride in the big litter she
reserved for the most pretentious occasions, as if my own feet would
no longer carry me. She thought it was beneath my dignity to walk
after the sun was low over the rooftops. Of course, the ostentatious
conveyance wasn't for the visit to Callista's, for which her everyday
litter was adequate. It was for the trip to Cleopatra's.

Not that everyone was riding. Two of Julia's girls were trailing
us, along with Hermes and a couple of my rougher retainers, men
handy with their fists and with bronze-studded truncheons tucked
into their cinctures. Anything could happen.

We found a small mob in the street outside Callista's house, and more gathered in the courtyard. There were litters like ours and slaves and attendants and bodyguards more numerous and rougher-looking than mine.

"That's Servilia's litter!" Julia said as we were carried into this carnival. "And there is Atia's!"

"This should prove to be an interesting evening," I said as the bearers set us down on the pavement of the courtyard. I got out and helped Julia from the elegant but awkward vehicle. As I did this I gazed around the courtyard. Callista's servants circulated, carrying trays of refreshments for the attendants who had to wait without. Greater houses than this one might not have bothered.

I hoped that the presence of these scheming women might add interest to what promised to be a dull evening. Much as I esteemed the company of Callista, I had never been able to abide the droning lectures of philosophers, and I had endured many such, as Julia had dragged me around from one learned gathering to another. She had a wholly lamentable taste for such high-toned, edifying entertainments, whereas I much preferred a good fight or chariot race.

Hermes nudged me. "Look who's here now."

The litter that entered the courtyard was unmistakable. It was Fulvia's. The bearers were her usual matched Libyans with their outlandish, colorful costumes and their hair dressed in innumerable plaits. First to emerge was Antonius himself. The lady herself emerged, dressed, so to speak, in a gown of Coan cloth that resembled smoke drifting about her voluptuous little body.

"She's holding up well for her age," Julia observed.

"So she is. Shall we go in? It's getting a bit crowded out here."

Echo met us at the door and conducted us inside, with Antonius and his wife right behind us. The inner courtyard, with its small, tasteful fountain and pool, had been set with numerous chairs and couches. At a dinner party there would have been couches for nine, but there was no such customary limitation on salons like this. The women crowded together near the fountain to gossip and sound one another out while the men gathered in a corner to commiserate. I was headed that way when Antonius came up to me.

"Dreadful business eh, Decius?" he said, grabbing a cup from a passing servant. I did the same. "I wouldn't mind if it was like a Greek symposium, where everybody's drunk by nightfall, but Callista's little dos aren't like that. All very refined. I hope I can last until we go to Cleopatra's. Then things should liven up."

"This is the sort of thing we must do if we prize domestic harmony," I told him.

"There's such a thing as too much harmony, if you ask me," he groused, burying his beak in his wine. "Ahh, Corinthian. Haven't tasted it in years."

"I don't think I've ever tried it. I thought I knew them all." I tasted the wine and it was decent enough but it had that resinous flavor I've always found objectionable in Greek wines. "I thought so. It's the sort of stuff women serve to keep the men from drinking too much."

"It won't stop me," Antonius said. "Odd sort of group, isn't it?"

I studied the guests and was surprised that I knew many of them. Brutus was there, doubtless escorting his mother although he was a known habitué of these events. Marcus Aemilius Lepidus was there as well. Caesar had picked him as Master of Horse for that year, an office previously held by Antonius himself. As the dictator's second-in-command he supposedly held a powerful office, but Caesar was such a hands-on dictator in all his doings that the office was little more than an empty honor, pretty much reduced to presiding over the Senate on days when Caesar did not feel like attending. I noted with little joy that Sallustius was oozing his way among the more illustrious guests, ferreting out secrets, no doubt. Cassius Longinus was with his wife, looking like a man who wished lightning would strike him. I didn't spot Cicero.

"More politics here than philosophy," I agreed, "but at least there's that lot." I nodded to where the astronomers were chatting among themselves. Sosigenes was among them, along with the Indian and the Arab and the other Greeks. "Caesar just told me he's sending them back to Alexandria. Maybe this is Callista's send-off for them."

"If she keeps the wine coming I can endure it," he said.

"Stay by me," I advised. "Hermes has a skin of Massic under his toga."

"Good for you. I was wondering why he was wearing a toga." By that time men rarely ever wore the toga except for sacrifices and Senate meetings, voting, and other formal occasions. Antonius and I and most of the other men wore the much lighter *synthesis*, a garment popularized by Caesar back when he was setting the fashion for Roman men. Nevertheless, the toga remained better for concealing things. Besides the wine, Hermes had our weapons beneath his.

The general hubbub stilled as Callista made her entrance from the back of the house. She was dressed as usual in a modest Greek gown of the finest wool. It was deep blue, with a simple fret embroidered at the hem. Her hair was parted in the middle, gathered at her nape and hung to her waist in back. Her only jewelry was a pair of serpent armlets. The men in the room had eyes only for her. In her austere simplicity she outshone the great beauties of Rome.

"My guests," she said amid the silence, "please forgive me for not greeting each of you personally. Certain matters demanded my attention elsewhere. I pray you all be seated." We all took seats, women to the front, men to the rear. Some picked at snacks proffered by the servants, but more for the sake of form than from hunger. We all knew we would be gorging ourselves to stupefaction at Cleopatra's.

"As some of you may know," she went on, "the illustrious astronomers of the Alexandrian Museum, who have graced Rome these recent months, are soon to return to Alexandria. I wish to announce this evening that I shall be going with them."

This drew speeches of dismay and protest. Some of the women, it seemed to me, protested very lightly.

"I have enjoyed immensely my years in Rome, which I do not hesitate to name the center of the world." There were murmurs of agreement at this fine sentiment. "Being here, and knowing you all, has been an experience the equal of living in Athens at the time of Pericles." Like the rest I applauded and made noises of agreement until I remembered that the age of Pericles, while a golden age in terms of art, philosophy, and culture, had in many other ways been disastrous for Athens.

"I have come to this decision after long and hard thought. Rome has gone through turbulent times these past few years, but times of turbulence and ferment are stimulating as well, and bring about much that is good and new. It has been so during my time here. While there has been violence in the streets, there has also been fine poetry composed. There have been excellent histories written"—she nodded slightly toward Sallustius, who preened—"and many splendid edifices erected to the glory of the gods." She gazed about the room, joining eyes with all of her guests. She had the most beautiful eyes I have ever seen. "But now I believe that Rome is soon to undergo a period of terrible trials, and violence surpassing anything that has gone before."

This set off a great deal of shifting and shuffling as we wondered what this might portend. Worse than the days of Sulla and the proscriptions? Worse than the final, mad days of Marius or the slave

237

rebellion of Spartacus or the rioting in the time of the Gracchi or the atrocities of the Social War? Come to think of it, Rome had seen a lot of truly terrible times. Hannibal didn't even come close.

"It is of course unworthy of a philosopher to take notice of such things," she went on. "A true philosopher must maintain perfect tranquility despite what is going on around him. He should seek to instruct those who in their folly resort to war and violence to gain their ends. Even the uproar of a city under siege should not disturb his contemplation. The imperturbability of Archimedes at the siege and fall of Syracuse stands always as our example." Yes, and look what it got that old bugger, I thought.

She smiled sadly. "My friends, I confess to you that I am far from being a perfect philosopher. I do not want to see blood in the streets of Rome. I do not want to see my friends die, especially at the hands of other friends."

For the first time someone from the audience spoke. It was Lepidus. "Callista are you telling us you foresee civil war for Rome?"

"I am not a sibyl or an oracle," she said, "and I do not believe that the will of the gods is made manifest in signs and portents, nor that the future may be descried in the stars nor in any other way. The future lies beyond a veil no sight may pierce. However, the doings and words of men may be observed and studied and analyzed and from these inferences may be drawn, if not conclusions." To my astonishment, she raised her eyes to mine and I felt as ensorcelled as a rabbit in the gaze of a serpent. "Decius Caecilius, is that not your art?"

I was as tongue-tied as a schoolboy caught by an unexpected question from his master. "Why, ah, I suppose—yes, it's what I do."

"You've caught him sober," Antonius said. "That's always a bad idea." This got a chuckle, but the sound was uncomfortable. Nobody had come expecting this.

"I have been practicing that same art," she said, "but on a greater scale. My position here has given me access to Rome's mightiest as well as her wisest. Alas, these do not always overlap. Some of these have confided in me and I will never betray their trust, but what I now know fills me with grave misgivings." Then she brightened. "In any case, my decision is made. There will be plenty of time to take my leave of each of you individually. I hope that you will call upon me should your steps lead you to Alexandria. Now we shall proceed with what I intended to be the theme of the evening, our farewell to the departing astronomers. The esteemed and very learned Sosigenes will now address us concerning some new discoveries in the heavens. Please forgive my digression."

Sosigenes rose and faced the gathering and began a lecture about something utterly incomprehensible to me. While this went on, a number of men, myself included, surreptitiously edged our way into a corner where we could converse in low voices. Hermes got out the Massic and filled cups.

"Well, that's damned odd, isn't it?" Antonius whispered. "What do you think it's all about?"

"It's a good thing she's leaving," Lepidus grumbled. "I'd be tempted to exile her from the City otherwise, along with all the other doomsaying fortune-tellers. Talk like that gets people upset."

"Surely it's only the rabble we worry about being stirred up by prophecies," I put in. "What rabble listens to a Greek philosopher?"

"And to think," said Sallustius, "I've had a source like this right here in Rome, and I never tried to squeeze any information out of her."

"You wouldn't have gotten a word from Callista except on philosophical matters," Brutus said. "She's the most discreet woman who ever lived." He thought about it for a moment. "Maybe the only one."

Cassius looked at him sourly. "You can't trust anyone with secrets, man or woman." Brutus just brooded into his wine.

Eventually we made our way back to our seats. A couple of the other Greeks spoke on elevated matters, but not the barbarians. Romans will listen to a foreign king or envoy speak on diplomatic matters, but otherwise we have little tolerance for ridiculous accents. We are used to Greeks, of course.

In time Callista proclaimed that we would now all repair to Cleopatra's villa across the river and there was an audible, in fact downright loud collective sigh of relief. We went out to the courtyard and those who had litters piled into them. Callista wanted to walk but Julia all but forced her to ride in our litter. This pleased me not only because of the close proximity to Callista, but because we could speak in some degree of privacy.

"Callista," I said, "I beg you to reconsider this move. I feel that very soon Alexandria will be a far more dangerous city than Rome. We have a fine country estate well away from the uproar of Rome, please stay—" she held out a hand for silence.

"I do not go to Alexandria to be safe. I want the tranquil atmosphere of the Museum. I have studies to pursue and books to write. I don't fool myself that I am leaving the real world behind."

"Why do you think Alexandria will be dangerous?" Julia asked. "What do you know that you haven't been telling me?"

"I don't *know* anything, but as Callista said earlier I observe and put facts and inferences together. It's something that has come up repeatedly during my current investigation, things Caesar has said, and things I believe Caesar has planned." I looked at Callista. "I believe he's spoken to you of some of these things. What you've learned from Caesar is part of why you are leaving. Am I right?"

"Yes," she said, "and Caesar isn't the only one."

"Why," Julia demanded, "does Caesar confide in Callista thoughts and plans that he tells no one else?"

"Because Callista is discreet," I said, "and she is his only intellectual equal in Rome. Perhaps in the world." She acknowledged this with the very slightest of nods. "A man like Caesar must be very lonely. He has countless servants and lackeys and lovers and even a few friends, but very few peers. Very few he can speak with on even terms. Whatever he thinks, he is actually human. He will miss you, Callista."

"He will not miss me for long," she said enigmatically.

Julia punched me in the side, hard. "What have you learned?" she hissed.

"I can't testify to the truth of it, but I heard this from the tribune Helvius Cinna. This is Cinna the poet, not Cornelius Cinna."

"I know who he is!" she nearly shouted. "Tell me!"

"Keep your voice down," I advised. "People outside can hear." She fumed but kept quiet. In a very low voice I told her about the proposed law allowing Caesar multiple wives of whatever birth or nationality he fancied. She went pale. Callista did not change expression. She already knew. That was how I was sure for the first time that it was true.

"But this is monstrous!" Julia whispered. "How can he—" she trailed off, unable to admit her loss of confidence in her beloved uncle.

"I think that Caesar is very ill," I told her, "and that he is no longer quite sane. It hasn't yet affected his intellect, or his clarity of thought. Those are as outstanding as ever, but it has altered his"—I grasped for a word, for an expression of an unfamiliar concept— "his perception of reality. He no longer recognizes a boundary between what Caesar wants and what is permissible, or even possible."

I gathered my thoughts, tried to place things in order, the way Callista would have organized one of her philosophical tracts. "This is something we've seen coming, but we've all been so in awe of Caesar that we haven't wanted to recognize it. We are reluctant to believe he has the same weaknesses as any other mortal. A few days ago he tongue-lashed a foreign envoy as you would an insolent slave, in front of the whole Senate. He's planning a major foreign war without having quite finished the last one. He plans to completely rebuild Rome to his own liking without any really clear idea what to do with the Rome that is already here. He is bringing long-haired barbarians into the Senate without even Romanizing them first! All right, that last one could actually improve the tone of the place, but you get the idea. He isn't rational anymore, but he can carry it off because he seems so rational.

"Now he wants to be pharaoh, with Cleopatra's aid"—I looked at Callista—"and that is why I think you shouldn't go back to Alexandria. He wants to conquer Parthia but Egypt is the real prize in this game. Alexandria got badly damaged the last time he was there. It could be far worse this time."

"He is right," Julia acknowledged. "Stay at our villa. Or if you must leave Italy, go to Athens. You could teach there."

"I deeply appreciate your concern," Callista said, "but I belong in Alexandria. If that is where the world is to end, then that is precisely where I should be." She smiled. "Besides, they don't let women teach in Athens. There hasn't been any new thought in Athens since Aristotle. Ah, here we are."

We had arrived at Cleopatra's, and a greater contrast to Callista's house would be hard to imagine. Legions of slaves helped us from our litters as if we were a visitation of cripples. Golden cups brimming with rare vintages were pressed into our hands. Lest we grow bored between litter and doorway, jugglers and tumblers performed for us, bears and baboons danced, people in white robes strummed upon lyres and sang. Atop the wall, a line of near-naked men and women walked on their hands, tossing balls to one another and catching them with their feet in a bewildering yet seemingly orderly fashion. Julia and some of the other women gathered together, apparently for mutual protection and made their way inside.

"This is more like it!" Antonius proclaimed. "I thought listening to those astronomers would turn me to stone."

"You were listening?" Lepidus said coldly, but the prospect of a really degenerate party had put Antonius in such a good mood that he ignored the sour-faced Master of Horse. Brutus and Cassius were huddled together and Sallustius looked like a man about to reap a great harvest of drunken gossip. We passed inside where, though it was not quite dark, things had reached a truly demented stage. Antonius grinned. "I'm going to have to get to know Cleopatra better."

As intrigued as I was by the lively goings-on, I knew better than to participate too fully with Julia present somewhere. Besides, I was hungry. With Hermes in tow I went in search of dinner, keeping a wary eye out for homicidal pygmies. We went past a pond full of crocodiles. People tried to tempt the awful beasts with fish and other delicacies, but the scaly monsters remained torpid. Another pool was full of hippos that splashed guests with water and noxious fluids. Signs in several languages warned that hippos are far more ill-tempered than they look. Cheetahs wandered freely. I hoped our hostess didn't have lions in her menagerie.

It wasn't difficult to find something to eat. The main problem was locating something small enough to get into my mouth. There were tables laden with entire roast animals, many of them exotic African species. I found a skewer of small grilled birds rolled in honey and sesame seeds, and I began to pick them off one at a time.

"Look at these oysters," Hermes said, lifting a plate of them.

"There's a pearl in every one of them. Do they come that way naturally?"

"I don't think so. You can eat the oysters, but keep the pearls."

"Keep them where?" he said, downing an oyster.

"Tie them up in a corner of your toga. You have enough material there to hold the loot of Tigranocerta."

"I know," he said, downing another. "This thing is hot."

I finished the spit and looked for something else. The laboriously exotic items like flamingo tongues and camel's toes were tedious and often disgusting, but I found enough items fit for human consumption to stave off starvation. Hermes handed me a platter of small pastries stuffed with chopped ham and goat cheese and spinach. They were resting on oak leaves made of hammered gold, which I kept. Soon I was ready to see what was going on this night.

"Caesar is here," Hermes said, jerking his chin toward a fur-draped platform where the dictator sat on a huge chair. Unlike his usual curule chair this one had a towering back, against which Caesar lay heavily, an elbow on the arm of the chair, laurel-crowned head propped on a fist. There was an identical chair beside his but Cleopatra was nowhere to be seen. People of some distinction approached him, bowing and cringing.

"They aren't kissing the hem of his cloak," I remarked, "but I can tell that they want to."

"Not so loud," Hermes said.

"Why?" I snapped. "He's just another politician."

"That's not true and you know it. Be on your best behavior or Cleopatra will throw us to those crocodiles over there."

"That should liven them up," I grumped, but resolved to be more discreet. Damned if I was going to approach Caesar like a supplicant, though. We wandered through the numerous rooms of the sprawling villa and in each of them something was going on to suit every taste. In one room Spanish dancers from Gades performed their famously lascivious routines. In another an actor with a fabulous voice declaimed hymns by Agathon. In a small courtyard Gauls in checkered trousers fenced with their long swords and narrow shields. In a long hall pantomimes performed the tragedy of Adonis in eerie silence.

Finally, I found Cleopatra standing among the women I had arrived with, including Julia and Callista. They were laughing and chattering like a pack of Subura housewives loitering around the corner fountain. I was about to join them when I saw coming toward me a strange pair of mismatched guests, one huge, the other slight. It was Balbus and Asklepiodes, both of them grinning like loons and both obviously half drunk.

"We've figured it out!" Balbus cried, turning heads all over the courtyard.

"We know how he did it!" Asklepiodes chimed in.

This was the last thing I had expected to hear at this event, but welcome news nonetheless. "How?"

"You remember I told you I would pray to my household gods?" Balbus said. "Well, I've done that every night and last night I had a dream, and in my dream I saw Hercules chasing Hippolyta all over an Arcadian landscape. Looked Arcadian to me, anyway. Never been there personally. When I woke I somehow knew that this had something to do with our problem." He was talking loud enough to draw attention and all sorts of people were drifting toward us. I was so eager to know where this was leading that I did not admonish him.

"So," Asklepiodes said, "today Senator Balbus came to me and told me of his dream. I knew instantly that our problem was solved." He smiled with insufferable smugness.

"Well!" I said, ready to tear my thinning hair out. Even Cleopatra was coming our way.

245

"Do you remember why Hercules was sent after Hippolyta?" Balbus asked.

"He wasn't after her," I said. "As one of his labors he was sent to fetch her girdle, which I always thought was a rather transparent metaphor for something indecent."

"And in art," Asklepiodes said, "how is the girdle of Hippolyta depicted? As a sash!"

"This meaning?" I said.

"Let me demonstrate." He looked around. "Queen Cleopatra, do you have a slave I can borrow? A young male, by preference. Marvelous party, by the way."

"Certainly." She snapped her fingers and a sturdy young fellow stepped to her side. "Please don't kill him. He's an excellent bodyguard." She looked at me. "He's no replacement for poor Appolodorus, but who would be?" Appolodorus, her bodyguard since childhood and the finest swordsman I had ever known, had died of a commonplace fever some years before.

"Observe," Asklepiodes said. "Young man, turn away from me." He took a long scarf from within his tunic and in an instant whipped it around the slave's neck. "You see how I grip both ends and have crossed my wrists?" The slave's face darkened and his eyes began to bulge. Asklepiodes, small though he was, had hands like steel, as I knew to my sorrow. He had demonstrated his homicidal skills on me more than once.

"Now, see how, when I twist thus, the knuckles of my hands press against his spinal column from opposite sides, two above, two below, just as we saw the marks on the dead men." He jerked his hands violently and the slave's eyes all but popped from their sockets. "With just a bit more pressure, I could break his neck easily." Abruptly he released one end of the scarf and the slave dropped to his hands and knees, gasping and retching. People made noises of wonder and dismay. "The wide scarf immobilizes the neck and provides leverage to bring the full strength of the hands and arms against the victim's spine, but it leaves no ligature mark as a cord would."

"It occurred to me," Balbus said, "that you could save a second or two by tying a weight into one end of the scarf. Then instead of having to lower it over your victim's head, you could just whip it around from behind."

"A weight," I mused, things whirring and clicking inside my head, "something like this?" I felt around in the purse tucked inside my tunic and came out with the massive brass coin.

"That would do nicely," Asklepiodes said.

"It did," I told him. To my astonishment, Callista snatched the coin from my hand and stared at it wonderingly.

"Where is it from?" She turned it over.

"India," I told her.

She closed her eyes. "Senator, please forgive my stupidity. This is the lettering I was trying to remember. I saw it in some books in my father's library when I was a child. They were written on palm leaves and they were from India."

"And this is the sort of writing you saw on Ashthuva's charts?" I thought about the Indian astronomer, Gupta. I remembered how he stood over Polasser's body, his long hair streaming, his turban unwound.

I turned to Hermes. "'The easterner, the star man'! Domitius wasn't talking about Polasser, he was talking about Gupta!" But Hermes wasn't listening. He made a strangled sound and bolted through the crowd, pushing people aside right and left. His toga slowed him but he was making very good speed anyway.

"Must need to puke," Balbus said.

"No," I told him, "I think he just saw somebody he knew and wants to renew the acquaintance. I think he saw Domitius."

"Not Ahenobarbus?" Balbus said. "Is it Domitius the banker?"

"No, this is another Domitius, a very fleet-footed one. We'll see if he can run through a villa as fast as he can cross-country. Queen Cleopatra, the man Hermes is chasing is a spy planted in your house by some very evil people."

"I would very much like to know what this is all about," said that monarch. A moment later there came a tremendous commotion from another part of the villa, with roaring and splashing that boded very ill for someone. Hermes returned, drenched and looking disgusted.

"We won't be getting any answers from Domitius," he said. "I almost had him, but he slipped on some wet pavement and fell into the hippo pool. They had rare sport with him for a few seconds. I don't think there are any pieces left worth burning."

"I think we have most of the answers we need anyway," I said.

"What is happening?" The voice was quiet but unmistakable.

"Caius Julius," I said, "I am about to give you the man who killed Demadus and Polasser. He's here in the villa somewhere. He is the Indian astronomer, Gupta, and I believe he is the most highly skilled assassin I have ever encountered. He certainly has the deadliest turban in Rome. He also has an accomplice. She lives just up the hill from here, near the old fort."

"Ashthuva?" Julia said.

"Oh, hello, niece," Caesar said absently. "Your husband seems to be turning in results for me in his usual eccentric fashion. I've seen him at his work before, but it has never involved strangled slaves and rampaging hippos before." Then he amended, "I do remember an occasion with stampeding elephants, though."

While we spoke Cleopatra was barking orders in what I realized was Macedonian Greek, her native tongue. Soon hard-looking armed men were swarming all over the place. Caesar looked unsteady and Cleopatra became suddenly solicitous and tried to lead him off, but he insisted on staying until the guard captain returned with the news that Gupta was nowhere to be found and nobody reported seeing him leave.

"I know where he's gone, and it's not far," I told Caesar. "Let's not have any mob scenes. I'll take Hermes and Senator Balbus and a couple of your lictors if you'll permit me, and we'll arrest them."

"This man is deadly," Cleopatra protested, "and for all we know the woman is too. Take my whole guard."

"We don't need foreign soldiers," Balbus said, taking a sword from a guardsman. "Armed Roman men are an entirely different proposition from unsuspecting astronomers."

"Quite so," Caesar said, "and, Decius Caecilius, if you have to kill them, make sure you get the whole story first."

We left and the party continued behind us. Outside, Balbus took a deep breath of fresh air. "Decius Caecilius, this is outrageous fun! I am so glad I ran into you at the *ludus* a few days ago."

Hermes passed me my dagger and *caestus*. "Maybe a few guardsmen wouldn't have been such a bad idea, though," he said, "no sense taking chances."

"Cleopatra might have slipped them orders to kill our suspects. I haven't cleared her from suspicion yet. It was her steward that hired Domitius. He didn't just come up here and knock on the gate and ask for a job."

The two lictors, fasces shouldered, fell in behind us. We had been walking for a few minutes before I realized there were six of us, not five. I called a halt. "Who are you?" I asked the dark-swathed figure.

Callista lowered her shawl. "I feel terrible for not recognizing that writing instantly. I may be able to help, and I really feel that I must witness the end of this."

"I can't be responsible for your safety," I told her.

"Nor should you be. A philosopher is always responsible for his own life and his own death."

"Come along then," I said, too tired to argue. One more to worry about. I hadn't really cleared her of suspicion either.

It was a beautiful night and silhouetted against the moon I could see the banner drooping from the high pole above the old fort. We hardly slowed when we reached the house. The door was bolted, but with a single coordinated kick Balbus and Hermes turned it to firewood and we passed on through. I told the lictors to stay at the door and let nobody out.

"Gupta!" I yelled, "Ashthuva! Come with me to the praetor!" There was no answer. We proceeded room by room. We found them in the rear of the house, crouched over a chest, drawing out bags that clinked. It seemed a sordid activity for such an exotic pair, but I suppose some things are the same the world over.

"I arrest you," I said, "for the murder of the astronomers Demades and Polasser and suspicion of complicity in the death of Postumius."

Gupta smiled, his teeth startlingly white in his dark face. He uncoiled to his full height as smoothly and bonelessly as a serpent.

"You arrest me, Roman?" he said in his strange, singsong accent. "Do you arrest my sister, too?" The lady herself stood as well, her clothing somewhat disarrayed. Balbus made a strangled noise somewhere high in his nose. He was seeing her for the first time. I was having a hard time keeping my attention on Gupta myself. I hoped Hermes was keeping his head about him, but I doubted it.

"Your sister, is she? You must be close. You killed three men for her on your sea-voyage here."

"You learned about that?" he said. "I had thought Romans were far too stupid to deduce such things."

"Don't feel too bad," I told him. "I've been known to underestimate barbarians in my time. Now, you have little life expectancy left to you, but I can promise you a quick, easy execution if you will answer my questions. I'll clear it with the dictator. Otherwise you'll answer those questions under torture and your death will be in no way easy."

He kept smiling. "Torture. You Romans know so little of torture. Come to India some day. I will show you what torture is really like."

"I'm afraid you are all through with India," I told him. Ashthuva was fiddling with something at her waist. "What are you doing, woman?" she took her hands from her waist and in an instant her singular gown unwound and fell to the floor, leaving her as naked as a statue of Aphrodite and ten times as enticing. Balbus made another noise and so, I fear, did I. She was completely covered with intricate tattoos, and while I was stupidly studying these Gupta made his move.

When I regained my senses somewhat, he was almost on me. No scarf this time. He had a long, curved dagger in his hand and he was moving as fast as any human being I had ever seen. He had quite sensibly chosen to attack me instead of Balbus or Hermes. I looked older and easier and, indeed, I was. I blocked his dagger hand with my cestus and thrust at him with my own dagger, but he snaked around it with an ease that was positively insulting. He cut again and I would have died then, but Balbus was on him and swift as the Indian was, Balbus was almost as fast and he was bull-strong to boot. He got both hands on the assassin's arms and Hermes clouted him over the head with a small table. No sense taking any chances with this one. Seeing her brother down Ashthuva whirled and darted for a back door but found herself facing Callista, who had dropped her shawl there and stood as serenely as if she were about to address a gathering of academics.

To my amazement and horror, the tattooed woman leapt high into the air and her right foot lashed out in a kick of neck-breaking force. I thought to see Callista dead in an instant, but this was a night for surprises. Leaning back slightly, she slapped the leg aside with her open palm. Ashthuva came down lightly, but she was slightly off-balance. Callista stepped in and with a dainty foot swept the Indian woman's leg aside and she toppled. She scrambled to get up, but in that instant Callista was on her, cracking her beneath the ear with the edge of a palm, gathering both her wrists into one hand, the other pulling back on the long, black hair. One knee was pressed into the small of the woman's back with Callista's full weight upon it. Ashthuva was going nowhere. Callista knelt there easily, crouched in a position that would have appeared awkward in another woman, her shapely, white left leg bared to the hip. She took no more notice of it than of her slightly disarranged hair.

"I knew some Greek women learned athletics," I said, "but I never heard of one training at the *pankration*."

"My father insisted that I be fully educated," she said.

I turned to Gupta, now held tightly by Balbus. I nodded at Hermes and he grasped the man's hair and jerked his head back so that he was looking up at me. I laid the point of my dagger just below his left eye. "Now, Gupta, some answers, if you please."

An hour later we were closeted in one of Cleopatra's personal chambers, guards on the door, the sounds of the still lively party muffled in the distance. The queen was there, as was Caesar. Hermes and Balbus we had left outside to enjoy the festivities but Caesar had insisted that Julia and Callista be present to hear my report.

The chamber was unusually modest for this place and its inhabitant, but I supposed Cleopatra put on the extravagance as what people expected from a queen of Egypt. Her personal tastes were more modest. Caesar now wore a simple tunic and *synthesis* and he had set aside his wreath of golden laurel leaves. He was very tired and looked every one of his years.

"It was what Julia suggested at the outset," I said. "The infighting among the great ladies of Rome over who is to be heir to Caesar. That and your scheme to change our calendar."

Caesar frowned slightly. "How did I bring this about?"

"You brought the astronomers to Rome, and among them was Polasser. Gupta came on his own and joined them because he really was an accomplished astronomer, with a sideline in astrology. As I've said before, one rogue will know another, and they were joined by the confidence man Postumius. It doesn't take three such men long to begin hatching plans. First they tried the grain scheme. Fulvia was a client of Polasser and he steered her to Postumius, who got her to talk to the grain merchants and use her patrician prestige to convince them to buy or not as Postumius directed. They made a killing that way, but it was too small. By that time Polasser had tumbled to the big-time money game here in Rome, and with his connections among the highborn ladies, he had the means to exploit it." I sipped at my wine. "Incidentally, Fulvia had the house that had belonged to Clo-dius. She let Gupta and Ashthuva stay there while their much more impressive house was being built on the Janiculum."

"That was where Postumius was killed," Caesar said. "Was that Fulvia's doing?"

"I believe so," I told him. "You can't trust a thief. I think he tried to cheat her of her share of the grain scheme takings." I looked at Julia. "You were right in observing that his torture bore the marks of wounded patrician pride."

"Was she in on the rest of it?" Caesar asked.

"I don't think so," I said. "They made use of her in the grain scheme, but she was too volatile even for men like those three."

Caesar pondered a while. "It isn't worth alienating Antonius.

I need him too sorely." He glanced at me wearily. "Don't look at me like that Decius Caecilius. Some day, if you're ever dictator, a great many things that seem serious now will take on a new perspective."

"What about poor Demades?" Cleopatra asked. "Why did he die?"

"Big ears," I said. "He hated Polasser and detested the astrologers as a group. He was snooping around, trying to get any kind of dirt on Polasser that he could gather, and I suspect he got an earful, but Gupta saw him snooping. Then he was eliminated."

"And this Domitius person?" Caesar asked. "Where does he tie in?"

"He was an acquaintance of Postumius from his horse racing days. They wanted someone reliable to spy here in the queen's house where you spend so much time. Polasser had been here at the queen's gatherings and he bribed the steward to hire the man."

Caesar looked at Cleopatra. "I'll deal with him," she said.

I didn't want to think about what that might mean. "When I started snooping around here," I touched my nose, which was still a little tender. Cleopatra looked abashed. "When I started snooping here, Gupta sent Domitius to the house of Archelaus. He didn't realize I'd be checking out there, too. He hoped to sell Archelaus information about your intentions in Parthia—and in Egypt."

Caesar looked at me sharply, then to Cleopatra. "My dear, we really should check outside the windows before we engage in serious conversation." Then back to me. "It is a good thing you are a very discreet man, Decius, and that you are married to my favorite niece."

"Anyway," I went on quickly, "once Gupta had his sister, if that's what she is, established in the new house and ready to bamboozle Rome's richest ladies, Polasser became superfluous. All his clients became hers. Gupta even summoned the other astronomers to confuse things, but he wasn't expecting me to be there that day, and I saw a bit too much and found that coin."

"So," Caesar said, "thieves fell out?"

"That's what happened, but we seldom see thieves on such a scale, or so strange."

We were silent for a while, then Julia spoke up. "Uncle Caius, who is to be your heir?"

Caesar smiled with infinite weariness and great cynicism. "Let's keep them all guessing, shall we?"

Two days later Gupta was dead in his prison cell. I was sure he'd swallowed his tongue, but Asklepiodes examined the body and was of the opinion that he had meditated himself to death. Whatever the cause, he was not a normal man. His sister, if that was what she was, escaped. One morning a dead guard was found in her cell, his clothes off and his neck broken. They should have set eunuchs to guard her. She was never seen or heard from again.

It was all so long ago. I never expected to live this long. I've outlived all of them. I even outlived Callista, and she lived to be a very old woman.

Of course it was Atia's brat, Octavius, who inherited, and he showed his gratitude in a singular way. He made Caesar a god, his deification solemnly ratified by the Senate and the College of Pontifexes. In this way did Caius Julius Caesar, finally, surpass all other Romans since the time of Romulus.

These things happened in the years 709 and 710 of the City of Rome, in the dictatorship of Caius Julius Caesar.

The latter year has ever since been known as the Year of Confusion.

AUTHOR'S NOTE

In this novel the author has departed from his usual strict adher-
ence to chronology and has, for dramatic purposes, compressed two
years into one. The Year of Confusion was 46 B.C. During that year
Caesar was engaged in the final actions of the Civil War, crushing
the Pompeians at Thapsus in Africa. Early in 45 he defeated their
last major army at Munda in Spain and only then returned to Rome
to oversee his vast program of reforms and building projects, leaving
behind a remnant of holdouts. In that year, his last full year in power,
Caesar was joined in Rome by Cleopatra. The author hopes he will
be forgiven for taking this liberty, which permitted him to combine
several of the most riotous, colorful, and dramatic events of the era
into a single story.

GLOSSARY

(Definitions apply to the year 710 of the Republic.)

Aborigine, Aboriginal   In Roman legend, the earliest inhabitants of Italy, before the arrival of Aeneas from Troy.

arms   Like everything else in Roman society, weapons were strictly regulated by class. The straight, double-edged sword and dagger of the legions were classed as "honorable."

The *gladius* was a short, broad, double-edged sword borne by Roman soldiers. It was designed primarily for stabbing. The *pugio* was a dagger also used by soldiers.

The *caestus* was a boxing glove, made of leather straps and reinforced by bands, plates, or spikes of bronze. The curved, single-edged sword or knife called a *sica* was "infamous." *Sicas* were used in the arena by Thracian gladiators and were carried by street thugs. One ancient writer says that its curved shape made it convenient to carry sheathed beneath the armpit, showing that gangsters and shoulder holsters go back a long way.

Carrying of arms within the *pomerium* (the ancient City

boundary marked out by Romulus) was forbidden, but the law was ignored in troubled times. Slaves were forbidden to carry weapons within the City, but those used as bodyguards could carry staves or clubs. When street fighting or assassinations were common, even senators went heavily armed, and even Cicero wore armor beneath his toga from time to time.

Shields were not common except as gladiatorial equipment. The large shield (*scutum*) of the legions was unwieldy in narrow streets, but bodyguards might carry the small shield (*parma*) of the lightly armed auxiliary troops. These came in handy when the opposition took to throwing rocks and roof tiles.

augur An official who observed omens for state purposes. He could forbid business and assemblies if he saw unfavorable omens.

auxilia *See* **military terms.**

basilica A meeting place of merchants and for the administration of justice. Among them were the Basilica Aemilia (a.k.a. Basilica Fulvia and Basilica Julia), the Basilica Opimia, the Basilica Portia, and the Basilica Sempronia (the latter devoted solely to business purposes).

bustuarii The earliest gladiators. The name comes from *bustuum*, a funeral pyre. These gladiators fought at the pyre or tomb site of the deceased dignitary to propitiate his shade.

calends The first of the month.

Civil War 49–45 B.C. After Caesar had conquered Gaul, his consulship was nearly at an end. He was apprehensive about returning to Rome without some safeguards against revengeful judicial action and hostilities from Pompey's followers. He suggested that both he and Pompey simultaneously retire from their consulships, but the Senate demanded that he step down. He refused, instead he crossed the Rubicon River (the border of Italy proper, hence the jurisdiction of the Senate), with a legion, which was contrary to a

Roman law designed to prevent a coup d'etat. Despite an offer of peace from Caesar, Pompey and most of the Senate fled to Greece after being chased through Italy by Caesar.

Caesar began his fight against the Pompeian forces in Spain and managed to seize the passes of the Pyrenees, preventing Pompey's generals (Marcus) Petreius and (Lucius) Afranius from taking Iberia. Caesar then surrounded the Pompeian forces at Ilerda and beseiged them until they gave up. Because they surrendered, Caesar allowed all the Pompeian forces to go, provided that they did not take arms against him again. Both Petreius and Afranius foreswore themselves and, with whatever troops they could round up, joined Pompey in Greece.

Caesar hurried to Rome where he had been appointed dictator by the Senate upon the nomination of (Marcus) Lepidus. This bought him enough time so that eleven days later he was elected consul by the people and resigned his dictatorship. Meanwhile in Numidia, Caesar's legate Curio (Caius Quintus Scribonius Curio, husband of Fulvia) lost both a battle and his life fighting the *optimates* under (Publius Attius) Varus with his ally King Juba of Numidia.

Caesar then invaded Greece but initially was defeated by Pompey's army at Dyrrhachium. Pompey missed his opportunity to destroy Ceasar's army because he thought Caesar's retreat was a ruse. At Pharsalus, Pompey's more numerous army attacked Caesar's but were decisively defeated. Pompey, his senior staff, and the remnants of his army fled to Africa.

In Egypt a civil war had broken out between Queen Cleopatra (VII) and her younger brother/husband Ptolemy (XIII). The reason for the Egyptian civil war was that Cleopatra granted Pompey's request for ships and grain as well as sanctuary for his army. She was intimidated into doing so by Pompey's allies near Egypt. The Egyptian people resented the fact that Cleopatra had caved in to Roman demands and ousted her as queen. She escaped from Alexandria and raised an army.

Pompey had fled to Egypt and Caesar pursued him there. Caesar wanted to end the Roman civil war and go back to the status he and Pompey shared in the Triumvirate. Ptolemy, however, interfered with Caesar's plan by having Pompey decapitated and sent the head to Caesar as a gift. It is said that Caesar wept when he saw it (Pompey, after all, had been his friend and son-in-law). Angered by Ptolemy's unilateral act, Caesar sided with Cleopatra and defeated Ptolemy.

Caesar became Cleopatra's lover, but because she was not a citizen of Rome, he could not marry her under Roman law. While Caeser dallied in Egypt, the *optimates* gathered more forces and were led by Scipio, a.k.a. Metellus Scipio (Quintus Caecilius Metellus Pius Scipio Nasica), (Marcus Porcius) Cato (the Younger), (Marcus) Petreius, (Publius Attius) Varus, who was already the governor of Africa, and (Titus) Labienus Caesar's former legate. They were also allied to King Juba I of Numidia.

Caesar defeated Varus in a naval battle, and Varus took flight to Spain where he was later killed in battle at Munda. For three months Caesar skirmished with the *optimates*, all the while his army was increased by desertions from his enemy's ranks. At Thapsus in Tunisia, he came upon Scipio's and Juba's armies. He attacked Scipio, and Juba, watching the fight from the sidelines, saw Caesar's army kill ten thousand of Scipio's men; Juba hastily withdrew. Scipio and Labienus managed to escape to Utica (Tunisia) where Cato was in command. With the destruction of the *optimates* main army, Cato realized that their cause was no longer viable and committed suicide. Scipio was later killed in a naval battle off Hippo Regius, Algeria, while Labeinus died in the battle of Munda. Petreius had fled with Juba but their army was cut off. They made a suicide agreement and fought a duel whereby Petreius killed Juba and then fell on his own sword. Caesar mopped up the rest of the opposition and returned to Rome.

client, pl. *clientele*   One attached in a subordinate relationship to a patron, whom he was bound to support in war and in the courts. Freedmen became clients of their former masters. The relationship was hereditary.

colonia   Roman colonies were originally established as military outposts. At this period of the Republic, *colonia* were lands given to veteran soldiers as a reward for service.

consilium   Broadly, an advisory group.

crucifixions   The Romans inherited the practice of crucifixion from the Carthaginians. In Rome, it was reserved for rebellious slaves and insurrectionists. Citizens could not be crucified.

curule   A curule office conferred magisterial dignity. Those holding it were privileged to sit in a **curule chair**—a folding camp chair that became a symbol of Roman officials sitting in judgment.

duumvir, pl. *duumviri*   A duumvirate was a board of two men. Many Italian towns were governed by *duumviri*. A duumvir was also a Roman admiral, probably dating from a time when the Roman navy was commanded by two senators.

eagles   The standard of a Roman legion was a gilded eagle. The eagle was the tutelary deity of the legion and came to embody the legion itself. Thus, a Roman on military service was "with the eagles."

eques, **pl.** *equites*   These were originally "knights" who fought on horseback. At this time during the Republic, they were a social class below the patrician Senate and above the plebeians. *See* **orders.**

families and names   Roman citizens usually had three names. The given name (**praenomen**) was individual, but there were only about eighteen of them: Marcus, Lucius, etc. Certain praenomens were used only in a single family: Appius was used only by the Claudians, Mamercus only by the Aemilians, and so forth. Only males had praenomens. Daughters were given the feminine form of the father's name: Aemilia for Aemilius, Julia for Julius, Valeria for Valerius, etc.

Next came the **nomen.** This was the name of the clan (gens). All members of a gens traced their descent from a common ancestor, whose name they bore: Julius, Furius, Licinius, Junius, Tullius, to name a few. Patrician names always ended in *ius.* Plebeian names often had different endings. The name of the clan collectively was always in the feminine form, e.g., Aemilia.

A subfamily of a gens is the **stirps.** Stirps is an anthropological term. It is similar to the Scottish clan system, where the family name "Ritchie" for instance, is a stirps of the Clan MacIntosh. The **cognomen** gave the name of the stirps, i.e., Caius Julius Caesar. Caius of the stirps Caesar of gens Julia.

The name of the family branch **(cognomen)** was frequently anatomical: Naso (nose), Ahenobarbus (bronzebeard), Sulla (splotchy), Niger (dark), Rufus (red), Caesar (curly), and many others. Some families did not use cognomens. Mark Antony was just Marcus Antonius, no cognomen.

Other names were **honorifics** conferred by the Senate for outstanding service or virtue: Germanicus (conqueror of the Germans), Africanus (conqueror of the Africans), or Pius (extraordinary filial piety).

Freed slaves became citizens and took the family name of their master. Thus the vast majority of Romans named, for instance, Cornelius would not be patricians of that name, but the descendants of that family's freed slaves. There was no stigma attached to slave ancestry.

Adoption was frequent among noble families. An adopted son took the name of his adoptive father and added the genetive form of his former nomen. Thus when Caius Julius Caesar adopted his great-nephew Caius Octavius, the latter became Caius Julius Caesar Octavianus.

All these names were used for formal purposes such as official documents and monuments. In practice, nearly every Roman went by a nickname, often descriptive and rarely complimentary. Usually it was the Latin equivalent of Gimpy, Humpy, Lefty, Squint-eye, Big Ears, Baldy, or something of the sort. Romans were merciless when it came to physical peculiarities.

fasces   A bundle of rods bound around with an ax projecting from the middle. They symbolized a Roman magistrate's power of corporal and capital punishment and were carried by the lictors who accompanied the curule magistrates, the *Flamen Dialis* (*see* **priesthoods**), and the proconsuls and propraetors who governed provinces.

First Citizen   In Latin: *Princeps*. Originally the most prestigious senator, permitted to speak first on all important issues and set the order of debate. Augustus, the first emperor, usurped the title in perpetuity. Decius detests him so much that he will not use either his name (by the time of the writing it was Caius Julius Caesar Octavianus) or the honorific Augustus, voted by the toadying Senate. Instead he will refer to him only as the First Citizen. *Princeps* is the origin of the modern word "prince."

forum   An open meeting and market area.

freedman   A manumitted slave. Formal emancipation conferred full rights of citizenship except for the right to hold office. Informal emancipation conferred freedom without voting rights. In the second or at least third generation, a freedman's descendants became full citizens.

frigidarium   The cold-plunge pool at the baths.

genius loci   The spirit of a particular place. An altar to the *genius loci* was typically a squat pillar with a serpent wrapped around it.

gravitas   The quality of seriousness.

gymnasium   Roman exercise facilities. In Rome they were often an adjunct to the baths.

ides   The fifteenth of March, May, July, and October; the thirteenth of the remaining months.

imperium   The ancient power of kings to summon and lead armies, to order and forbid, and to inflict corporal and capital punishment. Under the Republic, the imperium was divided among the consuls and praetors, but they were subject to appeal and intervention by the tribunes in their civil decisions and were answerable for their acts after leaving office. Only a dictator had unlimited imperium.

impluvium   The pool of water in the atrium of a house.

insula, pl. insulae   Large blocks of multistory tenement housing (literally meaning "island").

Lapis Niger   A very ancient monument in the Forum, consisting of a block of basalt carved with words in extremely archaic Latin. It was already ancient during the late Republic and only a few words were recognizable. It bears to this day the oldest example of written Latin.

lares   The household gods, whose altar was usually in the atrium.

legion   Legions formed the fighting force of the Roman army. Through its soldiers, the Empire was able to control vast stretches of territory and people. They were known for their discipline, training, ability, and military prowess.

lictor   Bodyguards, usually freedmen, who accompanied magistrates and the *Flamen Dialis*, bearing the fasces. They summoned Assemblies, attended public sacrifices, and carried out sentences of punishment.

ludus*, pl. *ludi   Public religious festivals put on by the state. There were a number of long-established *ludi,* the earliest being the Roman Games *(ludi Romani)* in honor of Jupiter Optimus Maximus and held in September. The *ludi Megalenses* were held in April, as were the *ludi Cereri* in honor of Ceres, the grain goddess, and the *ludi Floriae* in honor of Flora, the goddess of flowers. The *ludi Apollinares* were celebrated in July. In October the *ludi Capitolini;* the final games of the year were the Plebian Games *(ludi Plebeii)* in November. Games usually ran for several days except for the Capitoline games, which ran for a single day. Games featured theatrical performances, processions, sacrifices, public banquets, and chariot races. They did not feature gladiatorial combats. The gladiatorial games, called *munera*, were put on by individuals as funeral rites.

maiestas   A crime against "the majesty and dignity of the Roman people." Not quite treason, but still a serious offense, it became a catch-all charge to use against one's political enemies in the late Republic.

Master of Horse   In Latin *Magister Equitum.* A dictator's second in command. In times of emergency, the Senate could appoint a dictator who would have absolute imperium. The dictator would appoint a Master of Horse who would carry out his orders. Marc Antony (Marcus Antonius) was Julius Caesar's Master of Horse.

military terms   The Roman legionary system was quite unlike any military organization in existence today. The regimental system used by all modern armies date from the Wars of Religion of the sixteenth century. These began with companies under captains that grouped into regiments under colonels, then regiments grouped into divisions under generals. By the Napoleonic wars they had acquired higher organizations such as corps, army groups, and so forth, with an orderly chain of command from the marshal down through the varying degrees of generals, colonels, majors, captains, sergeants, corporals, and finally the privates in the ranks.

The Roman legions had nothing resembling such an organization. At the time of the SPQR novels the strength of a legion was theoretically 6,000 men, but the usual strength was around 4,800. These were divided into sixty centuries. Originally, a century had included one hundred men, but during this period there were about eighty. Each century was commanded by a **centurion,** making sixty centurions to the legion. Six centuries made a cohort. Each centurion had an *optio* as his second in command. The centurionate was not a single rank, but a complex of hierarchy and seniority, many details of which are obscure. We know that there were first-rank and second-rank centurions. The senior centurion of the legion was *primus pilus,* the "first spear." He was centurion of the first century of the first cohort and outranked all others. Centurions were promoted from the ranks for ability and they were the nearest thing a legion had to permanent officers. All others were elected or appointed politicians.

Legionaries were Roman citizens. They fought as heavy infantry, fully armored and armed with the heavy javelin (*pilum*), the short Spanish sword (*gladius Hispaniensis*), and the straight, double-edged dagger (*pugio*). They carried a very large shield (*scutum*) that at that time was usually oval and curved to fit around the body. Besides holding the center of the battle line, legionaries were engineers and operated the siege weapons: catapults, team-operated crossbows, and so forth.

Attached to each legion were usually an equal number of *auxilia,* noncitizen troops often supplied by allies. These were lightly armed troops, skirmishers, archers, slingers, and other missile troops, and cavalry. The legion had a small citizen cavalry force but depended upon the *auxilia* for the bulk of the cavalry. Through long service an auxiliary could earn citizen status, which was hereditary: his sons could serve in the legions. *Auxilia* received lower pay and had lower status, but they were essential when operating in broken terrain or heavy forest, where the legions could not be used to advantage. In battle they often held the flanks and usually, with the cavalry, were charged with pursuing a broken and fleeing enemy, preventing them from re-forming or counterattacking.

There were other formations within a legion, some of them obscure. One was the ***antesignani,*** "those who fight before the standards." Already nearly obsolete, they were apparently an elite strike force, though how it was manned and used is uncertain. It seems exceptional bravery was required for assignment to the *antesignani.*

In Decius's time the legions were still formed as a unit, served for a number of years, then discharged collectively. Even when on many years' service, they were ceremonially disbanded, then re-formed every year, with the soldier's oath renewed each time. This archaic practice was extremely troublesome. When a few years later Augustus reformed the military system, legions became permanent institutions, their strength kept up by continuous enlistment of new soldiers as old ones retired or died. Many of the Augustan legions remained in service continuously for centuries.

The commander of a legion might be a **consul** or **praetor,** but more often he was a **proconsul** or **propraetor** who, having served his year in Rome, went out to govern a province. Within his province he was commander of its legions. He might appoint a **legate** (*legatus*) as his assistant. The legate was subject to approval by the Senate. He might choose a more experienced military man to handle the army work while the promagistrate (proconsul, propraetor, proquaestor, or procurator) concentrated upon civil affairs; but a successful war was important to a political career,

269

while enriching the commander. For an extraordinary command, such as Caesar's in Gaul or Pompey's against the pirates, the pro-magistrate might be permitted a number of legates.

Under the commander were **Tribunes of the Soldiers,** usually young men embarking upon their political careers. Their duties were entirely at the discretion of the commander. Caesar usually told his tribunes to sit back, keep their mouths shut, and watch the experienced men work. But a military tribune might be given a responsible position, even command of a legion. The young Cassius Longinus as tribune prosecuted a successful war in Syria after his commander was dead.

mundus, pl. mundi   Literally, "mouth." A cave or opening in the ground believed to lead to the underworld and used to contact the dead.

munera   Special games, not part of the official calendar, at which gladiators were exhibited. They were originally funeral games and were always dedicated to the dead.

nefasti   The eighty-four days when business was prohibited.

nones   The seventh of March, May, July, and October; the fifth of the remaining months.

October Horse   On the ides of October a rite to Mars was celebrated in a two-horse chariot race on the Campus Martius (Field of Mars). The October Horse, i.e., the outer horse of the winning pair (the strongest runner), was sacrificed to Mars. The tail was cut off and taken to the Regia (the traditional home of Numa, Rome's second king who established the office of pontifex maximus, and the home of subsequent pontifexes maximus) where the horse's blood was dripped on its hearth. The blood from the sacrifice was collected in a bowl and given to the Vestal Virgins to use in other ceremonies. The horse was also decapitated, and two teams, one from the Subura district and the other from the Via Sacra, fought for the horse's head. The winner who brought back the head to his district was then a local hero who supposedly brought good luck to the area.

offices   The political system of the Roman Republic was completely different from any today. The terms we have borrowed from the Romans have very different meanings in the modern context. "Senators" were not elected and did not represent a particular district. "Dictator" was a temporary office conferred by the Senate in times of emergency. "Republic" simply meant a governmental system that was not a hereditary monarchy. By the time of the SPQR series, the power of former Roman kings was shared among a number of citizen assemblies.

Tribunes of the People were representatives of the plebeians, with power to introduce laws and to veto actions of the Senate. Only plebeians could hold the office, which carried no imperium. **Tribunes of the Soldiers** were elected from among the young men of senatorial or equestrian rank to be assistants to generals. Usually it was the first step of a man's political career.

A Roman embarked upon a public career followed the **cursus honorum**, i.e., the "path of honor." After doing staffwork for officials, he began climbing the ladder of office. These were taken in order as follows:

The lowest elective office was **quaestor:** bookkeeper and paymaster for the Treasury, the Grain Office, and the provincial governors. These men did the scut work of the Roman world. After the quaestorship he was eligible for the **Senate,** a nonelective office, which had to be ratified by the censors; if none were in office, he had to be ratified by the next censors to be elected.

Next were the **aediles**. Roughly speaking, these were city managers, responsible for the upkeep of public buildings, streets, sewers, markets, brothels, etc. There were two types: the **plebeian aediles** and the **curule aediles**. The curule aediles could sit in judgment on civil cases involving markets and currency, while the plebeian aediles could only levy fines. Otherwise their duties were the same. The state only provided a tiny stipend for improvements, and the rest was the aedile's problem. If he put on (and paid for) splendid games, he was sure of election to higher office.

Third was **praetor,** an office with real power. Praetors were judges, but they could command armies, and after a year in office they could go out to govern provinces, where real wealth could be won, earned, or stolen. In the late Republic, there were eight praetors. Senior was the ***praetor urbanus,*** who heard civil cases between citizens of Rome. The ***praetor peregrinus*** (praetor of the foreigners) heard cases involving foreigners. The others presided over criminal courts. After leaving office, the ex-praetors became **propraetors** and went on to govern propraetorian provinces with full imperium.

The highest office was **consul,** supreme office of power during the Roman Republic. Two were elected each year. Consuls called meetings of the Senate and presided there. The office carried full imperium and they could lead armies. On the expiration of their year in office, exconsuls were usually assigned the best provinces to rule as **proconsul**. A proconsul had the same insignia and the same number of lectors as a consul. His power was absolute within his province. The most important commands always went to proconsuls.

Censors were elected every five years. This was the capstone to a political career, but it did not carry imperium and there was no foreign command afterward. Censors conducted the census, purged the Senate of unworthy members, doled out the public contracts, confirmed new senators in office, and conducted the *lustrum*, a ritual of purification. They could forbid certain religious practices or luxuries deemed bad for public morals or generally "un-Roman."

There were two censors, and each could overrule the other. They were usually elected from among the exconsuls.

Under the Sullan Constitution, the quaestorship was the minimum requirement for membership in the Senate. The majority of senators had held that office and never held another. Membership in the Senate was for life, unless expelled by the censors.

No Roman official could be prosecuted while in office, but he could be after he stepped down. Malfeasance in office was one of the most common court charges.

The most extraordinary office was **dictator**. In times of emergency, the Senate could instruct the consuls to appoint a dictator, who could wield absolute power for six months, after which he had to step down from office. Unlike all other officials, a dictator was unaccountable: he could not be prosecuted for his acts in office. The last true dictator was appointed in the third century B.C. The dictatorships of Sulla and Julius Caesar were unconstitutional.

orders The Roman hierarchy was divided into a number of orders (*ordines*). At the top was the **Senatorial Order** (*Ordo Senatus*) made up of the senators. Originally the Senate had been a part of the Equestrian Order, but the dictator Sulla made them a separate order.

Next came the **Equestrian Order** (*Ordo Equestris*). This was a property qualification. Men above a certain property rating, determined every five years by the censors, belonged to the Equestrian Order, so named because in ancient times, at the annual hosting, these wealthier men brought horses and served in the cavalry. By the time of the SPQR novels, they had lost all military nature. The equestrians (*equites*) were the wealthiest class, the bankers and businessmen, and after the Sullan reforms they supplied the jurymen. If an *eques* won election to the quaestorship, he entered

273

the Senatorial Order. Collectively, they wielded immense power. They often financed the political careers of senators and their business dealings abroad often shaped Roman foreign policy.

Last came the **Plebeian Order** (*Ordo Plebis*). Pretty much everybody else, and not really an order in the sense of the other two, since plebeians might be equestrians or senators. Nevertheless, as the mass of the citizenry they were regarded as virtually a separate power and they elected the Tribunes of the People, who were in many ways the most powerful politicians of this time.

Slaves and foreigners had no status and did not belong to an order.

optimates   The party of the "best men." Patricians were all but extinct, only a few families left. Caesar was a patrician, but he was a in the popular assemblies.

palestra   Greek exercise facilities. *See* **gymnasium.**

patrician   The noble class of Rome.

peculium   The savings of a slave with his master's consent put toward his manumission.

pedagogues   Greek for a slave who accompanied children to school.

pomerium   The sacred boundary of the City of Rome.

popular assemblies   There were several of these. They were nonsenatorial and had varying powers. The *comitia centuriata* included the entire citizenry. The *consilium plebis* was restricted to the plebeians. The *comitia tribute* consisted of the citizenry organized in "tribes" (voting groups.)

populares   The party of the plebeians.

praetor peregrinus   *See* **offices.**

priesthoods   In Rome, the priesthoods were offices of state. There were two major classes: **pontifexes** and *flamines*.

Pontifexes were members of the highest priestly college of Rome. They had superintendence over all sacred observances, state and private, and over the calendar. The head of their college was the *pontifex maximus,* a title held to this day by the pope.

The *flamines* were the high priests of the state gods: the *Flamen Martialis* for Mars, the *Flamen Quirinalis* for the deified Romulus, and, highest of all, the *Flamen Dialis*, high priest of Jupiter.

The *Flamen Dialis* celebrated the Ides of each month and could not take part in politics, although he could attend meetings of the Senate, attended by a single lictor. Each had charge of the daily sacrifices, wore distinctive headgear, and was surrounded by many ritual taboos.

Another very ancient priesthood was the **Rex Sacrorum,** "King of Sacrifices." This priest had to be a patrician and had to observe even more taboos than the *Flamen Dialis*. The position was so onerous that it became difficult to find a patrician willing to take it.

Technically, pontifexes and *flamines* did not take part in public business except to solemnize oaths and treaties, give the god's stamp of approval to declarations of war, etc. But since they were all senators anyway, the ban had little meaning. Julius Caesar was pontifex maximus while he was out conquering Gaul, even though the pontifex maximus wasn't supposed to look upon human blood.

Princeps **(First Citizen)** This was an especially distinguished senator chosen by the censors. His name was first called on the roll of the Senate, and he was first to speak on any issue. Later the title was usurped by Augustus and is the origin of the word "prince."

scena A building or backdrop for a play.

Saturnalia   The feast of Saturn, December 17–23 (basically what we celebrate today as Yuletide or Christmas), a raucous and jubilant festival when gifts were exchanged, debts settled, and masters waited on their slaves.

Sibylline Books   Very ancient books of prophecy, kept by a priesthood called the *quinquidecemviri;* (board of fifteen men). In uncertain times, the Senate might order a consultation of these books to discern the will of the gods. The language was very archaic and obscure and the interpretation doubtful.

sistrum   A percussion instrument consisting of a handheld frame to which small metal discs are attached, rather like those on a tambourine.

Social War   A war fought from 91 to 88 B.C. between Rome and its Italian allies. It is called "Social" from *socii,* Latin for "allies." It is also called the Marsic War (from Marsi, the most prominent tribe). Unrest developed among Rome's allies when Rome stopped sharing wartime plunder. A political solution was first sought that conferred citizenship on the allies. However, when Marcus Livius Drusus, who was the chief sponsor of the measure, was assasinated war broke out. Rome won in the field, but still wound up giving citizenship to the allies, thus a share in war plunder plus voting rights.

SPQR *Senatus Populusque Romanus*   The Senate and People of Rome. The formula embodied the sovereignty of Rome. It was used on official correspondence, documents, and public works.

subligaculum   The Roman loincloth. Typically worn during athletic activity.

synthesis   A fashionable, brightly colored dinner costume put on over the tunic.

Tarpeian Rock   A rock above the cliff of the Capitoline Hill used for executions (from which traitors and parricides were hurled).

It was named for the Roman maiden Tarpeia who, according to legend, betrayed the way into the Capitol to the Sabines.

thyrsus **pl.** *thyrsi*   A wand wreathed with vines and tipped with a pinecone. It was part of the regalia of the rites of Dionysus/Bacchus.

toga   The outer robe of the Roman citizen. It was white for the upper class, darker for the poor and for people in mourning. The *toga candidus* was a specially whitened (with chalk) toga worn when standing for office. The *toga praetexta,* bordered with a purple stripe, was worn by curule magistrates, by state priests when performing their functions, and by boys prior to manhood. The *toga trabea,* a striped robe, was worn by augurs and some orders of the priesthood. The *toga picta,* purple and embroidered with golden stars, was worn by a general when celebrating a triumph, also by a magistrate when giving public games.

triclinium   A dining room.

triumph   A ceremony in which a victorious general (*triumphator*) was rendered semi-divine honors for a day. It began with a magnificent procession displaying the loot and captives of the campaign and culminated with a banquet for the Senate in the Temple of Jupiter, special protector of Rome.

Vestal Virgins   Virgin priestesses, chaste like the goddess Vesta; six of them served for thirty years, tending the hearth of Rome, and any violation of the vow of chastity was punished by burial alive. Vesta's shrine was the most sacred object of Roman religion.